RACHEL
versus
SEAN
with
Jackson in the Middle

RACHEL
versus
SEAN
with
Jackson in the Middle

WAYNE LOBDELL

ARCHWAY
PUBLISHING

Archway Publishing books may be ordered through booksellers or by contacting:

Archway Publishing
1663 Liberty Drive
Bloomington, IN 47403
www.archwaypublishing.com
1 (888) 242-5904

ISBN: 978-1-4808-8459-5 (sc)
ISBN: 978-1-4808-8460-1 (hc)
ISBN: 978-1-4808-8461-8 (e)

Library of Congress Control Number: 2019917443

Print information available on the last page.

Archway Publishing rev. date: 11/4/2019

INTRODUCTION

Weaving humor and presidential trivia in with discussions on serious political issues has been a fun challenge while writing this book. I spent a lot of time reading and viewing the media analysis of the American political landscape.

This story is about what happens when fictional characters, Rachel Paterson, the existential progressive, and Sean McCarthy, a classic conservative, become bogged down at a Washington pub in the company of an amazing, brilliant, self-educated African American bartender, Jackson Lewis. Rachel and Sean, equally attractive, intelligent, and articulate, are both struggling with the challenges of balancing the schedules of high-pressure jobs with family obligations. Humor and American presidential trivia are mixed into teasing suggestions of a possible romance.

One evening, while putting the finishing touches on this story, I listened to one of Joe Biden's opening campaign speeches. He opened with the traditional proclamation of America being the greatest country on the planet, with the strongest economy, the greatest technology, and a superior military. He proceeded to tell his audience what a terrible president we have in Donald Trump and then gave his vision of how he was going to make it all better with higher wages and more benefits for the middle class and the poor with laws and legislation requiring the wealthy to share.

That all sounds appealing to the majority because the majority of our population is either poor or middle class. All the while, Donald Trump is screaming at campaign rallies that he is the greatest president to ever lead our country and that he deserves all the credit for America's accomplishments.

This is all déjà vu political campaign stuff that happens every four years. And this campaign rhetoric and legislative battles between the Democrat and Republican parties has been going on for more than fifty years. As stressful as it has been at election time, our two-party system has, in fact, achieved some amazing success. We are the greatest nation in the history of planet earth.

The free enterprise, incentive-based capitalist economic system has worked because the two-party system has maintained an effective balance between those who want more incentives to grow and create wealth and those who want a more even distribution of wealth. In practice, our history, with thirty Republican administrations and twenty Democratic administrations over the past fifty years, has demonstrated that too much greed and unfair practices at the top is not healthy, creating a less productive economy. On the other hand, pushing up wages and welfare too fast creates obstacles to economic growth.

As we navigate through this volatile political season, I hope this story motivates you to listen to opposing views and generate some rational understanding of the need to evaluate the issues in depth from multiple angles.

CONTENTS

PART III

PART I

CHAPTER 1

RACHEL

The soup was simmering on the stove in the dimly lit kitchen as Jake Patterson stood over his Glock 29. He had just cleaned the handgun and placed it on the kitchen table when he heard the sounds of the garage door opening. He hadn't heard a car entering the drive, but after a slight pause, the garage door squeaked as it rolled back down.

Rachel Patterson had pressed the garage door opener just before turning into the drive. The sounds of the garage door muffled any noise from the vehicle as it entered the driveway of the three-bedroom, ranch-style home occupied by her, her husband, and their two children.

Pleased to be home after a stressful day, she eased into the tight space, reached across to the passenger seat for her briefcase, and removed her tired body from the Ford Mustang. She opened the kitchen door entrance and froze.

Jake, with his back to her, stood over his gun at the kitchen table, very still. He suddenly lifted the gun, spun around, held it with both hands, and pointed it directly at her.

Rachel stiffened, her face turned white, and she braced herself for a bullet to her face. *Oh, God, don't let him do this.*

Click. He pulled the trigger.

Rachel twitched, her mind preparing for the end of her life, and then she realized nothing had happened. Her first thought was a misfire, but then she heard him laugh. "What in the hell is the matter with you?" she shouted, her face turning red. "Have you gone crazy?"

"I was just cleaning the gun. I knew it was empty. Calm down."

"You want me to calm down? I should call the police."

"Don't be ridiculous."

"You say I'm being ridiculous?" Rachel was shaking and had tears in her eyes. "What you have done is irresponsible, and—as a matter of fact—it's a crime."

Jake placed the gun back on the table. "Okay, okay, sorry. I was trying to be funny. It was the wrong thing to do."

"Funny? You think pointing your goddamn gun at my face and pulling the trigger is funny? It's not funny. It's crazy."

Rachel moved past the table through the kitchen. "That's it. That gun's gotta go. I don't want it in my house."

"Oh, really? You don't want ... and *your* house? This is my house too."

Rachel turned back to Jake. "I'm not living in this house another day with that gun here."

Jake proceeded to his office space. "Okay, okay. You're overreacting, but I get the picture. I'll lock it in my desk drawer right now."

Rachel, still shaken, walked swiftly up the stairs to their bedroom. It was nine fifteen.

Jake locked his gun, returned to the living room, and plopped down on the couch to watch Hannity on Fox News.

Fifteen minutes later, Rachel entered and sat down on the opposite end of the couch.

Jake turned toward her. "Now that you've had your say about the gun ... I saw you and Steven having lunch at Rockwell today. Were you waiting for another couple to join you—or was that a romantic lunch?"

"Don't be ridiculous. We were reviewing plans for a presentation. I moved over to his side of the booth so we could both see the proposal. We have a big event coming up."

"I saw you were looking at some papers, but he seemed to be admiring you."

"That's crazy. Why didn't you join us?"

"I was embarrassed and didn't want to cause a scene."

"This is crazy. First, you scare the hell out of me with a gun, and now you're accusing me of having something going with a coworker? I'm not done talking about the gun. I absolutely hate having that thing anywhere in this house. Do you know how many people die every year from gun accidents—not to mention deaths when it's not an accident? School shootings, drug dealers, robberies, temper tantrums? More than thirty thousand every year. It's crazy! America is the gun capital of the world. They should make them illegal for everyone except the police or authorized security workers."

Jake put Hannity on pause, ready for his own debate. "With all those political books you read, and all the time you spend watching

MSNBC, I'm sure you remember the second amendment. You and your liberal friends will never get rid of the right to bear arms. The problems come from not enforcing gun laws. And people have a right to protect themselves. What if a bad guy enters our house with a gun? What are you going to do? Chase him away with a broom? I'll never be without a gun."

Rachel got up and walked away, still shaking. Upstairs, she quietly looked in on her six-year-old twin sons, Jason and Jamie. Thankfully they were sound asleep. She then returned downstairs to the master bedroom. She still felt too shaken up from the gun incident to sleep, and she turned on CNN just as her cell phone rang.

"Hi, this is Rachel."

"Rachel, boss lady wants us to make a three-day trip to DC, leaving here Sunday night."

"I know. She called me this afternoon too. I was already in DC this week. I told her I'd have to check my situation back here. It's getting tough at home. Steven, I've been traveling too much lately. I don't think I can do this one."

"We gotta do this one, kid. It's a big deal, and it could lead to more events."

"I know, Steven. Scope Public Relations puts on a lot of events."

"Yes, they do some internationally."

"Yikes, about all I need to end my once-happy marriage is to start traveling out of the country. My family thinks I'm deserting them. My twins gave me a lecture yesterday—not to mention how Jake would take this."

"I understand, but if you can't come, she wants me to take Andrea. I don't want Andrea with me on this job."

"Aw, you sure? Andrea adores you."

"Look—we could get a nice bonus if we put together a successful event. I need you as my partner, not Andrea."

"I could use a bonus, but my kids need me home more. And Jake—"

"You know I've got the same problem at home. Think about it. The problem is that I have to know tomorrow morning. Not my timetable; it's the boss's."

"Okay, you don't need to wait. I'll go."

"I'll book the flight, reserve the rooms at the Marriott, and take you to the airport."

"Okay, thanks. Good night."

"Good night, Rachel."

Rachel dropped into her bed. She felt like she had finally fallen asleep when Jason and Jamie came piling in on her. It was seven in the morning.

"Mom, Jamie and I got a ribbon for the drawing he did."

"And I scored a goal in Tuesday night's game," Jason said.

"Yeah, Mom, he only got the goal 'cause I passed it to him."

"That's good. You got the assist," Rachel said. "Did your team win?"

"Nah, we lost 3–1."

"But it was a good game, and you had fun."

After setting the boys up with bowls of Fruit Loops, Rachel approached Jake in his office. "I have the boys ready for school and fed them breakfast. Can you drive them?"

"I have an eight fifteen meeting at the company office; you'll have to take them."

"How is that not a surprise? I guess now is the best time to tell you, but I have to go back to DC on Sunday afternoon. I tried to get out of it, but I have to be there. I'll come back Wednesday."

"Ya know, Rachel, I don't ever remember agreeing to be a stay-at-home dad. I'm trying to build a business. Why can't you get a day job?"

"We've been through this so many times. I can't find a nine-to-five job that pays enough to pay our bills. Why don't you get a job that we can count on?"

"I'm building my business. Real estate sales take time to build clientele."

"I've been hearing that for two years. You shouldn't have quit the Bridgestone job. At least you brought home a regular paycheck."

"You were sarcastic about my job and complained that I wasn't making enough."

"And now you make less. That wasn't what I had in mind."

"I don't want to talk about this anymore. I'm going to work."

CHAPTER 2

SEAN

Sean McCarthy had that usual feeling of relief and anxiousness while landing at the airport. As he lifted from his seat, he reached up to open the overhead bin, pulling out his carry-on bag from the jammed space. He was happy for the end of his flight from DC to Fort Lauderdale after a two-hour delay at O'Hare and then squeezed into a coach seat between two large passengers. The overbooked flight couldn't honor his business class reservation. The gentleman in the window seat wanted to chat. Sean wasn't in the mood, so the big guy chatted across him with the lady in the aisle seat. Sean wanted to ask them to shut up, but instead, he just put his seat back the short distance it would move.

Sean's attitude improved as he felt the Florida sunshine while walking at a swift pace from the terminal exit door. Looking at his watch, he was pleased with his good Uber timing. He tossed his suitcase in the back seat of the SUV, and looking up, he immediately recognized the driver by name. Sean was good at names. He could address, by name, most key staff members at all twenty-seven of his restaurants in South Florida.

"Good timing, Roberto. Take me to my office on Hillsboro. And if you can, wait ten minutes, then you can take me home."

Roberto smiled. "Sure enough. Your home is in Royal Palm, right?"

"You got it."

Sean pulled his phone out of his back pocket and dialed.

"McCarthy residence." Sean recognized the voice of his sixteen-year-old neighbor, Lisa.

"Hi, Lisa. Can I speak to Beth?"

"She's away at a meeting. I was just putting the kids to bed."

"Okay, I'll be there in ten minutes."

Fifteen minutes later, after a quick stop at Sean's office, the Uber driver pulled into the driveway of the McCarthy home, located on the Royal Palm Yacht and Country Club golf course in the Royal Palm subdivision. It was one of South Florida's elite gated communities, with seven hundred multi-multimillion-dollar homes. The McCarthy's had built their 5,900-square-foot, three-car garage home seven years ago, just before the birth of their first child, Ricky.

Sean entered through the front door, put his briefcase in his office, and moved to the bedrooms of seven-year-old Ricky and five-year-old Lucy.

Lucy, a prolific talker, lifted her hands and started toward Sean. "Mommy's mad at you, Daddy. She says you work too much. I was late for school this morning, and we had a squirrel on the porch."

"We missed you, Daddy." Ricky jumped ahead of Lucy, rushing to hug Sean. After lots of hugs and a couple of stories, Sean tucked them in, paid and excused Lisa, and then settled down to his favorite tilt-back chair to tune into Fox News while enjoying a cold beer. Just as he was about to doze off, he heard the garage door open.

"Did you pay Lisa?" A grim expression accompanied Beth's first words as she entered the living room, briefcase in hand.

"I did—and I tucked in Ricky and Lucy. Lucy says you don't like my work schedule."

"I don't."

"And I don't like yours. You're a sociology professor. Why are you getting home at nine?"

"I had a TEA Association meeting. That's 'Teacher's Education Association,' in case you forgot."

"I know who they are. We've talked about this before. Many of the members are socialist advocates. And your sister was on Facebook, posting about boycotting fast-food restaurants. We have five fast-food restaurants. They pay for this house and helped her pay for her daughter's education. That's absurd. Maybe she should pay us back."

"Let's not start this again," Beth said. "And can we watch something else? That Hannity guy gives me the creeps."

"We're not watching CNBC. I'd think you got enough left-wing socialism at your meeting."

"It's not socialism. It's progressive. And I'd appreciate it if you were a little more understanding about what I do—and the things

I stand for. Where my friends and I work, we see all the poverty, prejudice, and unfairness to the poor and even the middle class. And we care about it. We see how skin color impacts opportunity and how people are mistreated."

"What specifically is it you want me to understand?"

"That we just want workers to earn a living wage and have decent health care." She raised her voice before Sean could respond. "Another thing, can you just avoid talking politics when we're with my friends? Last Saturday at the Bronsons' cocktail party, you spent the whole night arguing, and you even called Reeves an off-the-wall left-wing liberal. The host!"

"Not true. He asked me out of the blue about what I thought about an open border, and I said opposition comes from off-the-wall, left-wing liberals. I had no way of knowing he was one of them."

"You should have assumed he was progressive and been less offensive. I'm sure he sees you as an off-the-wall right-winger. And at this point, all my friends do."

"Can we talk about this in a more civil way? Without insults?"

"I'm just giving you some obvious observations and facts."

"Let me give you some facts," Sean said. "The restaurant industry is the largest employer of students. It's a learning experience that young kids need. What's better for a kid: blocking traffic while carrying some protest sign or working in a restaurant, learning responsibility, and earning money? Your friends want to open borders. As I see it, and it's obvious when you consider the consequences, an open border is an absurd idea. Millions of poor, half-starving people living in Mexico and South America want to come here. I can sympathize, but we can't provide for all those people, millions of them, especially when we already have homeless right here."

"I know we can't take in millions. The numbers aren't that big," Beth shot back. "If the numbers start to get out of hand, we can always have a quota. This country was created for immigrants. Our ancestors were immigrants. Today, we need some policies in the government that make for a more even distribution of wealth."

"You think maybe we should turn this six thousand-square-foot home with a three-car garage into space for some poor homeless?"

"Now you're getting sarcastic."

"What about drugs and crime?" Sean asked. "Drugs and human trafficking are coming across the border, killing citizens, and that ends up costing our government hundreds of millions. At the same time, our country's big cities have thousands of homeless sleeping in the streets."

"The answer is in immigration reform, though, not building immoral concrete walls."

"This conversation isn't making any sense," Sean said. "Enjoy your MSNBC socialist talk. I'm going to bed. And by the way, I fly out Sunday afternoon. I have an NRA board meeting in DC. I'll be back Thursday afternoon." Sean rose from his chair and turned toward his office, a converted first-floor bedroom.

"So I go to Newsome's Sunday reception by myself?"

Sean responded, walking away, "I guess so. You don't expect me to miss that opening on Monday morning of an important NRA meeting, do you?" That's the 'National Restaurant Association,' in case you forgot."

Sean closed the door firmly before Beth could respond.

CHAPTER 3

FILIBUSTER'S PUB

Several days of uncharacteristically warm January weather on much of the East Coast, including Washington, had left road surface temperatures above freezing. The snow melted into slush. Then a rapid drop in air temperatures, overwhelmed by the cold air above, turned the slush mixture to ice. The streets were not drivable, but this awareness was delayed for the ever-bustling activity on the streets of major cities on the East Coast. As darkness set in, forecasts were either missed or disregarded. Subways were jammed with the pushing of anxious throngs. Hotels were suddenly overbooked. The DC fire department realized its trucks couldn't move. The weather bureau announced a near-record twenty-five inches of snowfall. Drivers were stranded on the George Washington Parkway.

Rachel Patterson found refuge at a familiar bar, Filibusters. She saw the storm coming too late to find a ride to her hotel room at the Marriott. Comfortably seated on a bar stool, reality had finally set in. As her eyes surveyed the bar and surrounding booths, mostly empty, she realized it was going to be a long evening. She didn't realize, however, what the evening's experience had in store for her.

Located on Massachusetts Avenue, the dimly lit Filibusters was within walking distance of the White House. Its walls were lined with big-hitting politicians' caricatures, including the unlikely pairings of Tip O'Neill with Ronald Reagan, JFK with Barry Goldwater, Lyndon Johnson with Richard Nixon, and Jimmy Carter with George Bush. This popular lower-level speakeasy was known among Washington insiders as an ideal spot for private meetings.

Outside the bar, also taking relief from the storm, Sean McCarthy moved cautiously down the slippery concrete steps to the entrance, glancing at the familiar sign on the door.

Welcome to Filibuster's Pub
Have a Casual Caucus

Pausing a few steps inside the door, Sean lifted his iPhone from his trench coat pocket and called DC Taxi Service one more time. *Wishful thinking.* No answer. And he had already tried for an Uber several times.

It's obviously the weather, Sean thought. *Might as well wait it out with a couple gin and tonics.*

Sean's demeanor was noticeably impressive. His dark brown hair was thick and lustrous. A strong face defined his features as molded from granite, and his dark brown eyes sloped down into a serious expression. Wearing a dark blue suit and a classic silver and blue tie, Sean walked with classy, upright confidence, radiating the appearance of unassuming class.

Making his way to the bar, Sean couldn't help but notice Rachel, sitting alone on a barstool. She wasn't classically beautiful. With no flowing, golden hair or ivory skin, no piercing eyes of green, she wasn't the sleek, catwalk model type—but she was stunning. Something radiated from within that rendered her irresistible to both genders. Men desired her, and women courted her friendship.

Rachel wasn't looking for conversation, only an escape from the weather where she could review her day's notes and sip on a gin and tonic. Appearing not to notice Sean, though, required a little self-control. She glanced in his direction, trying not to be impressed, and then quickly turned her head back to look at the bartender.

"Good evening, Mr. McCarthy," the bartender said, as Sean slid into a bar stool two seats from Rachel.

"Jackson, you responsible for this weather?"

"No way. This is Minnesota weather," Jackson said as he mixed Sean's regular gin and tonic. At six foot one, Jackson conveyed a friendly but direct presence. He wore dark-rimmed eyeglasses, and his curly dark hair was streaked with gray as if giving away his sixty-five years of age that would otherwise be undetectable. He still moved swiftly and displayed a brilliant smile.

"Why Minnesota?" Sean asked.

"This weather always makes me think about Minnesota. I've never actually been there and wouldn't want to go to that part of the country this time of year, but they tell me this is common in

Minnesota. Congressmen and women and their staffs like to talk about it. I've talked to all of them here, going back to Humphrey, McCarthy, and Mondale."

"Humphrey? Come on, Jackson. You're not that old." Sean turned his head to include Rachel in the conversation. "Jackson is a celebrity bartender in this town; he knows more about what's going on in this city than Congress does. And he's also the best storyteller in DC. Probably has a lot of stories that will just stay inside this bar."

Rachel looked from Sean to her drink and smiled.

"Now, Mr. McCarthy," Jackson said, "I'm not any kind of celebrity, just a happy, humble bartender who loves his job. Of course, with as long as I've been here, I do have some spicy stories. Many of which I would never repeat."

Sean grinned. "Since you're talking about politicians from the sixties, how about you tell us a story from those days."

"Sure, I always got a little story to tell." Jackson tilted his head toward Rachel. "If the lady doesn't mind. The one I'm thinking of could be considered a little inappropriate for a proper lady."

"Go for it. I'm a big girl," Rachel said, smiling.

Jackson leaned his forearms against the surface of the bar, settling in for his favorite part of the job. "You need to be able to remember the era to really appreciate this," he said.

☆   ☆   ☆

"It was a hot Saturday evening in the summer of 1961, and Billy had a date with Peggy Sue. He arrived at her house and rang the bell."

"Oh, come on in!" Peggy Sue's mother said as she welcomed Billy. "Have a seat in the living room. Would you like something to drink? Lemonade? Iced tea?"

"Iced tea, please," Billy said.

The mother brought the iced tea. "So, what are you and Peggy planning to do tonight?"

"Oh, probably catch a movie, and then maybe grab a bite to eat at the malt shop, maybe take a walk on the beach ..."

"Peggy likes to screw, you know," the mom informed him.

"Uh ... really?" Billy replied, with raised eyebrows.

"Oh, yes!" the mother continued. "When she goes out with her friends, that's all they do!"

"Is that so?" asked Billy inquisitively.

"Yes," said the mother. "As a matter of fact, she'd screw all night if we let her!"

"Well, thanks for the tip," Billy said as he began thinking about alternate plans for the evening.

A moment later, Peggy Sue came down the stairs looking pretty as a picture, wearing a pink blouse and full circle skirt, and with her hair tied back in a bouncy ponytail. She greeted Billy.

"Have fun, kids!" the mother said as they left.

Half an hour later, a completely disheveled Peggy Sue burst into the house and slammed the front door.

"The Twist, Mom!" she yelled at her mother. "How many times do I have to tell you? The damned dance is called the Twist!"

☆　　☆　　☆

"That's funny, Jackson." Sean glanced at Rachel as she joined in the laughter. "Pour me another gin and tonic. What's your best gin?"

"Just got in some Gentleman's Cut—a hundred dollars a bottle."

"Come on now, Jackson. You're pulling my chain."

Jackson laughed. "How about Beefeaters?"

"That will do."

"The lady here seems to like it. Looks like she's ready for another."

Sean decided it was time for an introduction. "I'm Sean, came in on United from Fort Lauderdale this afternoon. And you?"

"Probably on the same flight," she replied. "Eleven-seventy-nine?"

"Yup. Is Fort Lauderdale your home?"

"No, I live in Coral Springs. And you?"

"Royal Palm in Boca."

"Nice area," Rachel said, obviously impressed. "Beautiful homes, and I hear a real nice golf course." She motioned to Jackson. "Guess I will need one more."

"Might as well. Cabs and Uber aren't moving," Sean offered.

"I know. I had Uber on the way an hour ago. I guess he went back home."

"How long you lived in Florida?" Sean asked.

"Twelve years now. Six years after my six years while a resident at Yale."

"Your major?"

"Social science. And you?"

"Hospitality management at Michigan State."

"Huh, I'm an events planner. We work with a lot of hospitality management people. Where did your MSU degree take you?"

"Restaurant operations in South Florida. I have my own company."

"What restaurant?" Rachel asked.

"Actually, I have twenty-seven," Sean replied. "You're probably familiar with Pronto's, one of my Shenanigan's locations, some breakfast-lunch locations, five Taco Bell franchises."

"Impressive, I love the Shenanigan's on Hillsboro. What are you doing in DC?"

"NRA meeting."

Rachel sighed. "Sorry, I hate guns."

"That's NRA, as in National Restaurant Association," Sean said with a laugh.

"Oops. I misunderstood."

"No problem. Excuse me. I gotta make a trip to the boys' room."

"And excuse me," Jackson said. "I need to check on my other customers—all four of them."

Rachel finished her drink and checked for Uber. No movement.

THE FOURTH POWER

Jackson returned and first served Rachel her gin and tonic and then Sean. "Enjoy. It looks like we're going to be here a while."

Two of the tables in the back side of the bar were occupied by couples who were conversing seriously. The TV above the bar was on Fox News, and Hannity was giving his opening monologue.

Rachel looked up at the TV screen with a disgruntled look. "Excuse me, sir," she said.

"You can call me Jackson."

"Okay, Jackson. I don't wanna sound rude, but I've been here five minutes now and have tried to ignore what's coming out of that program. Could you either turn the TV down as low as possible or switch to another channel?"

"No problem. I was about to switch," Jackson replied. "I try to change every half hour between Fox and CNN. Let's face it: CNN favors the Democrats, and Fox favors the Republicans. Some make an effort not to be biased. Andrew Cuomo. He makes an effort to recognize Republican positions on CNN, just like Harris Faulkner recognizes Democrat positions on Fox. Some others do the same. I agree though that we see a lot of bias on both CNN and Fox."

Sean joined the conversation as he returned. "I can attest to that," he said with a smile. "Jackson's pretty much neutral."

Rachel frowned. "It's impossible to be neutral if you listen to that guy." Hannity was reiterating Trump's determination to build a wall on the Mexican border. "I doubt if Hannity even knows the meaning of the word *neutral*."

"Kind of like Cuomo on CNN coming from the opposite direction," Sean interjected.

"You can't be serious."

"Oh, I'm serious. Cuomo and Tapper are consistent with their attacks on the right, never criticizing the left."

"Come on now. That's not accurate," Rachel replied. "Cuomo and Tapper have a lot of Republican guests and are not as obnoxious as Hannity."

"The last time I watched Cuomo interview a Republican, he had his guest seated at a desk in a low-level chair, while he parked himself in a conspicuously higher chair. The objective was obvious."

"Smart move by Cuomo."

"I call it a chicken shit move."

Rachel frowned as Sean continued.

"Let me give you a good example. This past summer and fall, during the 2020 presidential election campaign, the media, especially CNN and Anchor Andrew Cuomo, came down on Trump with a story about Trump and his legal counsel, Rudy Giuliani, calling on Ukraine leader Zelensky to probe Joe Biden and Biden's son, Hunter, for Hunter's involvement in a Ukrainian financial scandal. The incident happened while Biden was vice-president. The scandal involved Biden informing Zelensky that the US would not accept a Ukraine request to guarantee a loan to Ukraine unless Zelensky fired the prosecutor who was investigating his son.

"It certainly was a question about a candidate for president that should be addressed. Biden did an interview earlier boasting that he got a Ukraine prosecutor fired, not articulating the circumstances. So which is the real newsworthy story, that the president and his personal attorney, as part of a campaign strategy, inquired about the president's potential opponent having involvement in an illegal financial matter with a foreign country, or the actual illegal behavior of Biden while he was vice-president?"

"Okay," Jackson cut in, "Reporters have a job to do: to attract an audience. So when they find a story, they put it out there. Trump's behavior was news at the time. The Biden story was history."

"But the Biden and son story was never covered at the time reports first surfaced. The Democrats get all the bullets with the media. They have all the networks, except Fox, and most of the newspapers. They just tell half the story, the half that favors the Democrats," Sean added.

"Aw, come on," Rachel said. "As Jackson just pointed out, the Biden and son story was old news. Trump's behavior was current news at that time."

"Give me a break, Rachel, fact is they only emphasized the part of the story that helped the Democrats."

Rachel flipped her hands up. "No, no, the real story is that President Trump tried to use the leverage of his office with a loan guarantee to get Ukraine's Zelensky to interfere in a US election with the manufacture of a corruption story about Trump's political opponent, Biden."

"Not exactly, you're changing words, like Committee Chair Adam Schiff," Sean replied. "At one of the hearings, Schiff sat there in his chair and quoted Trump with words Trump never used.

"Look, I will agree that was an improper move on Trump's part and he needed to be criticized for it. Being improper is one thing, but impeachment is carrying it a little too far, especially if you consider all the circumstances. Furthermore, he didn't ask him to 'manufacture' as the Democrats have said. He asked Ukraine to investigate. Big difference. What gets me is that Trump's actions became the big story for weeks, while the clearly illegal behavior of Biden was ignored. This was what Jackson referred to as the fourth power in action. Like I said Trump didn't ask Ukraine to manufacture illegal acts by Biden, he asked them to reveal the facts."

Jackson took over. "Okay, let's move on. I don't think the whole matter ever solved anything. Just more of our government spinning their wheels and not getting anything done. The way Congress is structured, as long as the Senate and the House have different majorities, they are not going to impeach a president. That is, unless a 'high crime' is committed. Trump's actions rise to the level of a misdemeanor, not a high crime."

Rachel anxiously interjected "Trump has committed multiple crimes."

"No way" Sean shot back. "It's all political crap. The founding fathers had hesitation about having impeachment in the constitution, especially Governor Morris and Charles Pinckeny, because they saw the possibility of it just being used as a political tool. They were right on. That's what is happening now"

"OK back to the media, I'm a channel switcher at home," Jackson offered. "I watch CNN more than Fox. I do think Harris Faulkner, on Fox, is good. She tends to tilt conservative, but she reports both sides of the issues without apparent bias."

Sean smiled. "CNN has outnumbered token conservatives." He

displayed a sarcastic grin. "Do you realize that Hannity continually tops Cuomo in the ratings—by a wide margin? And by the way, you can't accuse Fox of being totally biased to the right. Fox has some regular contributors, like Donna Brazile and Juan Williams—just a couple of examples of fierce Democratic party advocates—as regular contributors. Oh, and the daytime guy, Shepard Smith, attacks Trump viciously sometimes."

Jackson stepped in. "Let me ask the two of you a question. Do ya ever make a point of analyzing and comparing the Fox and CNN coverage of the same political event? It's crazy. It's like they didn't listen to the same event. You can often see that the newscasters personally like or dislike a person just by the expressions on their faces and the words they use when they talk about someone affiliated with a political party."

Rachel smiled. "The liberal audience is divided between CNBC, CBS, and CNN. That's the obvious reason for Fox having a higher rating on political news. Combine them, and Fox comes up the loser."

"Okay, I will buy that," Sean said with another arrogant grin. "It takes three liberals to match one conservative."

"How about this one?" Jackson said. "What are the four primary policy influential powers of our country?"

Rachel rolled her eyes and smiled. "This is a trick question, right? The founders created three branches of government: legislative, executive, and judicial." Rachel tapped one finger on the counter for each branch. Then, tapping her pinkie, she continued, "Let me guess, let's see … you must mean the media is the fourth."

"You got it. Our founding fathers' intent was to create the three sources you just mentioned, with the real power coming from the voters through elections. They knew that a free press would have influence through the process of reporting the news. However, the intent and expectation was that they would report facts and not distort them with personal bias. Report, not create. Over the past few decades, especially in recent years, the press has become an opinion source primarily. Where do conservatives and liberals, or Democrats and Republicans, form their opinions? Does it come from spouses, family, work, schools, or the media?"

Sean took a sip of his drink and answered, "I'd say conservatives' opinions come from their family foundation and the church. And liberals from friends and schools."

"Which means, and I agree," Rachel said, "liberals have educated opinions from schools and listening to friends who form rational opinions. Conservatives come from family and profit-motivated business."

Jackson took a rag from his back pocket and began wiping the counter, out of habit. "I think you have it on the key sources, but you haven't mentioned the media. The news stations have massive audiences. The political coverage comes mostly from Fox, CNN, and MSNBC. Fox, as the leader, reaches close to three million listeners a night, and CNN and MSNBC together are roughly another three million. And, of course you know, Fox is biased to the right, and CNN and MSNBC are biased to the left."

Sean shook his head. "The media gain in power has been an eventual process."

"They have always had a powerful influence," Rachel said.

"I understand that. My point though is that in recent years, they have become more powerful than they were in the past. We have not only the press and TV, but we also have smartphones, computers, wristwatches. There are so many ways for the media to influence, and they do."

Rachel and Jackson both nodded their heads.

"Remember the Supreme Court hearing for Kavanaugh?" Sean continued. "When he was going through his nomination hearing for the Supreme Court, those accusations emerged about his behavior in high school, and that became the number one national news story for weeks. Then, when absolutely no evidence or corroboration was discovered, and one of the accusers actually admitted she fabricated her story, the media was very quiet."

Rachel perked up. "Do you know how many women are afraid to come forward—and how many are pressured to recant when they do?"

"But that doesn't change the fact that the media wanted the story to continue no matter what," Sean said. "And another one, the big one: the falsely created story and special prosecutor investigation of Trump collusion with Russia in the 2016 election. It was a total hoax by a group of partisan Democrats who were cheered on by most Democrats across the nation. Two years, hundreds of media feature headline stories, more than thirty million dollars, and a whole lot of reputations-scared prosecutors had to give complete exhortation. I realize Trump irritates Democrats by boasting on Twitter and his poor use of the English language, but that whole investigation process was absurd. What I think was really bad was the Democrats' behavior in the whole investigation's final report process. They wanted to find Trump was colluding with Russia and were disappointed by the report. Why would anyone want to see and find that our president was colluding with a foreign country, especially Russia? No one should want that to be true. That's how partisan our politics have become. It's downright mean-spirited. The media should have a responsibility to cover the news in America without bias. The problem is that 90 percent of the media is left biased, and that affects their coverage of the news."

Through Jackson's smile came a little smirk. "I feel the need to point out that Republicans wanted Clinton impeached as well. They wanted him to be found guilty. That's just politics today."

"Appointing a special prosecutor was meaningful and productive," Rachel said. "More than thirty people and quite a few companies were indicted. Do you want to tell me that Trump, knowing the wheeler-dealer, win-at-all-cost person he is, that his people, including his son, didn't correspond and even meet with the Russians, that you don't think he would do anything he could do to hurt Hillary Clinton's campaign."

"I've heard so much contradiction I can't be sure of anything," Sean replied. "But this I do know: all the so-called spying went on while the Obama presidency was still in place, and this includes the attorney general and the FBI. It's all crazy. Earlier in 2018, I heard James Comey, the director of the FBI under Obama, say they weren't spying, just doing surveillance with wiretaps. That's absurd. If wiretapping is not spying, I don't know what is."

Jackson jumped in before Rachel could make further comment. "Let me just make a point. I know what I am about to say is not of the generally accepted opinion, but I think the vast majority of legislators have good intentions." Jackson paused for a restart. "I have a full bookshelf about the American presidency, all by renowned historical authors ... and, I might add, I have read all of them. I have studied all past presidents. Donald Trump is certainly the most unusual president this country has ever had. He is very unique in many ways. He has the least amount of government experience and is hated by the opposing political party with more passion than any other past president. He totally lacks professionalism in his communication and messaging to Americans, and he shoots himself in the foot with all his tweeting, which makes everything he wants to accomplish more difficult than it should be. Instead of trying to work with his opposition, he attacks them for not agreeing with him. But irrespective of all the problems he has created for himself, he is intelligent, and a hardworking person, and man of action doing many things that past presidents failed to do."

"I think you are being a little tough on him," Sean said, somewhat defensively.

"Not by my standards, Rachel said. "So, Jackson, you're familiar with all the presidents?"

He nodded. "Through books."

"Okay, who was president in the spring of 1845?"

"John Tyler. He took over as president for William Harrison, who died of pneumonia one month after being sworn in."

"Very good."

"That was quick."

"Since we are on presidents, let me hit you two with a couple of presidential trivia questions."

"Gonna make me pay for asking you that question I asked you?"

"No, this is an easy one. Which president gave the longest speech at his inauguration? It was a dry, cold day, and consequently, he fell ill and died after only thirty-three days as president."

"While you are thinking about that, who was called a party pooper when he banned booze, card playing, and dancing from the White House."

Rachel answered, "The long speech was by William Henry Harrison. He died before he hardly got started as president."

"I knew that, but I got the second one. It was James Polk," Sean responded.

"Okay, one each. You guys are quick. Here's one more. Which president was known for skinny-dipping in the Potomac River every morning. A reporter took advantage of this information and sat on his clothes until he would grant her an interview."

There was a long pause.

"Okay, I'll let you think about that one for a few minutes."

"And by the way, the skinny-dipping president was John Quincy Adams. I'm one up." She gave Sean a friendly poke in the shoulder.

"How about some more, Jackson?"

"Later, let's finish with the media."

"I agree that it's important. They certainly have power. But should we define them as the fourth power from the perspective that the founding fathers perceived power? What bothers me is that the founders had expected the media to be a check on the government, not to try to determine elections, which they certainly do. They need to be independent, give us the facts, and let us decide how those facts influence our thinking. Instead, they have become partial, one way or another, and they skew the way the information they present is perceived. We all know Fox supports Republicans and CNN supports Democrats. The three network outlets are less obvious, but they clearly lean to the left. The irony of all this, though, is that the media can be used. Trump used the media masterfully in his presidential campaign. His campaign spent zero dollars on the media, while super PACs spent thirty-seven million on Hillary—and Clinton's campaign spent another fifty-two million on their own campaign ads. That's eighty-seven million on Clinton media—and zero spent by Trump. We all know how that turned out.

"In reality, most candidates welcome any opportunity for media coverage, for office at any level, under just about any circumstances," Jackson continued. "As long as the candidate has a chance to present themselves positively. The media gets ratings by presenting the unusual, the surprises, good or bad. Trump is unusual, in my opinion, in a creepy, unsophisticated way: simple sentences, repetitious, and inaccurate. Exposure is exposure, good or bad. The media negatively presented Trump, but they did it so much that everyone on the planet recognized him. The result of that was that enough voters liked him enough to get him elected. It didn't hurt that Hillary ran a lousy campaign."

"I hear ya, Jackson," Sean said. "But don't you think that was an exception?"

"Yup, almost everything about Trump is an exception."

"Okay, we can all agree he's an exception," Rachel said. "The difference is I see it mostly as bad exceptions."

"Ya know," Jackson said, absentmindedly folding his arms across his chest, "if you say something enough times to the whole world, it's gonna sink in as true to some people. Trump called the media 'fake news' so many times that he created this tendency for people to question what they hear in the news. Or maybe they believe what they wanna hear and call it fake news if they don't like it. It got so the people Hillary called deplorable reveled with joy at everything Trump said and cussed at any negative comments. Again, don't get me wrong, Trump is not my idea of, by any means, the person I care to see in the Oval Office. I can't agree with the far right—nor can I agree with far left."

Rachel frowned softly.

"I know, I know, I don't sound like the stereotypical black voter," Jackson said. "Close to 90 percent of black people are Democrats. I'm actually an independent, and I realize that puts me out of mainstream black America, but how we are ever going to make any political progress if we all stick to what we think we're supposed to believe? I realize that, historically, black people have been mistreated horribly in this country. I also realize that we are still not getting a fair shake, but how are we gonna fix that? Not by everyone stubbornly sticking 100 percent with a political belief just because their friends tell them they should. During his administration, President Obama accepted the proposal of three Republicans to cut his proposed stimulus package by a hundred billion because that's what was needed to get some results. He conceded to get the Dodd-Frank Wall Street Reform Act passed. One of our greatest American leaders, Dr. Martin Luther King, practiced compromise when he advocated nonviolence in protesting.

"Black Americans need to keep working for equality, while at the same time, we work to pave the way for equal opportunities and elect progressive leaders. I tell my progressive friends, don't just block me out because I don't sound like a total progressive. Sometimes a compromise can equate to progress. I've been chatting with legislators for years. I think most of them want to do the right thing. The problem is they are influenced by campaign funding from special interest groups, even though the funding is necessary. Organizations like the NRA on the Republican side and the unions on the Democratic side have a powerful influence on the elections. They can eliminate a primary candidate from becoming a nominee if the candidate doesn't support their organization. For instance, in practice, supporting the NRA's positions is a prerequisite for becoming a Republican. The same is true with the Democrats and the unions. Did you ever hear of a Republican win an election who opposed the NRA—or a Democrat win who opposed unions? That is just the way it is, and radio, newspapers, the internet, and social media all add fuel to the fire. For the most part, Fox News and most high-audience radio stations support the conservative Republicans. CNN, the majority of social media, and the other TV networks mostly support the liberal advocates, but these media sources just end up promoting a hostile environment between the two parties. It's nothing new, but media exposure to the public has grown leaps and bounds with the internet and cell phones. Bottom line, despite their good intentions, when they're first elected, once in office, our legislators become a part of the problem." Jackson looked to his right across the bar. "Excuse me. I think that table over there needs a drink. I'll be back to finish that thought."

Sean looked at Rachel. "He's got some valid points. What concerns me is where this country will be for the next two generations. What's in store for our sons and daughters and nieces and nephews—and our grandkids? Are we going into socialism? We have presidential candidates with large followings, like Bernie Sanders and a couple of dozen other candidates, who have agendas ranging from liberal to socialist. It sounds appealing to a lot of people to have a free college education, free health care, and more welfare programs. The problem is this: Who's going to pay for it? Higher taxes on the wealthy sounds like an easy answer, but when you increase taxes on those who create jobs, you take away the incentive for business owners to expand and create those jobs. Socialism has been a failed form of governing a nation, when you look at history: the Soviet Union, Cuba, the Middle East, Korea, Venezuela, and North Korea. The intent always looks good, lots of goodies through wealth redistribution, but the fact is that the money runs out because business stops growing. I think it was Churchill who said something like, 'Socialism is a philosophy of failure, the creed of ignorance, and the gospel of envy. Its inherent virtue is the equal sharing of misery.' We have a twenty-nine-year-old first-term congresswoman, Alexandria Cortez, or AOC, who has spiraled into the limelight big with promoting the Green New Deal, a totally unrealistic socialist plan. President Trump called it like a high school paper, quite accurately. He said something like, 'It would be great for the so-called carbon footprint to permanently eliminate all planes, cars, cows, oil, gas and the military—even if no other country would do the same.'

Brilliant! A quick question to give you a chance catch up, Rachel. Who was supposed to be in Lincoln's theater box on the night of his assassination—but changed plans at the last minute?"

"Ulysses Grant," Rachel snapped.

"You got it. Back to even."

"Okay. Let's get back to today's politics."

"Our county, formed approximately 230 years ago has an Executive branch led by the people's elected President, 535 elected Congressmen and women, 435 in the House of Representatives and 100 Senators. In addition to Congress we have a judicial branch, the Supreme Court to interpret the laws. This system of government has struggled many times over the years, but they have always survived.

I think, and I have spent a lifetime reading about and following American history. I think we are in unprecedented times,

Rachel cut in "Yes, because in 2016 we elected the most corrupt, dishonest, foul spoken President in the history of our country.

"Whoa, whoa, that's the far left socialist seeking view that were so shocked and angry at the 2016 results that they committed to do whatever it would take, irrespective of reason and the laws of our country to remove the President from office.

What are you talking about? Where have you been the last two years. Trump has colluded with foreign countries, committed treason and generally been an embarrassment to our country.

I would say what's embarrassing to our country and a disservice to our people is the Democrats witch hunt of our President. First it was Russia, Russia, Russia and then Ukraine, Ukraine, Ukraine. When the Russia allegations failed after two years of a Special Prosecutor digging, subpoenas and hearings they went after Trump for inquiring about the dishonest behavior of Democrat Joe Biden.

OK, I think your both stretching the issue. It's not totally resolved yet. History will record it someday. We have another election coming; let's talk about the specific issues.

CHAPTER 5

GETTING POLITICAL

Rachel jumped in first. "Let me reveal my political identity. I am not advocating a socialist government. Progressives advocate democracy. We just want to eliminate the huge inequality in income. We need more government control to protect the consumers from the greedy and unfair practices of the big corporations. Our America, the land of the free, should be a nation of equal opportunity—and it's not. Why do the top 1 percent own two-thirds of the wealth? How does it make sense to have billionaires and homeless people living in the same city? Education and health care should be free and managed by the government."

Sean replied, "I have some answers for you, but we need to talk about that when Jackson returns. By the way," he said, leaning in, "I've chatted with him many times. He is one brilliant guy, like a walking encyclopedia."

"Why is he just a bartender? He certainly has a better vocabulary than Donald Trump."

Sean agreed. "Trump's vocabulary is very unpresidential."

"Not even good at a junior high level."

Jackson came back and said, "I find the guy to be a paradox. I wholeheartedly agree with Rachel that his vocabulary is what you might expect from a construction worker or a teenager at a sports event: very unsophisticated. He is clearly a narcissist, believing his own misrepresentation of the facts. Seems to have to have praise. If he doesn't get it from others, he praises himself. On the other hand, he has, I have to admit, done some pretty impressive things."

"I don't recall what he has done that's impressive," Rachel replied. "I would never have thought someone could be elected president who could say all the dumb things he says." She looked at her cell phone. "Allow me to read you these: 'I think I am actually humble. I think I'm much more humble than you would under-stand.' That was on a *60 Minutes* interview on July 17, 2016. I have some on my iPhone. 'The beauty of me is that I'm very rich.' 'I will be the greatest jobs president that God ever created.' That was announcing his campaign for president. 'All of the women on *The Apprentice* flirted with me—consciously or unconsciously. That's to be expected.' 'Let me tell you, I'm a really smart guy.' 'Sorry losers and haters, but my IQ is one of the highest—and you all know it! Please don't feel so stupid or insecure. It's not your fault.' Then, about his body, he says, 'My fingers are long and beautiful, as, it has been well documented, are various other parts of my body.' Then during the presidential debate, he took precious time to counter a joke about him that his rival Marco Rubio had said: 'He referred to my hands, if they're small, something else must be small. I guarantee you there's no problem. I guarantee it.' At a rally in Toledo: 'We should just can-cel the election and just give it to Trump.' When asked whether he'd accept the election outcome, he said, 'I will tell you at the time. I'll keep you in suspense, Okay? I've had a beautiful, I've had a flawless campaign. You'll be writing books about this campaign.' And then, of course, the Russia thing."

Sean shook his head. "Rachel, you don't really believe that, do you? What a hoax that was. There's more evidence that the Sasquatch is real or Santa Claus is real than there was for Trump colluding with Russia. They spent two years and cost taxpayers more than thirty million and never found any serious violations. Even though some aspects are still being contested, and the Democrats are still digging!"

"I realize they didn't get impeachable offenses—just a lot of inappropriate contact between Trump's people and the Russians."

Jackson smiled as he moved away to check on his customers, commenting as he walked away. "I agree with Rachel when it comes to the appropriate use of language. Trump's not the sharpest knife in the drawer when it comes to vocabulary. In fact, it's pretty bad."

Sean looked back at Rachel. "I will never defend Trump's lan-guage. It's often embarrassing, but I just feel we have to give credit where credit is due, and he has done some good things. I wanna go back to your comment where you said 'just a bartender.' Jobs are as important as you make them. Jackson loves his job and is great at it. He's a very smart guy. From what he has told me, school was easy for him, but he wasn't serious about education, so he didn't get a scholarship for college. He had jobs and missed school a lot, so he chose a job he thought he would like and become the best at it, and he has achieved it. He knows he could find a higher-level job if he wanted to. He sees his job as important, and it is. More young men should approach life the way he does."

"You say he is smart, brilliant. How did he get so smart without going to college?"

"The same way guys like Ben Franklin and Abraham Lincoln did: self-education, reading lots of books, and an aptitude for absorbing knowledge."

"He appears to be a smart guy. Comparing him to Franklin and Lincoln is a pretty big leap."

"I'm just saying Jackson is a very intelligent guy and capable of doing anything he wanted in life. He just chose to be where he is happy." Sean decided to change the subject. Looking directly at Rachel, he asked, "Do you have a family?"

"Husband and twin five-year-olds."

"If you don't mind my asking, what do you do and what does your husband do?"

"He's in real estate sales. As I said, I am events planner."

"Real estate sales are dependent on a strong economy," Sean replied. "We can't raise taxes, increase wage rates, provide free health care and free education, and expect a growing economy. Same with events. It takes a strong economy for companies to be able to afford events."

"You're assuming we can't have a growing economy with a progressive economy. But the difference is that a progressive economy includes all the people, not just the rich," Rachel said. "What about your family?"

"I have a wife who is a social worker, and I also have two kids. As you might guess, my wife would be on your side."

"Smart lady."

"Yes, she's smart and a good mom. She also enjoys the benefits of the successful business I have built, but she doesn't understand why I have to travel and work long hours. It comes with success. She wants me home, helping with the kids more often while she works and becomes active in socialist organizations. We are in two different worlds; she watches CNBC and reads liberal publications, and I watch Fox, belong to the other NRA, and read conservative publications."

Jackson returned and said, "Where was I? Oh, yes. Well, I was talking about how our presidents and how legislators are so engaged in contentious accusations and controversy that they can't seem to get anything done. Day in and day out, all we hear about is lawsuits, special prosecutors, investigations, and hearings on accusations of bad behavior. Often it involves digging up something as far back as high school. Ya know, as I said, I really think they wanna do what's right. With President Trump, for example, certainly, his style of shooting from the hip, being reckless with facts, and his excessive and irritating self-promoting has helped fuel this hostile environment. I couldn't and have not voted for him, but I believe he wants to do what he sees as best for America. He works a tremendously long schedule and has made some excellent decisions, like creating a robust economy and forcing NATO nations to pay their fair share for defense.

Rachel said, "Republicans like to ignore the fact that Obama got us out of the 2008 recession and created a robust economy to build on."

"Sorry, that's not an accurate assessment. The economy certainly was not robust in 2016. I don't know who the Democrats have to offer now who's gonna be an improvement over Trump," Sean said. "They have all gone to the wild wild left. The one who has boosted herself into the limelight is Alexandria O. Cortez, better known as AOC. She is only twenty-nine—not old enough to run for president—but she gets more media attention than all the other Democrats. The others have to be scratching their heads and wondering where she came from. At some event, I can't recall where, she suggested Reagan and FDR were racists and said capitalism is a practice of racism and greed for gain. She doesn't think the economy is doing well and says unemployment is low because everyone has two jobs.

"On a PBS interview, she said our capitalism is hyper and like the Wild West, no-holds-barred, with profit at any cost. She insinuated that capitalism wouldn't last. She also referred to the situation in Palestine as an 'occupation' by Israel, then added that she favored a two-state solution. The essence of her PBS interview was an insult to Israel and favored Palestine. Of course, her remarks got a lot of media attention. Calls came out for Congress to take some type of action against her. The Democratic Party procrastinated and waffled and finally approved a resolution that … Let me read it."

Sean looked at his cell phone.

"'It encourages all public officials to confront the reality of anti-Semitism, Islamophobia, racism, and other forms of bigotry, as well as historical struggles against them, to ensure that the United States will live up to the transcendent principles of tolerance, religious freedom.' It was an obvious move by the Democrats to avoid criticizing AOC directly. What do you think would have happened if a Republican had said something prejudicial against a minority race? To me, AOC is an off-the-wall socialist. I'm amused by her comment that automation is good because we will have more time to do fun things. Art, reading, exploring? I guess she thinks we can all stop working and live off government freebies."

Rachel jumped in and said, "You're distorting the meaning of what she said. She is a progressive, and she wants more equality and elimination of prejudice against minorities."

"I don't think she has been very supportive of Israel, whose people have suffered massive persecution."

"As I said, I don't view Trump as an appropriate president. He scares me with his snap decisions, misquotes, and distortions of the facts. I find it scary having him in control of decisions that could bring about World War III. Having said all that, though, I have to admit he seems to be trying. He's all in, totally dedicated to what he believes is right. Few men or women in their seventies can work as long and or as hard as he does. I'm not saying I agree with him or would forecast that all of what he is doing is or will be successful. I just don't see him as the evil monster that should be impeached. Impeachment proceedings are such a waste of time and energy unless indisputable crimes are involved. The voters should have the president they elected in office for the term he was elected for. Our election process with year in and year out campaign battles have become so bitter that our government has become ineffective. We need to make an overhaul of the system or devise a new one. Our two-party system isn't working. I'm not left wing. I'm not right wing, Republican or Democrat. I evaluate issues and the person, and I always end up voting for some I don't totally agree with. Most people decide if they are Republican or Democrat and vote for whoever that party's candidate is. I vote for the candidate who I feel is an advocate for the most issues I support.

"I supported Bill Clinton, and then he disgraced the Oval Office and lied about it. Not only did he have Monica crawl under his desk, but they also discovered other affairs he had before being elected. Too much time and money was spent on impeachment proceedings that didn't accomplish anything. As I see it, Clinton led the country to a strong economy. He compromised with Newt Gingrich to pass beneficial legislation. He wasn't my favorite. My favorite was Barack Obama. Yet, as his presidency progressed, I thought he had some weak points. He certainly had the media on his side. I was amazed and not pleased when he sent one hundred and fifty billion in American dollars, boxed in cash, to Iran, one of our most dangerous enemies. Yes, he got a nuclear agreement for it, but the value of that agreement is very questionable. That situation also helps me understand why the Trump administration and most Republicans were astounded when the same Democrats, who support that one hundred and fifty billion shipment to Iran, opposed Trump's request for five billion for border wall construction. I want to consider the facts. When a president is elected by the people, he or she should be allowed to enact most of their agenda—subject to issues requiring congressional approval, of course."

Jackson looked across the bar and saw a hand waving from a table. "Excuse me for a moment," he said with a nod.

Rachel, seeing an opening in the conversation, turned to Sean. "I get some of what Jackson is saying, but Trump has been an embarrassment to our country nationally and internationally. He has the Republican agenda for the wealthy on steroids. He said he was qualified for the presidency because he was a successful businessman. The media has exposed the real Trump; he inherited a million or more from his father, which was a lot of money fifty or more years ago. He has avoided taxes, and when one of his corporations failed, he just filed bankruptcy and moved on to another deal. That's not management skills—just greed and dishonesty."

Sean grinned. "Wow. It sounds like you really like the guy. Let me just say ... I realize he gets a little wild with his tweeting. I know he had a fast-moving lifestyle, and I wish he wouldn't say some of the things he says. Some bad behavior just seems to come with the presidents we elect; how about the Clintons and Nixon? What we should look at is results. He made massive cuts in wasteful regulations. Look at our economy, the progress with fair trade, getting other NATO nations to pay their fair share, more manufacturing jobs, and minority employment is the best it has been in decades. Google the list of his accomplishments; it's impressive. He's a man of action, not all good, but certainly a lot of beneficial results. An especially good example is moving the American embassy to Jerusalem. Presidents in the past fifteen to twenty years campaigned on moving that embassy to Jerusalem and then didn't do anything about it when they came to the White House. Trump promised it, and he did it. He has probably worked harder on delivering his campaign promises than any past president."

"Well, I guess we are far apart in our opinion of that guy. What you refer to as his accomplishments were mostly for the wealthy. You say he cut regulations. Regulations build economic stability. He is beholden to the NRA. We need more gun control, not less. Trickle-down economics don't trickle down. We need to fix our racist justice system, invest more in public education and twenty-first-century energy, spend more on environmental protection, provide more funding for domestic violence victims, enact trade agreements that protect workers, increase the minimum wage, ban assault weapons, and go to universal, single-payer health care. You Republicans like to praise Reagan's military spending. The more we spend on the military, the less we have for textbooks. Trump calling Elizabeth Warren 'Pocahontas' was a racial slur. The wealthy need to pay higher taxes. We need higher minimum wages. I can give you more. Do you want more?"

"No, that's okay. I get the picture." Sean shook his head. "No, no, I don't mean *the* picture. I mean *your* picture. The Democrats are all about more giving and raising taxes on business at the expense of job creation. Problem is, when you increase taxes on business developers, they can't create jobs. The eventual result is a recession."

"Not true. When you benefit the middle class, they spend more, which stimulates the economy and creates more jobs."

Jackson said, "I will be right back." He proceeded to check his other two customers.

As Jackson walked away, Sean nodded toward him and looked at Rachel. "Interesting guy."

"Yes, he seems very knowledgeable—and professional."

"He is an amazing guy. His views on the issues are from the heart, you'll see. Not a liberal or a Republican. His loyalty is to the issues that he feels are best for this country."

Rachel scrunched up her face, unconvinced. "I think he leans conservative."

"And I see him leaning liberal. He votes for Democrats."

"I would think a bartender would want to avoid talking politics or expressing his opinion on issues that might offend a party loyalist, and that's almost everyone in Washington. They are totally behind whatever position the party they have chosen is rallying for."

Sean picked up his empty glass in a salute to Jackson and held onto it while he talked enthusiastically about his friend. "Jackson has the unique talent of analyzing and talking about the issues that divide the country, and without alienating either liberals or conservatives, he comes up with what you might call compromises. As he says, he likes to create solutions so that both sides gain something. Not all they would like to have, but enough so that both sides can accept that they have made progress. Not without measured reluctance, but that's par for the course." He then quickly changed the subject. "Have you been in here before?"

"I've been here a few times," Rachel said, looking around. "A couple of times by myself to just wind down before I go back to my room. Once for a meeting, when we sat in a booth to review an agenda. I think that booth over there," she said, pointing. "I've never actually met Jackson until tonight. I take it you come here often." She laughed a little at the innuendo of the last line.

Sean smiled, pretending not to notice the unintended innuendo, so as not to make Rachel uncomfortable. "It's convenient for a break on an open night. And I enjoy chatting with Jackson."

Jackson returned, and Rachel wondered if he'd been having similar conversations with the other two customers.

Sean turned in his stool to face the counter. "Jackson, after all these years, and all that you've heard and seen, how do you see the effectiveness of Washington today? What kind of path are we on now compared to past years?"

"You really want to know?"

"Go for it," Rachel said.

Sean agreed. "Let's hear it."

"I have a lot of ideas," Jackson started, "not that they will ever be used. The best idea is how to solve deadlocks on legislation. I would give the proposed legislation to three Democrats and three Republicans, lock them in a room and not let them out until they came to an agreement."

Sean laughed.

Rachel smiled. "I doubt any legislator would agree to take on that challenge."

"Okay, that's enough from me. I'm more interested in hearing you two debate the issues. However, I will give you my humble opinion on where I see the country today. I find that whenever I get involved in talking policies and issues, I have to recognize that we have a ghost in the room, just as we do tonight. I'll make my comments brief. After all, what does a black bartender of forty years know?"

Rachel leaned in. "And the ghost is?"

"I will tell you when we get on the topic it mostly applies to."

"I think you might know more than anyone in DC," Sean said.

"I'm impressed with your political knowledge," Rachel added. "Have you ever run for office?"

"Look," Jackson said, "I don't have the recognized credentials to offer solutions on complicated political issues. Note that I said I recognized credentials, such as a law degree. I've never been elected or even worked on a campaign. What I have done is spent forty years, actually sixty years, if I count high school, listening to and talking to the so-called experts on the issues, listening to media … and I have read hundreds of books. I am also a logical thinker without a political party affiliation. I try my best to look at the issues logically. I see logic as the foundation for my ideas, not political party, and not seeking office. I have absolutely no agenda."

Sean said, "Will you ever run for office in the future? I mean, Trump didn't have a law degree either."

"No, not likely. There are a lot of smart people in Washington. Let me put it this way. I'm worried about what kind of nation we'll have for my grandchildren and yours. Our government is dysfunctional. As I said earlier, many of those elected to office want to do what's right. The problem is, we are not the nation that was founded some 220 years ago. The founding fathers created a nation that has survived four horrible wars—the Revolution, the Civil War, World War I, and World War II—and numerous other conflicts we were involved in. The Korean War, Vietnam, the Iraq War, and the Cold War. Some opposed them, yet we held together as a nation, in spite of many disagreements and lost lives.

"How is it different today? For one thing, we are becoming

divided into ethnic lines again. Diversity should make us stronger. Unfortunately, that has not been the case historically. No nation has survived with racial diversity to the extent that the United States seems to be headed in the coming years. Not saying that diversity is bad, just that we don't have a government that is ready to take the necessary steps to cope with it.

"We need a president who has the experience, the management capability, and the character that our citizens can be proud of. Should we elect a president just because he or she is a businessman, because of his color, because he looks good on TV, or because he or she runs a good campaign? I don't think so. We need to find a way to elect the most qualified person, a real leader who we can be proud of. Looking back, we don't need presidents who have their aides sneaking a Hollywood sex symbol into the White House to service him while the First Lady is out of town. Have their secretary service them under the desk, authorize a break-in into the opposing party's campaign office, or try to manage the country with snide remarks on Twitter. A president should have character and conduct himself professionally.

"Congress is made up of people who are committed to political parties and special interest groups. They are united and effective in passing legislation to help themselves. They are provided with a life-time pension for serving six years in Congress. The salaries are about $170,000 annually for members of the House of Representatives and $193,000 for Senators—plus full benefits for life. We could live with those salaries and benefits if they made decisions for the best interest of their constituents.

"If you take the time to follow what they are doing, it becomes obvious. So much of their time is spent on name-calling, investigating their opposing party and candidates, appointing special prosecutors, consulting with lobbyists ... just plain old dirt digging. Remember that conversation last winter about the border wall? It went something like this:

Trump: I want a border wall. I promised it to the people who voted for me.

Nancy: You're not getting money for a border wall. I thought Mexico was paying for it.

Trump: Mexico will pay for it with lost tariffs.

Chuck: You're not getting a wall. Walls don't work.

Trump: Okay, I will leave the government shutdown for weeks, months, years.

Nancy: I'll give you a dollar.

"And so on. Meanwhile, we have ten million illegal immigrants in our country. More than 250,000 more coming in every year. They commit thousands of crimes, including murders. Millions of South Americans want to come to the United States Most are good people who just want a chance to work. And we need workers. But we need to make sure they are coming here for the right reason. We need control at the borders: walls, fences, patrols, something. I could go on and on, but I want to hear you two discuss and debate these issues." Jackson looked over his shoulder. "Okay, I'm gonna check on my two other customers, and then I want to listen to you two."

Rachel turned to Sean. "Jackson sounds like a Republican."

"And to me, he sounds like a Democrat," Sean replied. "A big part of our differences is that today's government has four powers. You know the original three: legislative, judicial, and executive. The fourth, the media, has gradually worked its way into power through influence. They can greatly influence the outcome of elections and the passing of legislation. CNN reported a sexual assault claim against Brett Kavanaugh when he was running for the Supreme Court but didn't mention that it was later retracted. In 2018, the *Washington Post* published a story about a seven-year-old child who they said died in border control custody, which created a lot of excitement against border control. The story was not true, but they retracted with far less fanfare. And it goes both ways. The *Boston Globe* reported that Elizabeth Warren's DNA test showed she was only one-thirty-second Native American. Then it later reported corrections showing even less Native American DNA, and that by the way, Warren had, in the past, used her DNA claim to help her get a job."

Rachel sighed. "Trump and the Republicans have beaten that one to death. Hannity and O'Reilly, before he was accused of sexual harassment—and Limbaugh on the radio—have shown their influence on policy and elections."

"I know it goes both ways. My point is that the media—newspapers, TV, and radio—have too much influence on elections and government policy. Why do they do it? Let's face it, the media is admittedly 90 percent Democrat. And they are careless with reporting because there are no consequences for what they do—other than credibility—but who cares about credibility in the media today?"

"I think you're exaggerating the impact and the frequency. You have conservative papers as well. Radio, Fox News, and how about the *Washington Post,* the *New York Post,* the *Pittsburgh Tribune-Review,* and the *Washington Examiner?*"

"Very good, Rachel, you have the big conservative papers memorized."

Rachel smiled. "I just have a good memory. I had to earn three degrees in six years at Yale."

"It seems to me that CNN has had an ongoing battle with Trump, and it grinds CNN to have him call them liars using fake news. Then they retaliate by seeking out every person they can find who is willing to berate Trump. The worst is Michael Avenatti. A camera seeker and a crook of all crooks. Tucker Carlson on Fox calls him the creepy porn lawyer. I guess because he represented Stormy Daniels, the stripper. He was in almost every kind of trouble you can imagine: thirty-one counts of bank fraud, lying to federal authorities, and so on. With all that going on, he actually said he was considering running for president. I can't understand why CNN would even talk to someone like that. Yet, CNN advanced his fake storyline that he was a candidate for president."

"Well, I'm certainly not going to defend Michael Avenatti's character. CNN was just reporting the news."

"I don't think nutcases should be covered."

"Be right back, but before I go, here's another trivia question. We have had a few nuts in the White House. Here's the trivia for you. One of our hefty presidents was rumored to have often gotten stuck in the bathtub. He also owned toy teddy bears that he would replace from the manufacturer when they begin to fade."

"Teddy Roosevelt?" Rachel said in an uncertain voice.

"Nope."

"Howard Taft?" Sean guessed.

"You got it."

"I'm coming to get you, Rachel."

"Okay, Sean's up one now."

Jackson returned to the counter and listened to the last part of

Sean and Rachel's conversation. "The media reports that really get me are the stories from unidentified confidential sources. How do we know if they have a source or not? What's to stop them from just making up a source? And why does just about everyone accept the validity? I don't get it. Okay, I'm done talking. I just want to listen to you two discuss the issues. Did I detect a little debate coming? You're in the right place to make your case. Liven my evening up a little. Hope you don't mind if I listen. Maybe I can be the ref." Jackson moved to a comfortable position, leaning back against the bar sink and halfway between Sean and Rachel.

"Okay, let's carry on," Sean said.

"That sounds like work," Rachel said with a smile. "I've been working all day. Not sure I want more."

"Your work and travel schedule brings up a good question," Jackson said. "I'll put it this way. Life has changed in homes and business since I first started working. Women going to work and many times being half—or the main source—of family income has created some big changes in the home. I watched a report on *Martha MacCallum* last year in which some professional analysts said women are less happy and have less sex because of the pressure of jobs and childcare. The point made was the stay-at-home moms who go to church on Sundays are more rested and are more accommodating to their husbands."

"So, you think women should stay home and service their husbands?"

"No way, I didn't mean that at all. I'm repeating observation of a trend."

"It's pretty logical. I'm the breadwinner in my family. My husband is trying to sell real estate, but he's not making any money. We sleep at different times and mostly in different rooms."

"Really, I would say *he's* got a problem," Sean said.

Jackson took over "Okay, before you go further with this debate, I would like to hear your vision of what you like to see in a President. Rachel, how about you?"

"Well, first of all I don't want a racist, narcissistic, arrogant crook with a reputation for womanizing and who is an international embarrassment. I want compassion for immigrants, women's right to choose, gun control, fair taxes, a living wage, a cleaner environment, and improvements in our education system.

"As our primaries for the 2020 election progressed, I saw Elizabeth Warren as the best person to provide us that leadership. She is bright, hardworking, and could lead America in a direction where we would see sharing of wealth and an enhancement of our reputation internationally. But I'm okay with Kamala Harris. I'm okay with Joe Biden. Any one of the candidates would be better than Trump. Seeing Trump defeated is my primary wish. I think the Democratic Party's choice will be a vast improvement over Trump."

"And you, Sean?"

"First I want to make a personal comment on Rachel's favorite candidate, Elizabeth Warren. Warren is proposing a wealth tax. I call it a success tax that will penalize those who have succeeded. Guess what that would do to all the charitable foundations that rely on gifts from successful people, those whom Warren calls wealthy. Those successful people, including myself, will cut back on or in some cases quit donating to charitable organizations with the rationale that the success tax takes all of their gifting budget. Charitable giving in the US from these so-called wealthy amounts to over 400 billion annually.

"My theory is that every US president is required to cope with domestic and international affairs while being opposed by a partisan media and the opposition of somewhere around 50% of the voters. Many of the leaders of foreign countries are dictators whose only interest is maintaining control of power. Coping with this environment requires an energetic, ambitious, sometimes risk-taking, tough-minded, thick-skinned, win-at-all-cost leader. Sound familiar?

"Donald Trump boldly stands up to anyone and everyone, although often crudely, in the process of achieving accomplishments that past presidents never attempted. We have all known for more than a decade that China has been taking advantage of, even stealing from, the US and its allies. Which past president dared to take on China? How many presidents promised to move the US embassy to Jerusalem while campaigning and failed take action once elected? How about deregulation, tax cuts and building a wall to protect our southern border? The list is long. Trump has worked tirelessly and boldly taking on issues that past presidents failed to attempt. I will put up with his character flaws to see him get results, as opposed to someone who will move us toward the disaster of socialism or a president who is indecisive.

"Okay," Sean continued, "your leadership vision follows your party's line. Let's talk now about the press and the social media. They have been elevated to be an increasingly powerful source of influence that can actually have a serious impact on economic conditions and world affairs. As examples, on the one hand President Trump's social media attacks on his political opponents, foreign counterparts, and the press create a negative atmosphere which impacts consumer confidence barometers, which in turn impact economic conditions in the US and around the world. On the other hand, Trump's opponents, including the press, seem to have so much disdain for the president that they seek to predict an economic decline and international turmoil, to the point that they can cause it to happen. An absurd but popular line of thinking today is that we are so politically divided and hateful that both sides actually wish for and promote failures that can be blamed on the candidate that they opposed in elections. What does this do for our nation as a whole? Wishing for a president to fail means wishing for a bad economy or possibly war. The consequence is damaging to everyone. It's not logical. Seeking to overturn an election or attempting to impeach a president, absent unequivocal proof of a serious crime, is an insurmountable task. It just isn't going to happen. It's a waste of time and very unproductive.

"Over 225 years ago, the framers of our nation's government created the three branches to work together, to compromise and seek solutions, not destroy each other. Checks and balances are meaningful and necessary, but spending the majority of political effort on seeking destruction is a recipe for a nation's failure.

"CNN covers positive developments for the Democrats and often disregards positive news on Trump and it's the opposite with Fox.

"I try to look at reality. When the conservatives and Republicans come out with something against Democrats and liberals, Fox covers it and CNN basically ignores it. Of course, the opposite happens with negative news on Republicans. CNN covers it and Fox ignores it.

"We'd better stick to politics," Jackson broke in. "You both sound very knowledgeable, and what else are we gonna do with the hours ahead of us? We have an excellent opportunity here with the two of you. Duel at Filibusters: Rachel versus Sean. I'm talking debate, not a battle, no anger. I repeat, politics today have become an all-out war of the Democrats versus the Republicans, conservative against liberal, no compromise. It's dividing workers, friends, and even families. It's all about misquotes and digging up dirt, some real, some exaggerated, and some fabricated. Both sides are doing it. It's dividing our country. It's getting worse, year after year. Gonna ruin our country. It's like an emerging civil war."

"Wow," Sean said. "You sound passionate about this. Let's talk about you, Jackson. I know you've been here for a long time. Bet you've' heard a lot."

"Been here more than forty years."

"You gotta be kidding me! Forty years? When did you start—in grammar school?"

"Thanks for the compliment. I grew up in a tough neighborhood near Benning Ridge area. Not in Ridge, but close to Fort Chaplin Park. I worked for chump change as a kid. My dad told me and my brothers and sisters, 'If ya want spending money, ya gotta get a job.' Got my first real job stacking shelves at the neighborhood grocery store. At twenty-one, I learned to bartend at a dive neighborhood bar. A few years later, a Benning Ridge politician recommended me to the new owner here. He hired me, and here I am, forty years later."

"If you've been here that long, you should own the place. The owner probably inherited the money to buy it and is at home having a few beers and watching TV."

"You sound angry," Sean responded.

"Not really. Just that I see too much inequality of wealth distribution in America; the rich are getting richer, and the poor are getting poorer. All these corporate people out there making millions and even billions while we have poor people living on the streets. Why are you still tending bar? After forty years, you should own it."

"I couldn't afford to buy this place, and I wouldn't want that responsibility. I'm happy just working here. They pay me well. I get by just fine. I would get bored if I retired. I'm a current event and legislative watcher. Get a lot of inside stuff from my customers. Very few Washington lawmakers who I haven't talked to. Of course, most of them are very guarded in what they say. They like hearing my point of view. Now, I'm pretty neutral. I watch the news, read three newspapers daily, and read a lot of books as well. I sometimes go through two or three books a week. Talk issues with these politicians who come here. Try not to be biased. Don't want to piss anyone off." He grinned. "Oh, pardon me. You must be hungry." Jackson handed Rachel and Sean menus. "You can eat at the bar, or Sara can take care of you at one of the tables. We have a limited menu and a small kitchen, but Maggie is a good cook. She leaves soon, but she has time to take care of your order if you're hungry."

Rachel and Jake scanned the menu, chuckling at the names of the selections: Bully Pulpit Beverages, Filibuster Burgers, Muckraker Chicken Sandwiches, Grass Roots Salad, and Silent Majority Desserts.

"If you like a healthy sandwich, try the Gerrymandering. You build your own with your personal selections from the list."

"Cute, but I'm really not hungry."

"And I had a late lunch. I'll pass also."

"Just thought of an easy trivia question. One of our past presidents had three hundred wrestling matches and only lost one."

"Lincoln," Rachel shouted quickly.

"Abraham Lincoln. Ya gotta get the first name."

"Get out of here."

"I think the last name is good enough. All even."

"Okay, let's get the discussion going. I have to make an admission. I'm taking a political science class online through Lake Geneva University. I have to do my final paper on the political divide in America. I'm thinking, as we are talking here, that the two of you could help me with this debate on the issues and the intensity of the debate between the two parties. The foundation of my paper involves the need for a greater effort for compromise.

"In this final course, which I'm in now, I have to ... let me read it word for word: 'Demonstrate mastery of program outcomes in political science and government by applying a scientific method and research analysis to create a professional research paper examining a current and relevant political issue.' The prerequisite is 'successful completion of the general education capstone course,' which I have done.'"

"Maybe we should just listen to you," Rachel offered.

"Nah, I'll participate, but I want to hear what you two have to say. Could I ask for your help in doing this paper?" Jackson asked. "I just need to do an extensive interview. Do you think you have time?"

"Maybe Rachel is qualified, but not me," Sean answered. "You need experienced politicians."

"Not true. I need people who have the knowledge and a feel for what the public needs are. You guys are perfect. I want to do it on the growing divisiveness in our country—how it affects our lives and the concerns we should have for the future of this nation."

"I think I can sum up our differences in one sentence," Rachel said. "Liberals believe that we have societal forces at work today that make opportunities fundamentally unequal for certain classes of people, while conservatives believe the foundation of our constitution gives the wealthy power to expand their wealth. Conservatives lack compassion. They are not bothered by the sight of so much poverty in the cities—or across the country for that matter."

"I don't think you understand basic conservative principles," Sean argued. "We think that people should be free to succeed and fail according to their own actions, choices, and abilities. Of course, every system has some flaws; free enterprise results in some people becoming very wealthy as a result of luck or inheritance. Not that many though. Success mostly comes from hard work, creativity, leadership, and taking risks. The results are not always good, bringing about some failures. Many don't have the personality to take that risk. For the most part, business development brings about success and job creation, helping the poor and the middle class, and creating more opportunity for more ambitious people to climb the economic ladder. We have to have the freedom to succeed. Take it away, and you will begin to have a stagnant economy with fewer jobs. These are all the principles this nation was founded on, and that's why we have become the most successful nation in the history of the planet."

"If I might make a point again, that record of success is in jeopardy, Mr. McCarthy," Rachel said, swiveling her stool to face Sean.

Sean turned his chair as well. "You can call me Sean."

"Okay, Sean. You're not recognizing the difference between freedom and privilege. Privilege creates opportunity and wealth by taking advantage of the middle class and the poor. Finding opportunities is not out there for everyone. People with wealth are in a position to get inside information on the best investments and money-making business opportunities. We need higher wages, free health care, and college education for everyone. A higher living standard for the poor and middle class will create a stronger, more balanced economy. What do you think, Jackson? You've heard it all in this bar. Let's just listen to your views."

"No, my talking would be boring. I will just add a few jokes. I like listening to a good old-fashioned conservative-liberal debate. From what I hear here in this bar, Washington has too many so-called experts getting too little done. I once read a Princeton University research report that found smaller groups actually tend to make more accurate decisions. When I see the gridlock in Congress, I wonder if the massive number of people involved in government legislation is the problem. In addition to a hundred senators and four hundred thirty-five members of Congress, we have more than twenty-five-thousand various types of staffers. The total number of government employees working in DC is over a million, and the total government payroll is over two billion nationally."

"Damn, Jackson," Sean said, whistling. "You're really on top of this."

"You got it. I keep myself informed. More people should do the same. We need a new type of leader in this country, and we need it soon. This country is slowly falling apart. We can stop the slide if we can only find the right leader: Democrat, Republican, or Independent. I don't care. I just want to see sound leadership debating the issues and coming up with solutions through compromise. I have often thought that a good business leader would make a good president. Trump is a businessman, but he's not a good one. His success came from inheritance and impulsive, reckless decision-making that resulted in some great successes along with some bankruptcies. He solved his failures by taking advantage of flaws in our legal system along with timely deal making, which resulted in huge financial success. That's not the kind of businessman we need to lead this country. He has worked hard and made some bold and successful decisions, but he has divided the country with his impulsive rhetoric, battles with the media, and massive staff turnover. His behavior has not set a good example around the world. America's leadership reputation has declined under Trump."

"You're kind," Rachel interjected. "It's worse than that. He should be impeached for collusion with Russia to help him win the election, all his lies, and his disgraceful behavior."

"No, no, I'm not saying anything like that. You're going too far. He was elected with a well-designed campaign and hard work. He was elected by the vote of most Republicans and many working-class Democrats. I disagree with his rhetoric, his divisiveness, and his leadership style, but I have to give him credit for many good and bold decisions. I actually preferred Obama. Even though he was often indecisive and slow at making decisions, he was well regarded by the majority of Americans and around the world." Jackson paused and shook his head. "Here I go again, talking too much. Go ahead, Sean."

"Come on now, Rachel," Sean said. "What was the alternative? The Clintons? What would more of that duo have done for the country? And they would have been a team. Talk about dishonesty and embarrassing behavior. Bill had numerous illicit encounters, had Monica crawling under his desk, lied, and finagled personal wealth from foreign countries. And, by the way, the Democrats spent a fortune trying to uncover that Trump was involved in collusion with the Russians. Not being able to find anything, they kept the investigation going on whatever else they could find in Trump's background."

"Hillary Clinton was her own person and would have been a far better president than Trump," Rachel argued. "She was possibly the most qualified person to ever run for president ... eight years in the White House, New York senator, and secretary of state."

"Oh my, are we living in the same world?" asked Sean.

Jackson said, "Can I make a point before you two go on? The problem you are having here is that you're bringing out the same old trash talk that defines the political party system year after year, trash talking between the two parties, creating ineffective leadership circumstances and little progress solving the nation's problems. It's getting worse year after year, to the point of taking our country down a path toward disaster. Some of it is true, some is not, and some is just exaggerated. When one or the other party comes into power, they start investigating the other party with hearings and appointing special prosecutors. And what a great job that is: an unlimited budget, a salary, nice benefits, and, most important, national name recognition. Every politician wants name recognition and fame. Being appointed special prosecutor is a career gift from heaven. Who wouldn't want that job? Had you ever heard of Ken Starr or Robert Mueller before they became special prosecutors?

"Before we go on with debating the qualities and failures of our recent presidents, I want to know what you think of my idea, namely that the political party nomination process for selecting candidates for president is flawed to the point that it doesn't provide Americans with the most qualified candidate for the public to vote for. Too often, voters are not happy with either candidate. In our desperate need for leadership, we need a new plan. As long as we are throwing out big ideas, I have an idea that I wish could be considered. It involves selecting an independent challenger to be a candidate for president. I said I wanted you two to do the talking. I would like to renege on that for a few minutes to tell you about my idea."

"Great, let's hear it," Sean said.

"But another trivia question before we move on. Here's a tough one. Which president had a morning ritual of having someone rub Vaseline on his head while he ate breakfast? By the way, he also extended this procedure to his choice of pets—two raccoons, Reuben and Rebecca, that would sometimes run around the White House." After a pause, Jackson said, "Let's move on with the discussion. One of you will think of it."

Rachel propped her elbow on the counter and rested her chin on her hand. "I'm listening."

CHAPTER 6

THE PERFECT CANDIDATE

"I realize this would be difficult to achieve, but it would be neat if we could find a means of taking on an initiative to bring together a leadership committee of seven individuals from various parts of the country and who have knowledge and experience in a variety of national and international affairs. They should be selected from a cross section of experienced and successful leaders, possibly in business, education, international education, military, science, history, technology, and economics. This group could undertake an unbiased search for the ideal candidate for president. The seven chosen, while having basic knowledge about domestic and international affairs, should not have held, run for, or campaigned for state or federal-level political office that would obligate them to any politically biased organizations. Those selected should be independent of commitment to any political party or be aligned with any major controversial issues. They would need to be open-minded to all platform proposals from Republicans or Democrats.

"Most importantly, they must be highly regarded as energetic and innovative and have achieved results in their respective fields, possess a broad range of knowledge, be open to compromise, and have successful experience in building and organizing through teamwork and consulting with a management team in making decisions. Also, they should not have an interest in personally becoming part of any administration. The talent is out there. The challenge would be finding a qualified and experienced man or women with the flexibility to make decisions without an agenda.

"The process I am describing should be all about finding a candidate who would give voters an option other than the same old party and organizational influences. If they have the essential leadership qualities, experience in the so-called swamp is not necessary. This person could build a team of experienced leaders in their respective fields. What he or she needs are leadership skills to select the right people to consult with and serve on a management team where decisions are team decisions, and once a decision is made, they are all in. The practice of recent years where we see open disagreements among the staff and cabinet is not an effective way to govern. A president needs team players. I don't see how a president can do an effective job with a revolving door for his management team. Trump's turnover rate among his advisors is absurd.

"The campaign for this independent candidate would not engage in promises to organizations, political parties, or individuals. Rather, this candidate would commit to appointing staff and cabinet members who are prepared for and open to considering all reasonable positions on the major issues and consult with the departmental leaders to create operating plans and direction. Naturally, the candidate will make clear intentions concerning disavowing extreme positions. And they'll provide assurance that the new staff and cabinet will seek direction in all policies to create a government to serve the long-term interests of our citizens. The president will recognize the necessity to, at times, make bold decisions that may be controversial in the eyes of the media and public. This leadership approach comes with the knowledge that we can please some of the people some of the time—but not all the people all the time."

"Wow! I nominate Jackson," Sean said.

Rachel nodded her head in agreement. "I second that."

"Let's be serious," Jackson said. "I'm not qualified, and I do not want to be any part of the process. I would just like to plant the seed anonymously and sit back and watch. As far as my knowledge to prepare the fundamentals of a plan, I feel I know the qualities of successful leadership and what's going on with the issues in this town. I've been an avid reader all my life and have had exposure to the conversations of many successful leaders in government. What I don't have is adequate formal education or proven experience. In other words, I think I have a great idea, but making it happen would be a major long shot. It would take the initiative of a highly regarded and successful person who has the skills and willingness to undertake such a project. Not a person who seeks the presidency him or herself, but a person who has the capability and resources to start the ball rolling. I would just want to watch as an uninvolved bystander. Let's talk about the qualities we would like to see in a president. Rachel, what would you like to see?"

"I know I don't want to see arrogance, narcissism, or distortions of the facts. You can guess who I'm referring to. You have already named many of the important qualities. I would like to see integrity, concern for equal opportunity for all the people, a willingness to take a stand against and not be dependent on the wealthy. He or she should have a concern for our environment."

Sean added, "Let's not forget recognizing the need for a strong national defense and a strong economy with opportunities to succeed."

"Both of your points are good, but they represent political philosophy. I'm talking about the personal profile. The leadership selection team would have the awesome task of selecting a leader who has an established record of all the key qualities of leadership: rationale, confidence, creativity, a passionate ability to communicate a vision, integrity, a willingness to listen to and consider opposing views, the skill to properly delegate while being innovative, and a willingness to share success or take the blame for failures. And by all means, he or she should be vetted for any character flaws through a well-scrutinized examination of his or her life experiences. The person should be someone who has successfully succeeded in building and leading an organization, delegating, coordinating, and establishing respect from his or her organization. The president should inspire others, be respected and honest, have integrity, be a good decision-maker, and have crisis-management skills and the courage to make unpopular decisions. Oh, and let's not forget—"

Rachel interrupted, "Are you talking about God?"

Sean grinned. "Or maybe a person from another planet."

"Of course," Jackson responded, "we don't have the person on this planet who possess all those qualities; the objective would be to be confident the person has honesty and integrity and then as many of the other qualities as possible.

"Obviously we can't make such a selection," Jackson continued. "It's just that I have had this idea for a long time. You two are reasonable people with interesting, yet typical opposing ideas. You have the knowledge from which we could engage in an experimental test on compromising political differences. This is something America needs, certainly at a likely more challenging level than the three of us can do. However, everything has to have a beginning. We can engage in a … let's call it a minor league practice to develop a framework for the big-league players to develop a new style of leadership. The objective would be to find someone who would be a game changer in American leadership. You two have the ideal background and experience to help me frame a plan. Just maybe our little experiment, if passed onto the right people, could be the seed for a plan to find a leader to framework some possible compromises to the major issues that are dividing our country. Again, I know it's a long shot. Let's just try to talk through some compromises with a few issues and see what we come up with." Jackson looked at Rachel and Sean seriously. "How about we start with immigration? Just a minute … I need to check on my two customers. I'll be right back, and then we can get started. Let's see if we can agree on an immigration policy."

Rachel looked at Jackson as he walked away and smiled. "You think you are going to find a way for me to agree with this guy on immigration policy?"

"I'm willing to play the game," Sean said, smiling back. "Good way to pass the time and help Jackson."

"I have to say Jackson makes an impressive case," Rachel said. "Problem is, making what he's talking about happen would be next to impossible."

Jackson returned to the counter.

Rachel said, "Before we get started on immigration, I have a question. Do you think black Americans are getting treated fairly in this country?"

"We are all Americans. But yes, there is a big discrepancy. The average black household makes about half of the average white household. The opportunities are not the same. Certainly, black students are much less likely to graduate from high school and attend college than white students with the same family income. According to a *New York Times* report, black men raised in the top 1 percent—by millionaires—were as likely to be incarcerated as white men raised in households earning about $36,000. Poor white men graduated high school about 78 percent of the time, and black men whose families had the same income graduated only 70 percent of the time. Disparities for women exist too, but they were much smaller. If you were to show a chart of the progress of equal opportunity for women and people of color in this country, the chart would be very long, gradually improving from the Declaration of Independence to today, with more to go. I have to say, though, it's getting better year by year. We still have color, race, and appearance prejudices. In fact, you, Sean, are the model for opportunities. If we had a tall ladder to designate opportunities, you would be at the top of the ladder: white, handsome, tall, educated, and successful. Working down, we would next place a beautiful woman like Rachel. Then comes people who may be a little overweight, not so pretty, or handicapped. We people of color have, historically, had a disadvantage because of color prejudices. The same thing is true, although to a lesser extent, for Hispanics and Asians."

Rachel said, "You mean, if I had been a boy, I could be owning a bunch of restaurants?"

Sean shook his head. "I didn't inherit my business. I worked a lot of years doing seventy- to eighty-hour weeks, took risks, went deep into debt, had some down times, and finally made it all work. In my organization, we make an extra effort to hire black people. That can be done in the restaurant industry. In more technical fields, certain qualifications have to be there. So, we need to do more to improve the qualifications of minorities."

"I agree," Jackson said, "and for all the prejudices I have talked about, the equalizer is hard work and accomplishment. Of course, I assume you worked hard to get where you are. What I am saying is not an exact measure, and the three of us don't look at people in that way, but across the population as a whole, it happens. The one factor that defies personal prejudice is money. If you have money, you get respect—even if it's grudgingly. Of course, all of what I have said has lots of exceptions. More importantly, it shouldn't be that way. The three of us are not that way, but in the world as a whole, that's just the way it is. It is getting less as people become more educated."

"What about other members of your family—your parents and grandparents?" Sean asked.

"Not a problem for me. Over the years, I have noticed being treated or looked at differently. I just don't let it bother me. My dad felt it more than I do, and my grandpa more than Dad, my great-granddad more than my grandpa, and my great-great-grandfather was a slave. Or at least he was supposed to be my great-great-grandpa. An uncle told me that one of my great-great-grandfathers was a white slave owner. Probably true. I didn't get to look like this from all African blood. That happened a lot, and not by choice, either. Things were tough back then. A lot of progress has been made. Today, I think we, as an ethnic group, need to do more to help ourselves. Too many of us who do make it big forget where we came from. They need to create jobs for their black brothers. Do like the Jews. Historically, the Jews have been persecuted around the world, yet here in the United States, they create jobs for each other and for others. Man, those dudes own lots of buildings and businesses across the country."

"Prejudices have been with us forever, certainly not just in this country," Sean said. "It's worldwide and goes back to the beginning of time. It's an evolutionary process that has taken too long. Just think, women couldn't vote before 1920. It took the passage of the Voting Rights Act of 1965 before the majority of African Americans in the South could register to vote."

Rachel gave Sean a jab. "That's pretty good stat knowledge for a conservative."

"Hey, conservatives of this day and age are just as much in favor of equal rights as liberals," Sean replied.

"I wouldn't go that far."

"It's true. Our big differences come on economic policy, gun rights, abortion, and immigration."

"What about national security? What about nationalism?" Jackson asked. "This has become an issue with Trump's campaign slogans 'Make America Great Again' and 'America First.' I have heard a lot of Democrats backlash on those slogans with the concern that it is aggravating our friends in other nations. What do you think?"

"What's wrong with 'Make America Great' and 'America First?' Do we want America to be second or third? Nationalism is pride in my country—just as we have pride in our favorite sports team or pride in our team at work. Hey, I just thought of the answer to our last trivia question. It was Calvin Coolidge."

"You got it. Sean's one up."

"Hey, Sean, did you use your cell? No fair."

"Do you think I would do that?"

"I don't know. Would you? I don't trust conservatives." Rachel gave him another friendly poke.

"Sean, before you retaliate, I would like to hear each of you name a couple of your favorite modern-day political leaders."

"Tough question, Jackson, but I would have to say, let's see, how about Winston Churchill and Ronald Reagan?"

Rachel objected. "He said modern-day leaders. I could have guessed you would name a couple of cowboys from the past. I have to go with real modern-day leaders: the late Ted Kennedy and Barack Obama."

Sean shook his head. "In the school of leadership and political thinking, those two are models for the Democratic party, very liberal. They want more government, less spending on defense, welfare, and free, free, free."

"I hear typical political rhetoric from you guys. Let's get serious. As for me, I'd have to say Bobby Kennedy and Martin Luther King. We can talk more about our leadership choices later. I wanna hear your list of issues."

"We can only make the world better by working together," Rachel interjected. "Boasting and saying we are better than you might work in sports—but not in international relations. Trump's boasting only aggravates our allies when we say America first."

"I think we should always try to make America first," Jackson said, "but it certainly could be done in a more subtle way than what Trump does. He doesn't know how to do things in a subtle way. It's not his style. His style is abrasive, mean-spirited, and often inaccurate."

"As I have said previously," Sean said, "his messages are often inappropriate and downright embarrassing. All leaders have some flaws. That's just his personality. I have to add though, we should look at results, not personality."

"Personality?" Rachel said. "I would add *disorder* to that—or downright stupid and dishonest."

"We understand." Jackson laughed. "You can't stand him."

"Yup, when I see his face on TV, I turn the channel. And that leaves me with a lot of channel flipping. Sometimes my only option is to turn off the TV."

"Okay, I get the picture," Sean said. "Jackson, tell us a little about your family. You've done well."

"If ownership and money are the measures of success, I'm not all that successful. On the other hand, if it's the accomplishment of what I want in life and being happy, I've had lots of success. I love seeing my family do well, and I love working here. I hear what's really going on in DC: the debates, political battles, and scandals."

Rachel listened intently. "You've lived here all your life? What about the family?"

"I've been married to my wife, Wanda, for thirty-nine years. I had two jobs while we raised our family. I was a morning bellhop at the Ambassador Hotel and worked here at night. Now I just work here nights. Love the action at night. Wanda was a maid at the Hilton. Now she also works part-time. With both of us working back in the eighties, we decided we could afford to get married and have a family. I make good money with tips.

"As for my siblings and parents, there are seven of us. I have two brothers and four sisters. One brother moved to Florida and worked a tech job. The other was a firefighter but got let go when his drinking got too bad. Now he's a vegan and is getting back on track. My other brother quit drinking too. One sister is a cop in Atlanta. One had a nice government desk job that paid the bills, and she's now retired. Unfortunately, though, her daughter got into drugs, and she lost her house trying to sort out her daughter's mess. Her daughter is doing better now. My other two sisters are also mothers: one is a single mother on welfare after the father of her children left, and the other became a teacher at a private school, which allowed her children to attend free of charge. They were able to get into good colleges as a result. I always intended to go to college, but I always seemed to get busy and postpone it. By the time I was in my forties, I figured it was too late. Then when I turned sixty, I read a story about some senior citizens going back to school, and I decided to give it a try. I enrolled in Lake Geneva University part-time and did excellent in my classes, especially political science. So, I decided to go for a political science degree. I'm working on my final paper."

"What are you going to do with it?" Sean asked.

"No specific plans. At sixty-five, I'm a little late to get started in political life as a job."

"What's your final paper on?"

"The paper you're going help me with?"

"Hope we don't disappoint you," Rachel said.

"I'll give it my best shot," Sean added. "By the way, how's your family doing, Jackson? I know you have two boys, and both were doing well the last time we talked about them. Tell Rachel about your two sons."

"Still doing great. Jackson Jr. is a professor at Syracuse University, and Lenny is a cop in Albany. They both went to SUNY. Junior graduated, and Lenny quit to get married. He got a job on the Albany police force, and his father-in-law was the director of personnel. Junior got his BS at SUNY and then his master's at Syracuse.

"And that's enough about me. Let's get back to the issues. We're going to have lots of time. I want to hear what your views are on immigration, guns, health care, welfare, the economy and jobs, race relations, concern about terrorist attacks, war, wealth distribution, the homeless, crime and violence, and the leaders you do and don't respect. I do this a lot to guests here at the bar. My guess is you're both pretty good. I will tell you about an idea I have. An idea that will solve immigration and crime problems and save a lot of money."

"Let's hear it," Rachel said.

Jackson shook his head. "Not ready yet. Let's hear you two go at it first."

"Seems like we already started," Rachel said. "Although I feel like it is two against one."

"So do I," Sean said. "Jackson, if you had to choose, which would you rather be identified as: Republican or Democrat?"

"Look—as hard as I try to be party neutral, some people say I sound like a Democrat; others say I'm a Republican. I have been accused of not having principles because I try to please both sides. Those who really listen to what I am saying understand that I'm willing to bend on principles if the result is an improvement over a stalemate. Often we can accomplish greatness with compromise.

"Tell ya what. We will first agree on an issue to discuss, then the two of you debate it, and then I will propose a compromise. We will then all discuss it and talk until we can come up with something to agree on. To make it work, you have to be ready to accept the fact that a solution is not likely to meet all your goals, but will be an improvement. I will just be the moderator. Shall we start with the Russian investigation and the concerns over Trump's possible involvement with the Russians to defeat Hillary in the 2016 election?"

"Oh, come on." Sean moaned. "That's been a total witch hunt by the Democrats. The Democrats and the media were so shocked that Trump beat Hillary that they had to come up with something to blame it on."

Rachel said, "You can call it a witch hunt if you don't want to believe it, but the facts and indictments are there. Trump lied, his attorney lied, and his military leaders lied."

"You want facts?" Sean opened his hands. "Here is an exact quote from the Mueller report: 'Although the investigation established that the Russian government perceived it would benefit from a Trump presidency and worked to secure that outcome and that the campaign expected it would benefit electorally from information, released through Russian efforts, the investigation did not establish that members of the Trump campaign conspired or coordinated with the Russian government in its election interference activities.'

"Yet we heard all about 'Russia, Russia, Russia.' The media and Democrats pounded on it so long, without any meaningful proof, that they convinced the public that Trump was guilty. Yet there was never anything there—other than Mueller probing down every other alley he could find to look at. Mueller liked the job and wanted to keep it going as long as possible. His team went way off course, digging into the personal lives of Trump staffers to find personal mistakes and inconsistencies in their stories that had nothing to do with Russia. They had to go to the Russian route because there was no collusion between Trump and Russia."

"Trump was procuring a relationship with Russia so that he could build a Trump Tower there. Seems a little inappropriate and a shady deal for a president to have a personal real estate investment with our most dangerous enemy."

"That was before he became president. I don't think anyone, including himself, expected him to actually win the presidency. The proposed real estate deal never happened. Let me ask you this. Who is our worse enemy: Russia or Iran?"

"They both are," Rachel said.

"What do think the media reaction would be if Trump sent a hundred fifty billion dollars of cash in boxes to Russia? The media would go crazy. It would be the biggest news story of the year, with cries for impeachment. Yet few people are aware of the second- or third-page coverage of Obama doing that exact thing for Iran."

"Hardly a reasonable comparison. That Obama administration cash transaction was part of a nuclear arms control agreement."

"If you could call it an agreement."

Jackson interjected, "Seems like we are skipping all over. How about we talk about immigration?"

"That's a deal," Sean said. "How about you start with immigration."

"So, we will be talking about compassion for the underprivileged versus building a wall to protect our wealth?" Rachel asked.

Sean shook his head and smiled. "Tell me, Rachel, what are your thoughts about sanctuary cities? Let me guess—you think they're great."

"Yes, yes, and yes. We are talking about America and the value of freedom. Freedom from want, freedom of speech, freedom to worship any God, and, most importantly, freedom from fear. Too many immigrants live in fear, which goes against everything America has built and projected out to the world. Statistics show sanctuary cities are safer and perform better than non-sanctuary cities. They perform better because they are melting pots of different ethnicities working together, and these people don't live in fear of being deported to their home countries. The sanctuary movement protects against a purely bureaucratic enforcement system. That system can include long detainment and judgment without a jury, or even a judge, as an arbitrary arm of prejudicial policy instead of just law. No legal system can perfectly implement justice in every circumstance, of course. Sanctuary serves now—as it has in the past—as a corrective and a challenge to such imperfection though. We should remember that it was once a part of the law, and it remains an effective way to reform and strengthen it."

Sean said, "Wow, that's unreal. We have more than two million people in American jails at an annual cost of more than forty billion. More than twenty-five of that can be attributed to illegals. In California, it's 40 percent. We have more than 350,000 criminal immigrants in jails across the country who are eligible for deportation, mostly residing in sanctuary cities. Each prisoner costs the American taxpayer thirty thousand dollars per year."

Jackson said, "Let's do a little more trivia. I'm going to ask three questions, but don't respond until I have finished all three. One of our presidents met his future wife when he was six years old. Another of our presidents had a dog he named an honorary army private. No one was allowed to feed him but the president. The dog became the subject of a comic strip and two MGM movies. Another president loved bowling so much that he had a one-lane bowling installed in the White House."

"Nixon," Sean yelled.

"Sean goes two up."

"Roosevelt was the dog president. I mean, he had the dog you're talking about," Rachel says with a little laugh.

"Back to just one up for Sean."

Rachel grabbed Sean's hand, laughed, and said, "Put your cell phone in your pocket, Sean."

"I don't think you will get the third one; it was Harry Truman. He met Bess when they were six. That's it. Let's talk politics."

Rachel was still looking at Jackson, seeking support on the sanctuary city issue, and he responded, "Sorry, Rachel, I tend to agree with Sean on this one. We need to get real about this. I don't have a problem with taking in immigrants, regardless of color or nationality. The problem is that we have to have limits, and they have to be vetted to ensure they're not coming here to commit crimes or are a part of a terrorist group. I've heard some kind of number referenced that a lower percentage of illegal immigrants, as a group, commit fewer crimes than our citizens as a whole. That seems like a valid point, but I have to say, so what? We have enough crime from our own people. Why should we take on more?

"Let me put it this way. Most Americans came from immigrants and favor more coming here—I certainly do—but we have to get logical here. Government figures show that we have more than a half a million homeless people in the United States. Something like one out of ten Americans live on incomes that put them at risk for hunger. I think it's twelve or thirteen million American children rely on food banks for assistance. It seems like we should be taking care of our own citizens first. Millions of people from Mexico, South America, and other parts of the world want to come here. We just can't take them all. So, it's only logical that we have a system to place some limits. And, if we are going to limit, why not limit immigration to the non-criminals, preferably those who are in need of jobs we have a hard time filling?"

"We're all humans," Rachel said. "We all have a desire to eat and have a place to live. Are you saying we should make judgments as to which ones should have the privilege of surviving? Who is so righteous as to make that call?"

Sean said, "Tough question. I got the answer." He laughed. "Donald Trump."

Rachel shook her head with a little chuckle. "He probably thinks so. His wall idea is just a campaign promise to get votes from the racist segment of our society. Walls are immoral, and I'm not convinced they work."

Jackson pointed to the door. "I gotta get logical again. If you wanted to walk to that exit door now, you and anyone else in this room could do it easily. If I obstructed that path with a partial wall, it would be more difficult. At a minimum, a wall in someone's path increases the difficulty, and fewer people will use the path. If I put a fence around my garden, fewer people would come in than if I didn't have a fence. The bigger the wall, the fewer will get past it. With today's technology, we can make a wall almost impassable. Every border wall security guard I have heard interviewed says that walls work. Excuse me for putting it this way, but to say walls don't work is absurd. To say they are immoral is also absurd. We already have 650 miles of wall. I never heard those walls called immoral until this year when Trump wanted to build more walls to keep his campaign promise. I don't like the way he goes about doing things, but when he's right, he's right. Also, we have had walls all over the world. I think it's something like seventy-five or eighty walls around the world. How can you possibly say walls are immoral?"

"It's a matter of opinion," Rachel answered. "Some people still see them as immoral. Nancy Pelosi is not the first person to call walls immoral."

"Okay, we are beating this to death," Jackson said. "Let's just finish by saying the point is we need to have a reasonable and manageable system for monitoring who comes and goes from our country—for our safety, for our families. I don't want to sound like a Trumper because I sure as hell am not."

Sean said, "I've been quiet because Jackson has covered it quite logically."

Rachel sighed. "Well, I guess I'm outnumbered on this one. So, put up the wall and double the funds available to help the homeless."

"I think that brings us to the scary national debt," Sean said.

Rachel jumped in before Sean could respond. "Excuse me. I have a call coming in. Hello?" Then she put the phone down. "No luck—just another robocall. That reminds me, the Obama administration introduced a policy for curbing unwanted calls. In 2018, the Trump administration, in their infinite wisdom of pursuit of deregulation, got a Federal Appeals Court to overrule the FCC, concluding the rule was unreasonable."

Sean looked at Rachel. He pulled off his tie and stuffed it in the inside pocket of his sports coat as he prepared to respond. "Cutting back superfluous regulations has been a serious asset to accelerating our economy. However, effective policy changes are bound to have some flaws. Hopefully, they will fix that one."

"Aha, we agree on one point," Jackson exclaimed. "That's a start. Robocalls are a nuisance, and we need to control them. Maybe we can find more to compromise on. I would like to see more compromises in politics. The differences today are too extreme. I can tell you what I see here at this bar. Professions and backgrounds vary, but liberals are frequently younger, and conservatives are the older ones. Now come on, I wanna hear from you two."

Sean sported a confident look at Jackson and then Rachel. "Ever heard the saying, 'If you're young and are not liberal, you have no heart. If you are older and are still a liberal, you have no brains'?"

"That's not a compromising addition to our conversation," Jackson said.

"It was a joke."

"Oh, I like jokes," Rachel said. "As you know, Trump has been accused of sexual misconduct by a slew of women. Of course, that is a case of he said and then she said, she said, she said, she said, and she said." Rachel leaned back in her stool, folded her arms and grimaced.

CHAPTER 7

POLITICAL PARTIES

Jackson interjected, "If you don't mind, let's try to find a subject we can focus on instead of jumping from one issue to another. How about more on the contrast between liberal and conservative ideas for governing?"

"I proudly consider myself a liberal," Rachel said. "Liberals see the need for big income earners, those making five hundred thousand or more per year, to pay more taxes to pay for services to the less fortunate. How does it make sense for a schoolteacher, teaching our children, making fifty or sixty thousand per year, to live in a rented apartment and drive an economy car, while a burger franchise operator, making hundreds of thousands per year, drives a Mercedes to his multimillion dollar home?"

"Let me remind you that the teacher didn't invest money and take the risk," Sean said.

"Shush." Rachel smiled. "I didn't interrupt you. Allow me to ask this. Conservative businesses have an unfair proportion of benefits, and they vote for legislation that hurts the middle class and the poor. Guns are a good example. Why should we let anybody have access to guns while we have schoolchildren being shot in classrooms? Why should we try to tell a woman she has to give birth to a baby after she has been raped or is a victim of incest? Why should we tell two loving same-sex citizens, who are a law-abiding couple, that they can't get married? We are the wealthiest nation on the planet. Why can't we afford to have health care for everyone? And one more thing ... you know how I recognize a conservative?"

"They own a business and create jobs," Sean offered.

"No, they name their two kids 'deduction one' and 'deduction two.'"

Sean gave a sarcastic laugh. "Was that supposed to be funny? Let's let Jackson make the jokes."

"Sean, I have a difficult question for you," Rachel said. "I can't think of anything that conservative leadership has done to help make American a better place to live. Maybe you can help me."

"How about keeping Americans safe?" Sean said. "The Reagan administration won the Cold War for us. How about creating the most powerful military and the strongest economy ever on this planet? How about Eisenhower's creation of the Interstate Highway System and the Civil Rights Act of 1960? Would you like more?"

"Are you serious? Are we supposed to be pleased that our government spends more on weapons that kill people instead of providing health care, better education opportunities, and improving working conditions for our young people? It's a matter of priorities; you want the wealthy to increase their wealth and give as little as possible for the middle class and the poor."

"You apparently like Joe Biden," Jackson said. "Rachel, give me a Biden quote that has impressed you."

"Okay, I have one. 'The measure of a man is not how often he gets knocked down, but how quickly he gets up.'"

Sean came in "That's a good one, Rachel. We need to be reminded that the United States—a nation established by our founding fathers, a group of brilliant and courageous men, in the late eighteenth century—has been knocked down many times and not only survived but thrived."

"No founding women, of course," Rachel cut in.

Sean paused and held up his right index finger. "Hold it, three points. First, I have ascertained that you are very knowledgeable. Second, the point you are making about women occurred as a result of the circumstances of that time in our history. Jefferson, for example, saw more rights for women coming. At the time, though, it was the norm. Now as for the rules of our discussion, I listened to you without any interruption. I expect you should do the same for me." Sean looked at Jackson. "Do you agree, Jackson?"

"We've got rules now?" Rachel asked.

Jackson took a minute to think. "Well, we aren't exactly busy here, so we wouldn't be disturbing anyone if you two get into a shouting match, but I think it would be best if you take this on one at a time."

Rachel smiled. "I can live with that. And one more thing. Let me suggest that we focus on the issues, not personalities. Debating about Donald Trump and Nancy Pelosi would soon become irrelevant and boring."

"Thank you," Sean said. "Let me clarify your points. Clearly, it has been established from experience that private enterprise is more efficient in providing services than the government."

Rachel smiled, started to say something, and then quickly covered her mouth with her hand, allowing Sean to continue.

"Thank you. The founding fathers of this nation recognized that more than two hundred years ago. They didn't intend for the government to get involved in people's daily lives. As for taxes, those who have succeeded and become wealthy pay more than their share. They represent about 10 percent of taxpayers and provide roughly 70 percent of government tax revenue. Free enterprise, in the process of creating incentives for hard work and innovation, necessarily creates disproportionate income levels. As for teachers, union bargaining creates an environment where compensation is based mostly on seniority rather than performance. That's wrong. The restaurant operators you refer to have failures as well as those who make millions. Hard work, innovation, and often seventy-to-eighty-hour weeks are the difference. That's the free enterprise that makes America a great nation. Guns are protected by the second amendment as a right to protect our property. As for the institution of marriage, it has always been for a man and a woman. Men living together as a couple are not marriages; they are partners."

"Wow," Jackson interjected before Rachel had a chance to respond. He shook his head with a smile. "You guys are really good. I have been listening to these debates for decades and can tell this is going to be one of the good ones. How about you take it one issue at a time?"

Rachel smiled. "Sean gave the typical right-wing spiel."

The two other customers, a couple, probably in their early fifties, approached Sean and Rachel.

"Pardon me," the man said. "We have heard part of your conversation. Very interesting. Can I tell you my favorite scenes at the White House?"

"By all means," Jackson said.

The man continued. "My favorite scene at the White House,

broadcast by all the networks, a year or so ago, was an impromptu meeting called by President Trump with Pelosi and Schumer, who thought it would be a private meeting, except Trump opened it to some of the press, with cameras. I couldn't believe it. There was Trump perched in a chair, purposely higher than the chairs his guests were sitting in, his puffy hair flowing. The House Democratic leader, Nancy Pelosi, sitting in a low chair, wishing she wasn't there, and Senate Democratic leader Schumer, sitting on a stool scowling, also not wanting to be there. The conversation went something like this: 'I'm getting the wall.' 'No, you're not.' 'Yes, I am.' 'No, you're not.' Can you imagine JFK or Ronald Reagan being a part of something like that? Politics today are ridiculous."

"That's it," Jackson said. "Let's talk politics."

The man continued, "Revelations of secret sexual encounters by leading politicians, and even presidents and presidential candidates have become almost predictable—JFK, Clinton, Hart, Trump, and many more. Professional people of all sorts become involved as representatives of so-called political leaders. They come to Washington with excellent reputations and are soon involved in all kinds of controversies. Ever heard of a lawyer breaking the law because his client told him to do so? I thought attorneys served their clients to honor the law. Breaking the law because your client asked you to do so is incompetent malpractice. Whether he did or not is not as important as the attorney's behavior. And one more thing … Trump is an articulate and energetic speaker with the vocabulary of a garbage man."

Jackson said, "When I came to this bar forty years ago, I recall several people telling me, and I quote, 'Washington is becoming so combative they can't get anything done.' I would call that calm compared to what we have going on these days. I'm an independent," Jackson said to the new guests. "I have opinions, but I'm pretty much up the middle and love to offer compromises. Before we get involved in debating specific issues, let's talk about the fundamental differences between what are referred to as conservative and liberal views. As a matter of fact, for the most part, it's liberal Democrats versus conservative Republicans. Historically, we have had a crucial number of swing votes in Congress. Not so anymore. Very few swing votes. Mostly party-line voting.

"Most universities and colleges advocate liberal policies, free education, more help for the poor, and higher taxes for higher-income people. Some are more moderate in advocating those benefits, and some are more extreme. I heard one Democrat call for giving everybody a thousand dollars a month. Now that's absurd. That's like saying vote for me because I want you to get free money."

"When you refer to liberalism, I assume you're including the media?" Sean asked.

Rachel replied. "He's talking policy views, not the media."

"As I see it from reading a lot of history, we have always had philosophical differences on the role of government policy and the laws," Jackson said. "The battle lines and debates have evolved between those on the conservative side, who feel we should adhere strictly to the Constitution, and the liberals, who feel we should shift more to a socialist-type government. I realize that I am defining them broadly, when, in fact, many variations exist. The problem today is that the reactions to the differences have become bitter and vengeful. Compromise is disappearing. Political leaders, seeking elections, tell lies for what they consider the better good. Consequently, the government has become dysfunctional. I fear we are headed for disaster within the next five years. A recession along with a stock market crash like we had in 2008 and 2009, and it has happened every ten years for most of the past 220 years, will be a challenge too difficult for our divided government to manage. So, how about we start with the economy?"

"Too many issues to compromise on," Sean said. "We need to do something that has a more specific issue to deal with. We could do religion." He grinned.

"You're not serious," Rachel replied.

"Not really."

"Referring to religion does remind me of a little story," Jackson said. "A delightful angelic little boy was waiting for his mother outside the ladies' room of the gas station. As he stood there, he was approached by a man:

"Sonny, can you tell me where the post office is?"

"The little boy replied, 'Sure! Just go straight down this street two blocks and turn to your right. It's on the left."

The man thanked the boy kindly, complimented him on how

bright he was, and said, "I'm the new pastor in town. If you and your mommy come to church on Sunday, I'll show you how to get to heaven."

The little boy chuckled and said, "You're shitting me, right? You can't even find the post office."

Rachel and Sean both had a good laugh.

CHAPTER 8

THE MEDIA

Jackson asked, "If we are going to pass over religion, where then do conservatives and liberals, or Democrats and Republicans, form their opinions? Does it come from spouses, family, work, schools, or the media? The pastor at my church says, 'We are like computers—where the body is the hardware, the mind is the software, and the power cord plugged into the wall is the spirit. When we pass on, our mind moves to heaven as our software moves to the cloud.'"

"I don't think we should just skip over religion," Sean said. "Religion has had a very important role in America, and it still does. Many of Americans' political views are formed in churches. Conservative views on life come from a family foundation and the church. Liberals' come from friends and schools."

Rachel answered, "Which means, and I agree, liberals have educated opinions from schools and listening to friends who form rational opinions. Conservatives come from family and profit-motivated business. When we consider how much influence the church should have in America, we need to consider the expanding atheist population. When voting, they are often referred to as the *nones* because they are the people who list *none* on questions of religious affiliation. Recent polls have shown that approximately 25 percent have given up on religion and that about one-third of millennials are doing the same. This means, in rough numbers, America has about thirty-five to forty million people who do not consider themselves as part of a religion. And, that number is growing."

"But," Sean said, "that means roughly two-thirds of our population is still affiliated with some form of traditional religion. In other words, a strong majority of Americans still have religion as a foundation for daily living. And this stands for a better America. It represents honesty, integrity, and a life of good values. I have found, in working with a lot of young workers, those from religious families are more reliable and better workers."

Rachel shook her head. "You make it sound like atheists are bad, and that's not true."

"No, no, we would never discriminate in hiring or advancing an atheist employee. We don't make a point of giving our employees' religion a factor in hiring or promoting. I'm just saying that, from experience, we find workers from church-oriented families, as a segment of the population, have noticeably better work standards than others. We have atheists at all levels among our more than a thousand employees. Many workers identify themselves with a particular religion but are not churchgoers. The group I am referring to as generally being noticeably good workers are those who attend church regularly."

Jackson said, "I think you have it on the key sources, but you haven't mentioned the media. Why is it that networks each have one or two dominant players as far as audience size is concerned? And, of course, the audience size determines salaries. On Fox, Hemmer, Hume, Gutfeld, Perino, and Judge Jeanine are all in the two-to-four-million annual salary range. Chris Wallace, Tucker Carlson, Martha MacCallum are in the six-to-eight-million range. Bret Baier is at about fifteen million, and Shepard Smith makes about ten million. Hannity probably makes about double as all those ten combined. Fox, for the most part, is too conservative for me. Although, I do like Harris Faulkner. How much does she make?"

"She was at about four hundred thousand, but it's probably more now," Sean answered.

"She's underpaid. It's the same at CNN. Cuomo, Jim Acosta, John King, Erin Burnett, and Jake Tapper are all under three million, while Wolf Blitzer makes fifteen million. The moneybags on CNN is Anderson Cooper. My estimates are only estimates, but they're close."

"Let's move to the issue of abortion."

CHAPTER 9

ABORTION

Jackson clasped his hands together in front of his chest. "I am very curious to hear your views on the quiet issue: abortion. I call it the quiet issue because it doesn't get debated that often, relative to the impact it has on voting choices and determining what political party you belong to. If you oppose abortion, you can't very well be an avid Democrat. I've never heard of a Democrat who opposed abortion. I'm sure we have some out there, but it can't be very many. The opposite is true with Republicans."

"I think it's a very clear-cut issue," Rachel said. "My niece had an abortion ... a good kid who made a mistake."

"How far along?" Sean asked.

"I think about five months."

Sean grimaced but said nothing.

Rachel continued, "Women have the right to decide what happens with their bodies. Her fetus was not a human life, so it didn't have separate individual rights. The government should provide taxpayer-funded abortions for women who cannot afford them. The decision to have an abortion is a personal choice for a woman regarding her own body, and the government must protect this right. Women have the right to affordable, safe, and legal abortions, including partial-birth abortion."

Rachel looked at Jackson. "This one is going to test our temperament."

"We have discussed sensitive issues so far without any of us becoming upset," Jackson said.

Sean tried to keep an even tone in his voice. "I have a belief that human life begins at conception. Abortion is the murder of a human being. An unborn baby, as a living human being, has separate rights from those of the mother. I oppose taxpayer-funded abortion.

Taxpayer dollars should not be used for the government to provide abortions. I support legislation to prohibit partial-birth abortions, called the 'partial-birth abortion' ban.' My family supports efforts to end the killing of babies. Are you angry with me for that?"

"No, I'm not angry with you," Rachel answered. "You are expressing your opinion, an opinion you grew up with. I just think you are wrong."

"Can I come in here?" Jackson asked.

Rachel breathed a sigh of relief. "Yeah, help us out."

Jackson folded his arms against his chest and sighed. "This has been a controversial issue for many decades. Various state laws against abortion go back to 1900. We know laws against abortion occurred as far back as early in the 1800s. As I assume you know, *Roe v. Wade* legislation came in the early 1970s; I think it was in '73. Battles over the issue have continued; abortion clinics burned. Lawsuits and continued efforts on the part conservative legislators to reverse that law have been a part of the political landscape since the law went into effect. Personally, I can understand the desire for a rape case victim and family members to not want to raise the baby. I'm sure you have seen pictures of an unborn of four to five months. That's a human being, a life. While in the womb, the baby's body parts and gender are fully established. The difference is that the baby exists in the mother's womb and functions on the life of the mother. Not until the baby leaves the womb in the process of birth does the baby function on its own. What happens the instant it leaves the mother's body? Does it become a human with all the rights of a citizen at that point, or does the baby have those rights at conception, when fully formed in the mother for several months? We will never have a consensus on that question. I tried once to discuss the feasibility of a compromise with a Catholic friend. I think we can come up with a compromise on abortion laws. Many—if not all—Republicans would vote to abolish *Roe v. Wade*, but Democrats won't hear of it."

"That would be impossible," Sean said. "I can't compromise my views on human life."

"And I can't compromise on a woman's right to choose what to do with her body," Rachel said.

Jackson looked at Sean. "Okay, Sean, what would you choose if given the option of only allowing abortions prior to three months pregnant or allow them any time and enact laws to enforce it? I'm saying if you only had those two choices."

"Obviously, I would vote for three months. If enforced, that would save a lot of human lives compared to what is going on now."

"Okay, Rachel, if you had to choose between banning all abortions for any reason other than saving the life of the mother and only banning abortions past the first three months of pregnancy?"

"If I only have those two choices, obviously I would take the three-month limitation, but the law already allows abortions, under legitimate defined circumstances, up until birth, which I feel is the right thing to do. Let the mother decide. It's her body."

"And she's carrying a human life," Sean said.

Jackson raised his pointer finger. "Close to one million human lives are taken by abortion annually, and 98 percent of those occur within the first three months of pregnancy. Only 1.5 percent, or about 150, occur after three months. And if the law was set for three months, that percentage would likely be less than 1.5 percent because the mothers would be forced to make their decision within the three-month time period. You have almost everything you are looking for, and Sean's people would be saving 15,000 lives."

Rachel shook her head. "Not gonna happen."

"I expect you're right," Jackson said. "I am just trying to make the point that we need to find more ways to compromise. This is probably impractical, but why not solve those issues that are deadlocked with Congress establishing a procedure for coping with them. Not all issues could be resolved this way, but certainly, some could. They would select a compromise committee of seven, randomly selected, four from the majority body and three from the minority. A new randomly selected committee would be selected for each issue approved for compromise arbitration. Issues selected for this arbitration option would require majority approval of the Senate or House."

"By the way, abortions are already permitted and happening. Why do I need to accept a compromise?" Rachel asked.

"For the sake of progress," Jackson answered.

Sean countered, "That's not progress; it's regression."

Jackson jumped in before the argument could progress. "As long as we have time here, let's take some more issues, one at time. Maybe we can find a compromise that you both agree on. As I mentioned earlier, I have an idea that will save this country billions and save lives at the same time. Not now, though. Let's talk about some other possible compromises first.

"Okay, let's get back to … immigration? That's always a hot topic. Or maybe we start with the economy. I think you will both agree that a country cannot survive without a healthy economy, given an exception, of course, to some periodic ups and downs."

"I'm for talking about the economy," Sean said.

CHAPTER 10

THE ECONOMY

Jackson stretched briefly before diving in. "So, let's start with talking about the fundamental differences in how we best achieve a stable economy: as a free market or a socialist economy."

Rachel said, "The capitalist economy is basically flawed because it creates clear winners and clear losers. The winners have the right to accumulate a disproportionate share of wealth, and they also have the power to suppress the rights of those they employ. I'm for a progressive system where the government has more control over industry and the workers have more rights in collective bargaining, both of which provide a greater measure of equality."

Rachel expected Sean to jump in, but he let her continue.

"Progressives believe in shared ownership of resources and central planning, which support a more equitable distribution of goods and services. As they see it, workers are responsible for economic output and should have a right to a commensurate reward.

"Even though I'm not a Karl Marx fan, he made sense with his theory that low-income workers, faced with injustices, would inevitably revolt against the wealthy. Progressives today, myself included, and including Socialist Democrats in France and Germany, as examples, advocate reforming, rather than replacing, capitalism as the best approach to achieving greater economic equality. Progressive reform is what we need.

"The government's role in a progressive system is to determine output and pricing levels. The needs are synchronized with the needs of the consumers. This allows planners to respond to inventory levels, consequently avoiding production inefficiencies. For example, when stores experience a surplus of coffee, it signals the need to cut prices—or the opposite when inventory is low."

Sean raised his eyebrows in surprise. "Wow, you're actually a socialist?"

"No, you just don't get it. I'm a progressive."

"Would you admit that progressives have many similarities to socialism?"

"I don't agree with that comparison. We are just progressives."

"I know the difference. The similarity, though, is that they are both failures. In a free market economy, the law of supply and demand—as opposed to a central government—regulates production and labor. Large companies and small startup companies rely on the concept of supply and demand of the consumer to regulate production and labor. Goods and services are sold at the highest price consumers are willing to pay, and workers earn the highest wages companies are willing to pay. The profit motive drives commerce and forces businesses to operate as efficiently as possible to avoid losing market share to competitors."

Since Sean let Rachel keep talking, she returned the favor and allowed Sean to continue.

"As Congress enacts more regulations on pricing, free competition, and wages, the efficiency of the free market system is diminished. Of course, some laws, regulations, and reasonable minimum wages are essential to combat flagrant inequalities. Free market principles, however, need to be maintained to create the most productive economy and the highest level of employment, which the history of the American economy has proven. The performance records of countries around the world have shown that the profit motive drives commerce and forces businesses to operate as efficiently as possible to avoid losing market share to competitors. Socialist, sometimes referred to as command, economies are marked by communist and socialist tendencies. The government controls the means of production and the distribution of wealth, dictating the prices of goods and services and the wages workers receive. The whole process is not compatible with economic expansion.

"They are trying socialism in Venezuela. How's that working out? How about Cuba, North Korea, and East Germany. They have all demonstrated the performance of socialism. How has it worked in those countries? Would we really want socialism in the United States?"

"Conservatives want to weaken central government," Rachel

argued. "They are primarily concerned with a strong military and a conservative Supreme Court. They see a subservient role for nonwhites, leaving them with the worst jobs and lowest salaries. Conservatives see the woman's role as supporting and promoting their husbands while they bear children or maybe get a job teaching or nursing."

Sean scoffed. "Rachel, that's a total exaggeration. Your assessment is twenty to thirty years old—and even an exaggeration of that era. Women are now very close to equal pay for equal jobs and are in high-level management positions, managers, CFOs, and even CEOs. They are on police forces, in the military—"

"Still not on a totally equal plane. Check the numbers. What do you see, Jackson?"

"I think it's getting pretty close. What about in education?"

"Good example. I look at the Bureau of Labor Statistics once in a while. Females make up more than 90 percent of pre-K and kindergarten teachers, about 80 percent of elementary and middle school, and more than 50 percent of high school teachers. Again, the reason is simple: low pay. The education of our children is our future. Underpaying them is very shortsighted."

"I would favor higher pay for those who performed better—just like in business," Sean said. "The problem is the unions. They oppose merit pay. Teachers don't have any incentive to do a better job. Like any field of work, you have a wide variation in skill, job responsibility, and performance. Yet, they base pay on seniority—not on accomplishments. I have heard stories of terrible teachers who are widely recognized as terrible at their jobs, but they continue because they have tenure. That doesn't make any sense."

"I see lots of reasons why merit pay would not work. It gives too much power to management, and performance evaluation is impractical. Jackson?"

"I have to say that I agree teachers are underpaid, considering their education requirements and the importance of their jobs. They have a very significant impact on the future of our country. On the other hand, I think merit pay would be good. Nothing against unions, but I just think performance should determine pay level.

"You have to recognize that we are always going to have flaws in any form of government and their theories and policies. We will never achieve perfection. The foundation is free enterprise, and its success is promoting competition and reward for innovation, hard work, and success. If you place too many restrictions, limit growth opportunity, and penalize success with taxes that are too high, the economy will suffer from a lack of incentive to take risks to develop business and create jobs. Granted, we can find some situations that seem unfair when, in a robust economy, many businesspeople become wealthy while we still have poverty. The conservatives say when you try to correct what liberals refer to inequities that create the wealth gap, you take the risk of negative impact on the economy because you penalize growth. The answer is for Congress to work together to find ways to cut the cost of living, like health care and education, and eliminate waste like the costs involved from drug and alcohol addiction. What are your thoughts on that?"

"So, does that bring us to drugs?" Sean asked.

"How about we start with marijuana?" Rachel offered.

CHAPTER 11

DRUGS

"Okay, that's an interesting topic," Jackson said. "Legalization is increasing across the country. I think more than half the states have legal marijuana, and some limit it to medicinal use. In any case, it's readily available anywhere. Republican views on marijuana tend to be against legalization, with the opposite being true for Democrats. Support is highest in the East and West Coast, where the states are mostly Democrat, and lower in the South, where the states are mostly Republican. Much of the opposition comes from parents who don't want to see a marijuana store around the corner from their kids' schools. The Save Our Society from Drugs organization claims it's bad for education. It's dumbing down our kids. Rachel, what do you think?"

"Well, all attempts that I have read about trying to prohibit marijuana have failed to reduce access by any measurable extent. So, it ends up wasting billions of dollars and accounts for hundreds of thousands of arrests each year. The ACLU found that there are several hundred thousand arrests for marijuana possession each year. Black and white Americans use marijuana at similar rates, but black people are more likely to be arrested than whites for marijuana possession. On the other hand, when you legalize it, it allows people to use this reasonably safe substance without the threat of arrest. Also, when it's legal, the government raises money in tax revenue instead of wasting money on enforcing laws. This is money that could be used for other causes. Laws that authorize marijuana use for medical purposes are effective because it helps with some symptoms and diseases. For example, marijuana has been shown to decrease nausea and increase appetite, which can be essential for patients who are having difficulty keeping down food or maintaining adequate nutrition. Also, for glaucoma sufferers, marijuana helps lower eye pressure. Also, some types of pain, such as peripheral neuropathy, respond better to marijuana than conventional pain relievers. Some cancer and AIDS patients have found marijuana to be helpful. Marijuana is not addictive, like many other narcotic drug medications that can be considered addictive, dangerous, or that produce unpleasant side effects."

Rachel looked at Sean and paused.

He responded, "The concern I and others have is that letting for-profit businesses referred to as the Big Marijuana market and sell cannabis may lead them to market aggressively to heavy pot users, who may have drug problems. In fact, we already do. This is similar to what's happened in the alcohol and tobacco industries, where companies make much of their profits from users with serious addiction issues. Among alcohol users, for instance, the top 10 percent of users consume, on average, more than ten drinks each day. It gets out of control.

"Marijuana is not *prescribed* for anything. It can't be because the FDA has never approved it to treat any disease, and there is little evidence that smoked cannabis or THC extracts help any of the diseases you mention except pain. Physicians *authorize* its use, usually after very short visits by patients who have come to them specifically to receive an authorization card. By far, the most common conditions medical marijuana is authorized for are pain and self-reported psychiatric conditions, such as anxiety and insomnia, not diseases such as Parkinson's.

"I accept that marijuana may have some benefits when prescribed properly and responsibly by a doctor. The problem is prolific use creates abuse, and I don't have a lot of trust in doctors' use of proper discretion. After receiving an authorization card, *patients* can then buy as much marijuana as they like for a year for any reason they choose. Most users are recreational users before they became *patients*. And there is no difference between medical and recreational marijuana. They are the same drug. Further, the vast majority of physicians will not write authorizations, at least according to the states that keep track of physician authorizations. A tiny number of doctors—so-called pot doctors—write prescriptions for nearly all of them."

"I don't think the proliferation is nationwide," Jackson argued. "In fact, worldwide use of marijuana can't be stopped. It's here to stay. The best thing we can do is to educate the public about the need for caution. We need to have controls on its distribution and education about proper use. All substances that affect our bodies need to be carefully scrutinized. Educating the public won't stop abuse, but it will slow it down. What are your thoughts on CBD?"

Sean said, "CBD has exploded in its use, growing faster than marijuana, by far. From what research I have done, CBD is safe to use and has benefits. Not everyone agrees on its benefits, but I have yet to hear any credible reports on it being harmful in any way."

"I'm not quite clear on the specifics of the content and impact of CBD and THT. I understand CBD doesn't produce a high, so the content must be different."

"It's THC, not THT."

"Oops, I knew that. What can you tell us about the specific differences?"

"It's all to do with the cannabis plant," Rachel said. "THC is the psychoactive component, which gets you high. THC is referred to as a recreational drug. It modulates sleeping and eating habits, the perception of pain, and countless other bodily functions. It may be useful in helping things like multiple sclerosis, nausea, vomiting, chronic pain, and some others I can't recall. The terms *cannabinoids* and *cannabis* are a little confusing. While cannabinoids are present in several plants, cannabis is the only plant known to contain CBD. CBD has the same chemical formula as THC, with the atoms in a different arrangement. For CBD to qualify, it can't have more than 3 percent THC. My uncle, Wayne, has Parkinson's and uses CBD oil regularly. It has also been shown, in studies, to help with inflammation, depression, anxiety, diabetes, and others. Some even see it as helpful in heart disease. The sale of CBD is popping up across the United States—and around the world—at a fast pace."

"How long has CBD been used?" Sean questioned.

"Actually, I don't know exactly. It started somewhere in the forties, but it only became popular in recent years. I'm not sure why it took that long, but it's on a roll now. You can buy it online or in stores that are opening up in almost every city. What I see as an issue is a challenge to find the right CBD for yourself. It comes in different concentrations and differs widely in the way it's made. Most importantly, the quality and purity of CBD oils, and therefore their effectiveness, varies from one manufacturer to the other. Some list the amounts in milligrams, such as 250 milligrams, 500, or 1,000. Other CBD oil products might list the concentration as percentages instead, such as 4 percent, 10 percent, or 20 percent cannabidiol, or CBD. There are not a lot of experts out there. Best if you go to someone who has been in business for a while and is known to be reliable."

"Do you use it?"

"Yes, I started with a product with a low dosage and then gradually worked my way up. I think it was 250 milligrams. I'm now on 500, and it calms me down and just makes me feel a little better. The low dosage didn't seem to affect me. That's what you're supposed to do: take a low dose and observe the effects over the course of several days or a few weeks. If you don't see the desired effect after this period, you increase your dosage."

"Great, I learned something," Jackson said, smiling. "However, I feel pretty darn good already, so I don't think I'll try it."

"Since we're talking drugs, or at least something other than food that we put in our bodies." Sean paused for a second, noticing Rachel wanted to make a point.

"You said a *drug*, and you are technically correct. To me, though, CBD is not a drug; it's a supplement. Although you are correct because it doesn't qualify as a supplement by the FDA."

Jackson picked up on where Sean was likely headed. "Since we are on drugs, what are your thoughts about the huge addiction problem in this country? This is an issue that I think both political parties agree is a big problem. I'm talking about the horrific problem of serious drug and alcohol misuse. It has been covered in a shocking fashion by the surgeon general. There were more than twenty-five million people in America last year who self-reported the misuse of illegal drugs or opioid-based prescription drugs. Incidentally, another sixty-six million reported binge drinking.

"Those sorts of numbers are hard to fathom. The economic toll is beyond staggering. The yearly annual economic impact from the misuse of prescription drugs, illicit drugs, or alcohol is more than four hundred billion dollars. Think about that number for a second. That is an economy-wrecking number. That sort of number means that this problem is taking root everywhere."

"I don't think we will agree on the means to solve the problem," Rachel said.

Sean smiled. "I think you're right, but we have to try."

"You're right," Jackson said. "I said both parties agree that it's a huge problem, but they don't agree on how to deal with it. The parties are so divided now; it seems absurd that this is one important issue they appear to agree is a problem, and they can't come up with a solution. Marijuana is in the limelight, but it's not the big problem that prescription drugs are; neither is drinking beer on Friday night after work or on a Sunday afternoon."

"Having pretty much clarified our positions on marijuana, what are your thoughts about the drug problem in the United States? And it is a problem. Deaths from drug overdoses in the United States are reaching staggering new heights. I recall the annual numbers in the past couple of years were more than seventy thousand. Think about it: seventy thousand unnecessary deaths in one year. In the terrible Vietnam War, total casualties were fifty-eight thousand, and in the Iraq War, there were about four thousand.

"The National Council on Alcoholism and Drug Dependency estimates that more than twenty million Americans are addicted to alcohol and other drugs. According to the Substance Abuse and Mental Health Services Administration, more than two million receive care at addiction-treatment facilities. The American market for addiction treatment is about thirty-five billion dollars per year. Any research I've done on drug treatment shows that it lowers drug addiction and actually saves money on the total addiction cost.

"If you include the staggering costs associated with criminal justice, treatment, and loss of productivity, estimates are that the real cost of America's drug epidemic exceeds a trillion dollars. That's more than the annual military budget, which is around seven hundred billion or more than the cost of welfare, which is usually similar to the military budget. I'm sure drug addiction impacts our annual health care costs, which is, of course, the biggest of all costs at four trillion. By the way, gun violence costs about a hundred million annually."

Sean said, "I think it's ironic that Obama is considered—and is—well spoken, however, he said something to the effect that when he was a teenager, he used drugs, drank, and pretty much tried whatever was out there. Then he added and seemed to imply, as a legitimate reason, 'But I was in Hawaii, and it was a pretty relaxed place.' Trump, on the other hand, despite all his reckless talk and being considered a bad guy by the liberals, has claimed, and it has never been refuted that he has never taken drugs of any kind, never had a glass of alcohol, never had a cigarette, never had a cup of coffee, and has called the crisis a 'national shame and human tragedy.'"

Rachel laughed. "I have a hard time believing that given all the lies he has been caught in."

"That's actually not the issue."

"You brought it up," Rachel said, poking Sean's arm.

"My point is that the growing drug crisis sweeping across the United States is deadlier than gun violence, car crashes, or AIDS, none of which have killed as many Americans in a year as overdoses do. The Center for Disease Control and Prevention says the crisis is getting worse. It's not confined to a small number of states or to lower-income people. It has spread across the whole country. While there are regional differences in the type of substance, overdose deaths are happening everywhere.

"The problem is that illegal narcotics are more readily available than ever, and drug distribution networks have expanded to rural and suburban areas. Part of the reason illicit drug traders are able to proliferate so widely across the Midwest and other regions has to do with the market there. These areas are home to thousands of people who first developed an addiction to prescription pills. The medical sector is a leading consumer of opioids, which produce morphine-like effects. This has to do with the fact that opioid-based painkillers have become a common remedy for a variety of conditions, such as back pain and arthritis."

Jackson nodded his head. "I've heard that the pharmaceutical companies aggressively lobbied doctors to prescribe new drugs such as OxyContin, which they claim could provide effective pain relief with no real addiction risk—even to long-term patients.

"An interesting point here is that the American medical sector ranks second in the world for opioid use. We have more than seventy thousand opioid-related deaths per year. The worst states are Alabama, Arizona, California, and Florida.

"Drug task forces suggest availability has been a key factor," Sean continued. "A lot of it has been a diversion from people who were just selling a surplus, overprescribing, the pharmaceuticals, that type of stuff. Various mental health boards have reported high access in terms of doctors prescribing opiates—and us as a society not having a clear picture of what the impact of that would be long term."

"Wow, Sean, you have really studied this."

"I'm concerned. I've got a lot of young employees, and I have my kids' futures to think about."

"I'm with you guys," Rachel said. "The cost is enormous. There are so many other ways we could use that money. I read that substance abuse costs are approaching a trillion dollars a year, but I understand tobacco and alcohol costs still top the cost of drugs."

Sean nodded. "Treatment is a major cost, and detox facilities have become a huge industry, but they are much less expensive than the alternatives, like incarcerating addicted persons. According to several conservative estimates, every dollar invested in addiction-treatment programs returns positive funds to reduced drug-related crime, criminal justice costs, and theft. When savings related to health care are included, total savings are even more. Major savings to the individual and to society also come from fewer conflicts, greater workplace productivity, and fewer drug-related accidents, including overdoses and deaths."

"And, let's not let the big pharmaceutical companies off the hook," Rachel said. "They appear to be making huge profits, and they are saving on taxes. Let me make a point on a related issue, health care, where I favor a single-payer system, by the way. We have serious problems, and I don't see the Trump administration solving anything.

"Americans shouldn't have to watch their children suffer without health care or be forced to choose between buying food or the medicines they need to stay alive. This is happening every day, and the way drug companies do business is contributing to this tragedy. Drug companies are cheating governments out of tax revenues that could be invested in health care. The medicines they produce are out of the reach of poor people. And they are using their power and influence to eliminate attempts to cut the cost of drugs.

"Tax dodging is fueling the inequality crisis and widening the gap between rich and poor. When drug companies dodge taxes, the poor suffer the most since governments seek to balance their budgets by cutting essential services. Also, while tax-avoidance figures appear lower in developing countries, the impact can be more severe because poorer countries often have weaker public services. Governments should insist that companies publish financial information for every country where they do business so it is clear if they are paying their fair share of taxes."

CHAPTER 12

WAGES

"Can we do a little more presidential trivia? I'm confident I can beat Sean."

"Sure, let me see."

"Past presidents John Adams, John Quincy Adams, Rutherford B. Hayes, John F. Kennedy, Theodore Roosevelt, and Franklin Roosevelt all attended Harvard. The father of one of them advised Harvard that his son was careless and lacked application. Which one was he?"

"While you're chewing on that one, one of our presidents would never have been around to become president had he not had an urge to go to the restroom just at the right time. Who was he?"

"The first one was JFK. I have no idea on the second one," Rachel responded.

"You, Mr. McCarthy?"

"Don't know."

"It was Lyndon Johnson. He was on a bombing mission, and Lyndon got off on a fuel stop and missed the takeoff while going to the restroom. The plane crashed on a mission, and all aboard died. Had he been on the plane, he would never have been here to become president."

"Back to even again."

"I'm on a roll now."

"You're cute." Sean smiled.

"What about legislating a minimum living wage," Rachel offered. "How can a fast-food worker making ten to twelve dollars an hour be expected to support a family? We should increase the minimum wage to twenty an hour."

"This is where liberals are shortsighted," Sean said. "Using fast-food restaurants as an example, the business model for that business is to create a low-operating-cost food-service facility that can provide restaurant food quickly and at low cost. Successful fast-food restaurant operators make an average of about 8 percent profit. As that business model has developed over the years, they have used a large number of part-time student workers. These are not jobs intended to support families. They are students working part-time and, in some cases, even retired people working part-time to keep busy and have some extra income. That's the business model of fast-food restaurants. Change it by raising wages too high, and you will see prices rise higher and higher to cover the cost. That will be followed by restaurant closings and lost jobs."

"I call it using cheap labor. Underpaying workers to make big profits? How much do the owners make? I see some McDonald's and Taco Bell owners driving their Mercedes to play golf at their country club, while their workers ride home on a bike to some little apartment. And while low pay might make sense for students or those seeking extra pocket money, not everyone who works minimum wage in a restaurant fits this profile."

"Restaurant profits are all over the board. Restaurants have more failures than practically any other type of business. It costs two to three million dollars to buy the land, build the business, and pay for the franchise to get started. Most owners work long hours. Some, after taking the risk and putting in years of hard work, eventually make a lot of money. That takes us back to the success of the free enterprise system. You work hard, take risks, and if you are lucky, you make a lot of money. Without that incentive, you would have less business development and fewer jobs. Restaurant work provides an excellent format for young people getting their first jobs. They learn about responsibility and the importance of working with others. It's a beneficial part of their education."

Rachel sighed. "I don't support the concept that liberals believe in individual action and progressives believe in collective action. European liberals in the center-right generally favor limited government intervention in the economy. Most of them adhere to economic liberalism, conservative liberalism, or liberal conservatism. As far as I can tell, 'conservatives' want weak central government—just strong enough to keep the post office open and the army buying weapons. They also want a weak state government, just big enough to run the courts and bail out failing businesses. What they really want is a nation governed by businesses and churches. They want nonwhites to learn English and accept a subservient role in the nation. This means they get the worst jobs and poor salaries and get to take the brunt of any austerity measures or economic hardships. They want women to accept their roles as mothers, daughters, and sisters. They want women to do a lot of unpaid work built around the promotion of their husbands and sons, training their daughters just enough to work hard, bear children, and ... maybe, if they're above-average in smarts, teach or nurse."

"Wow, do you really think it's that bad? Maybe in the Middle East. Maybe a hundred years ago—but not today."

"I'm not saying all conservatives see it that way. That's just the vision of the far right."

"I guess I don't know any far-right people because I don't know of any conservatives who are that extreme."

"One point before we get on immigration. I have to tell you, Sean, I question your numbers on income tax. The middle class has taken a beating under Trump. Of course, all the while, the wealthy have seen their tax rates take a big fall."

"As I see it, nearly everyone has benefited from reasonable tax cuts, either from paying lower taxes or from the increase in job opportunities. Check it out sometime ... the high-income earners pay the bulk of taxes. Something like 95 percent of taxes are paid by 50 percent of the people. The other 50 percent pay around 5 percent."

"Those numbers are misleading. Of course, the high-income earners pay more in total. That's because they have such comparatively high incomes."

"Enough on taxes. Let's talk more on immigration," Jackson said. "I'm here because my ancestors came here as slaves. I'd like to hear your comments on immigration, all the hubbub about immigration reform, the millions of men, women, and children who are technically here in the United States illegally. Talking about immigrants reminds me of a story."

A Scottish woman goes to the local newspaper office to see that the obituary for her recently deceased husband is published.

The obit editor informs her that there is a charge of fifty cents per word.

She pauses, reflects, and then she says, 'Well, then, let it read: 'Angus MacPherson died.'"

Amused at the woman's thrift, the editor tells her that there is a seven-word minimum for all obituaries.

She thinks it over and says, "In that case, let it read: 'Angus MacPherson died. Golf clubs for sale.'"

☆   ☆   ☆

Rachel and Sean laughed.

"Okay," Jackson said. "Let's get back to immigration."

CHAPTER 13

IMMIGRATION

Sean said, "Those with long memories have recalled that prominent Democrats, including Senator Chuck Schumer and then-Senators Barack Obama and Hillary Clinton, were at one time heartily in favor of funding a barrier wall on the southern American border. You can find multiple records of their sentiments from back in the day when the earnest lawmakers embraced border security with enthusiasm. They funded a 287-mile wall in Jordan last year. If it's okay in other countries, why not on our border? Nancy Pelosi argued that 'walls are immoral.' Chuck Schumer called President Trump's stand against open borders a 'manufactured crisis.' But less than one year ago, Pelosi and Schumer approved funding for that long border wall in Jordan."

Jackson said, "You both agree that immigrants who want to come here and become good citizens are good for America. Your difference is whether or not we should be selective in a way to eliminate those who come and may break our laws. Making that determination is not possible. Some break laws out of desperation to feed their families."

Sean raised two fingers. "There are two kinds of people we don't like to see here: those who break the law and hookers. For lawbreakers, the reason is obvious. As for hookers, we should flat out tell them they are not welcome. Sanctuary cities are absurd. That's just plain protecting people who break our laws. I don't get it," he said, looking at Rachel. "Why do we want to protect people who break our laws?"

Rachel answered, "Sanctuary cities are safer because they encourage good relationships between undocumented immigrants and law enforcement. Murder rates went down in San Francisco after they became a sanctuary city."

"I would have to see those numbers; it doesn't make any sense."

Jackson came back and said, "First of all, when we talk immigration, as with other issues, let's try to look at it logically. Do we want open borders, letting anyone in this country who wants to come? I doubt very many Americans want to see that happen. At a minimum, we should try to keep out the felons and drug dealers. On the other hand, this is America; we are a nation of immigrants. We either came here as immigrants or our grandparents—or past generations—did. So, I see those two points as a given. Let's have some fun with this; how about you guys debate the extremes, and then we can talk about a compromise."

Rachel pointed her finger in the air with a grin. "I agree with Jackson. Let's stick with immigration. It's a good topic for us to discuss. I like it because Sean can't possibly defend the disastrous Republican policies. Parents separated from their children? Trying to build a wall like they do in communist countries? The founding fathers you refer to were immigrants. We have continued to be a nation of immigrants. How do you just start shutting them out, sending families back to starvation and chaos? Your favorite Republican, Reagan, said, 'Tear down this wall.' Donald Trump said, 'Put up this wall.'"

"Let me ask you this: do you think we should have laws in this country?" Sean argued.

"That's a loaded question. Of course, we need laws—if the laws are reasonable and properly enforced, yes."

"And who determines whether they are reasonable and properly enforced?"

"The courts."

"So, you're saying our laws should be enforced until such time the law is changed by way of legislation."

"Not always. One of our famous founders, your man Thomas Jefferson, said, 'If a law is unjust, a man is not only right to disobey it, he is obligated to do so.'"

"I don't recall saying I agreed with everything Jefferson ever said."

"Where we are going with this?" Jackson asked.

Sean said, "My point is if we have laws, we should enforce them; otherwise, why have them? The law says you need to go through the immigration process to come here. We have people coming from

South America, Mexico, and other countries, in violation of our laws, committing crimes, getting sent back home, and then coming back and breaking more laws. They are often protected by American sanctuary cities. What sense does that make?"

"Some people in this country have been the subject of prejudicial laws," Rachel said. "Sanctuary cities provide an opportunity to issue broad public challenges to injustices within the legal system. Federal immigration enforcement often limits local involvement. Sanctuary cities want to protect everyone who lives within their jurisdiction regardless of legal status."

"That's absurd. This is America; we are a nation, a nation of freedom with law and order. Immigration is a national issue. An issue that should be governed at the federal level, supported by the states, not different laws for every state. Allowing states to harbor criminals is absurd."

"Let me tell you a story I am familiar with. A family lived in Guadalajara, Mexico, where the father worked on a ranch, and the mother was a waitress. The family's oldest child stayed home to take care of the younger children. The town they lived in was dangerous. The father was shot and killed for no known reason. The mother wanted to move to America in search of a safer place for her family. They found their way to America, and the children got into a school while the mother worked as a waitress. The oldest son finished school and became a policeman. The whole family is thankful for America. They love America. Should this family have been denied entry to our country?"

Sean responded, "I understand your point, but—"

"Just a minute, and then you can respond, but let me mention one more that I recall. CBS News gave a report some time ago about a man named Armando, in his thirties. His situation was one of so many when he said, 'I just want my family to be acknowledged as human beings. I work hard every day while in fear of being separated from my family.'"

"I understand your point and sympathize with them. Your examples are not a problem. The problem is those who come here and commit crimes. And we have millions of American citizens living at poverty levels, living on the streets. We have thousands of Americans killed in the streets of Chicago. Those problems should take priority. What's the purpose of protecting illegal criminals in sanctuary cities? How would you like to lose a family member as the result of a gunshot from an illegal who has been deported and reentered this country?"

Rachel was on the edge of her stool. "Wait, I'm not done yet. We as humans should be born free, yet are often caged by walls, fences, and guns, limiting movement and opportunity. The issue shouldn't be political; it is economical and moral. The gifts of nature are not distributed evenly. These differences create variations in wealth and are often suppressed by types of government, religious prejudices, and closed borders, consequently sentencing families to lives of struggle and poverty."

"That's an impressive argument, and I commend your compassion, but the United States can't solve all the world's problems. We are a generous nation, providing more foreign aid than any other country while still having our own poverty to take care of. What do you want for the future of our children in America? Providing safe and healthy lives for our children should be priority one. Our resources are not unlimited. Unlimited immigration will impact our ability to provide opportunities for American citizens. Our welfare system will become overly burdened."

"I believe the majority of immigrants who want to come to America want to come here to work and be good citizens. We need to allow some of them in and can accommodate those who can fill jobs where we have a shortage of citizens to fill those jobs. Taking jobs at lower wages that would otherwise be sought by Americans, however, is not good for our country. It also promotes economic inequality and increases welfare costs. You refer to America being a nation of immigrants. That's not really a valid reason for open borders because today's immigrants don't assimilate and actually have become a major source of crime. They tax our welfare system and usually don't pay taxes. Add these concerns to the concern for exposing our country to easy access for terrorist, and you have the necessity to monitor, screen, and limit entry into this country. It's only common sense. Look at what's going on around the world. If you cross the North Korean border illegally, you go to prison and do hard labor for up to twelve years. In Iran, you are detained indefinitely. In Afghanistan, you are shot; in Saudi Arabia, you go to jail; in China, you just may never be heard from again. In Cuba, they toss you in jail for as long as they care to. Yet when you cross the US border, you get a job, a driver's license, and a Social Security card."

"Can I make a comment here?"

Sean and Rachel both motioned for Jackson to speak.

"I think we are in dire need of immigration reform. We are a nation of immigrants and desperately need to legislate proper policies. What we have now is nonfunctional. You can't have millions of people in two adjacent countries—with different laws, regulations, and welfare systems—exist with a shared border that's not managed and not have serious problems. We need some type of system of management for crossing that border."

"The problem is that our nonfunctional government can't work together enough to accomplish that 'not-so-difficult task.' The Republicans and Democrats just keep fighting over whether to have or not have a wall and what is a wall. It's all silly. They don't reason whether the wall is needed or not; they are for it or against it based on party line thinking. The logic of choice is just not there. I heard quotes that 'a wall is immoral.' Furthermore, how is it immoral between the United States and Mexico and not immoral in other parts of the world? Both parties funded and paid for a 287-mile wall in Jordan. The wall in Israel has been a lifesaver. We already have existing walls between the United States and Mexico of more than 650 miles, approved by Democrats and Republicans. Much of the current walls are fencing that is not too tough to compromise. A wall is a wall is a wall. If you have one, it should be a real wall that has an extremely high difficulty to get over or under. This is not difficult stuff; it is just common sense."

"These politicians often contradict themselves on the key issues if they think they need to switch positions to oppose a candidate in the other party. Both parties do it."

Rachel responded while attending to her cell phone. "I think that's a bit of an exaggeration. Excuse me for looking at my phone ... I'm keeping track of an Uber driver. He was twelve minutes away, then back up to fourteen, been there for twenty minutes. He must have stalled somehow."

"Which way are you going?" Sean asked.

"I'm at the Marriott."

"I'm there also. We should share a ride."

"You would share a ride with a left-wing liberal?"

Sean smiled and offered a toast. "Here's to sharing with a socialist."

"Nah, nah, a progressive, not a socialist." Rachel obliged with a less than enthusiastic bump of her glass.

"Uber's not coming until the roads are clear," Jackson said, "which is all right by me. I'm enjoying the debate. You both have good points. In my opinion, one of the big obstacles of these issues is cost. At some point, I want to tell you about a simple plan I favor that would save lives, crime, and billions in costs. That money could be used to help solve some of the issues you're talking about. I've explained what I think of as an 'American Foundation plan' to a senator and several congressmen. They just say they will check into it—then either they don't get back to me or they question the probability of ever getting enough support to make any headway with it."

"So, what's your proposal?" Sean asked.

"Not yet, maybe later. I want to hear more of your debate first, but I can tell you my proposal will be of value in this debate."

Rachel smiled. "Let's face reality. The United States is clearly a nation of immigrants. Immigration was taken into consideration when this country was founded in 1776. They were committed to open borders. Our charter document outlined our country's fundamental economic principles and how people should be allowed to move around the earth freely. As they conveyed it, the natural benefits are open to all. The majority of immigrants are seeking a better life and contribute to economic productivity and live life peacefully. Closed borders promote inequality and racial divide. In 1776, America was coping with a huge debt. They debated about immigration and questions about dealing with foreign trade. The Declaration of Independence established the new republic's fundamental economic principles. Closing borders threatens those achievements. When America declared independence, they set forth to pursue policies of free trade and free immigration. A committee, including John Adams, Thomas Jefferson, and Benjamin Franklin, condemned England for 'cutting off our trade with other parts of the world.'

"The resources of the earth are not evenly divided. Wealth and income created by these differences are magnified by the nations that suppress entrepreneurship and promote religious intolerance, gender discrimination, and bigotry. Closed borders increase those injustices, creating inequality. The argument for open borders is both an economic and a moral argument. All people should be free to move about the earth—not limited by the lines we refer to as borders. The overwhelming majority of immigrants want to make a better life for themselves and their families. Geographical differences in wages also signal an opportunity for migrants, increasing world output. Some economists project that a world of open borders would bring about a huge increase in world productivity."

"And massive crime and terrorism," Sean blurted out. "Sorry—go ahead and finish your thoughts."

"You're underestimating why the vast majority want to come here. Ellis Island officially opened in 1892, subsequently processing more than twenty million immigrants from around the world. These people were seeking a better life in America. The goal was to create a melting pot in which immigrants successfully assimilate and become representative of our national identity, while also proudly retaining some aspects of their ethnic past. We are all Americans whose ancestors came from Italy, Russia, Poland, Germany, Ireland, Yugoslavia, Mexico, Australia, Nigeria, Pakistan, Egypt, and other countries."

"Wow." Jackson shook his head and smiled.

"Yes, that was impressive." Sean leaned back in his stool, swung around to Rachel, and placed his hand on hers in a brief gesture of respect.

Rachel felt her cheeks warm.

"Yet, I have to correct you on some misguided assumptions and comments," Sean said. "The biggest problem of your open border defense is that we are a much different country today than in the times you are referring to. It was less than four million then, and it's more than 330 million today—plus we have guns and drugs. Allow me to clarify some other points."

"Excuse me. So you want to look to the principles of the founding fathers when we talk about gun laws—but not when we talk about immigration?"

Jackson interrupted, "We're going to be here for a long time. Could you pause while I check on my customers?"

"Sure, Rachel's going to tell me a little about herself and where she acquired all that knowledge."

"Thanks for the compliment. I work for an events planner, did my undergrad at Yale, and got my master's there as well. I've always been an avid reader."

"And your husband?"

"Married my high school boyfriend, a high school and college football player—not good enough to get drafted by the pros and just got by enough in school to stay eligible for football. Jake is a gun lover and watches Fox News and sports on TV. He quit his job as a security guard two years ago to get into real estate sales. We have twin six-year-olds at home. Going through a divorce. It will be final in a week or two. I married for what I thought was love. Turned down a rich boy for a stud muffin. Big mistake. I need to be home with my kids, but I have to work to pay the bills. Interestingly, I was hired on the ninetieth anniversary of the 1920 passing of the legislation for women's right to vote. Can you believe that only that short of a time ago, women couldn't even vote? When my parents were married in the sixties, women were expected to stay home or maybe get a job as a teacher—if the husband was okay with the idea. Okay, that's enough for me. Sean, can I guess you are happily married, you have three kids, and your wife is at home taking care of the kids?"

"Not exactly. She's a sociology professor. You would like her left-wing political philosophy. She belongs to a local political group. I share in homemaking—even though I'm the majority owner and CEO of a restaurant company with close to a thousand employees. I have built the company to a point where I have a solid management team, and some have equity in the company. We have two kids, a boy who's seven and a girl who's five. My wife wants me to help more with the kids so she can spend more with her liberal friends. I'm not comfortable with that. I've given her an alternative to quitting the job—or we quit our marriage. I'm active with our Association, the NRA, that's National Restaurant Association, not the gun guys. I read a lot of books on management, economics, and politics. I also follow the news, mostly on Fox late at night. My wife and I argue more than talk."

Jackson returned with a sly smile. "My customer says he can't have another drink because he's scheduled to go to confession next Sunday. That reminded me of a little story you might enjoy."

☆   ☆   ☆

A woman takes a lover home during the day while her husband is at work. Her nine-year-old son comes home unexpectedly, sees them, and hides in the bedroom closet to watch.

The woman's husband also comes home. She puts her lover in the closet, not realizing that the little boy is in there already.

The little boy says, "Dark in here."

The man says, "Yes, it is."

Boy: I have a baseball.

Man: That's nice.

Boy: Want to buy it?

Man: No, thanks.

Boy: My dad's outside.

Man: Okay. How much?

Boy: Two hundred and fifty dollars.

In the next few weeks, it happens again that the boy and the lover are in the closet together.

Boy: Dark in here.

Man: Yes, it is.

Boy: I have a baseball glove.

The lover, remembering the last time, asks the boy, "How much?"

Boy: Seven hundred and fifty dollars.

Man: Sold.

A few days later, the dad says to the boy, "Grab your glove—let's go outside and have a game of catch."

The boy says, "I can't. I sold my baseball and my glove."

The dad asks, "How much did you sell them for?"

Boy: A thousand bucks.

The dad says, "That's terrible to overcharge your friends like that. That is way more than those two things cost. I'm taking you to church—to confession."

They go to the church, and the dad makes the little boy sit in the confessional booth and closes the door.

The boy says, "Dark in here."

The priest says, "Don't start that shit again—you're in *my* closet now."

Sean and Rachel, both chuckled.

Jackson got back to business. "Okay, you guys are great. You disagree, big-time, and are not getting angry. I'm enjoying this, but

I'm anxious to hear your positions on guns, health care, climate change, education, crime, welfare, taxes, drugs, race relations, and foreign policy."

Sean looked at Rachel. "Rachel, my first thought is on your reference to immigrants assimilating here. That's very idealistic. Assimilation has been a part of past history. Unfortunately, more and more immigrants today, especially illegals and criminals, are not assimilating. They are creating separate neighborhoods. Our founders have written and publicly spoken about their concerns about mass immigration. They advocated the purpose of allowing foreigners into our young nation was to preserve, protect, and enhance the republic—not to recruit millions of new voters or create permanent ruling majorities for political parties. They put their lives on the line to achieve their objective.

"It's a different world out there today. I don't think any civilized countries have fully open and free borders, welcoming all comers. Since you quoted Jefferson, let me give you some other founder quotes. I can read them off my cell phone. In 1790, James Madison said: 'We seek inducements as possible for the worthy part of mankind to come and settle amongst us, and throw their fortunes into a common lot with ours.' Notice he said the worthy part, meaning we need to filter out the unworthy. Madison clearly argued that America should welcome the immigrant who could assimilate but exclude the immigrant who could not readily 'incorporate himself into our society.' How about this one: 'By an intermixture with our people, they, or their descendants, get assimilated to our customs, measures, laws: in a word soon become one people.' That was none other than George Washington.

"Alexander Hamilton, apparently with a concern for the future, wrote in 1802: 'The safety of a republic depends essentially on the energy of a common national sentiment; on a uniformity of principles and habits; on the exemption of the citizens from foreign bias and prejudice; and on that love of country which will almost invariably be found to be closely connected with birth, education, and family.' Research of the founding fathers will verify their opinion that applicants wanting to immigrate to our nation don't have the constitutional right or civil right to demand entry into the United States. It's a simple fact that it is essential to have supervised and restricted borders to protect the sovereignty of our own citizens.

"I talked about this in my economics club; we meet every Thursday for two hours. The government has numbers on the impact of illegal immigration. Although I don't recall exact numbers, I can be close; we have more than fifty thousand illegals in federal prisons and more than two hundred fifty thousand in local jails, and they estimate that, in total, they accounted for more than a million and a half arrests or seven times per person. I don't know what that costs us, but we, as law-abiding citizens, are paying for it.

"As our founding fathers intended. They expected—they looked forward to—millions of immigrants coming to America to partake in this new nation conceived in liberty and dedicated to the proposition that all citizens are created equal. By all means, to the founders, immigration was a mutually beneficial process. For the first time in their lives, immigrants would benefit from an open society in which they were encouraged to participate in the nation's political and civic life, while also enjoying the fruits of their labor and a standard of living beyond expectations.

"In exchange, ethnic groups coming to America would, by way of their unique customs and traditions, contribute to the evolving American character, changing it and shaping it in ways that benefited everyone. A melting pot includes many flavors and ingredients. So to with America's character, which delights in its German beer, Irish music, French architecture, Italian architecture, African art, French literature, Latin American cooking, and many other historical, cultural, scientific, and educational contributions. But the founders also insisted that immigrants assimilate in ways that resulted in them having American opinions and beliefs, including loyalty to their new country that exceeds the loyalty to their old one."

"Let's hear what Jackson has to say," Rachel said.

Jackson suddenly lit up. "I am very impressed by your knowledge. What I am not hearing are solutions to your differences. Of all the nationalities, my African American heritage has faced the most difficulty being accepted. I realize Irish, Jewish, and others have had challenges, but nothing like African Americans. It has taken a long time for us to go from slavery to second-class citizens to today. We have all the rights of citizenship, but we still see problems with acceptance.

"The leadership in the black communities has not done a good job. They need to get more involved in improving the qualifications of people of color to get better educations and create more jobs. Better yet, African Americans need to develop business and become more a part of the free enterprise system.

"I was lucky; I had a father at home. He and my mom encouraged and helped me get through high school and two years of college. I could have gone on, but I liked my job at this bar so much that I decided to make it a career. And I'm not sorry about that. I love it here. In my opinion, what we need is a clearly defined immigration policy. Completely open borders, without regard to controlling drug trafficking and the return of those who have committed crimes, is unrealistic. On the other hand, we are a nation created from immigration, so we need to welcome and accept those who seek to come here to make a better life. So, the question is not about open or closed borders. We do need to screen out those who create problems and place added burdens to our welfare and justice system. It's a management problem. A very difficult management problem."

"So, what's your solution?" Rachel asked.

"Nobody wants to hear my ideas. I want to see you guys come up with a compromise idea. My foundation plan would be helpful. As I said earlier, I'll talk about it next time we meet."

Sean startled. "We're doing this again?"

Rachel laughed. "I don't see that we're making enough progress to call for another meeting."

Sean continued, "US Census data shows that the overall population of immigrants is at an all-time high, of more than forty million. As many as seven million immigrants entered the United States during President Obama's presidency; two million came illegally by crossing the border or overstaying their visas. Californians, as a whole, oppose population sanctuary cities, big-time. A UC Berkeley study verified these findings for the reading public. Nearly 80 percent of those polled from all political leanings opposed policies that declined cooperation between local law enforcement and federal agencies. What's the surprise here? These sanctuary city policies amount to nothing more than dangerous posturing from desperate, self-serving, predominantly Democratic politicians and left-wing groups.

"The California Values Act ensures that police and sheriffs don't help ICE round up and deport immigrants in California, and it's without consideration of crimes they have committed. The

American Civil Liberties Union supported the law's passage and has advocated for similar measures in other states. This bars essential contact between California law enforcement officers and Immigration and Customs Enforcement. It's ludicrous. The appropriate and logical policy is for ICE to issue detainers to go to local jails, and law enforcement officers to release the names of convicts before turning them over to ICE.

"Following revisions from Governor Brown, jurisdictions may report heinous crimes to ICE—only if they want to! The law prohibits state and local law enforcement from reporting criminals to federal immigration authorities unless the criminal has been convicted of a serious crime. The list of offenses is lengthy but includes felonies like rape, kidnapping, stalking, various forms of abuse, possession of an unlawful weapon, felony-status DUI, and involvement in drug trafficking. The California law requires the state attorney general's office to create model policies limiting the extent that public facilities like schools, hospitals, libraries, and courthouses can aid immigration authorities. The law also subjects law enforcement agencies to produce annual reports on how many immigrants they send to federal authorities."

Rachel said, "In 1776, American patriots were coping with problems of crushing sovereign debt, debates about immigration, and questions about managing foreign trade. The Declaration of Independence outlined the new republic's fundamental economic principles. Closing borders threatens those achievements. When Americans declared independence, they wanted to pursue new, independent economic policies of free trade and free immigration. A committee of five, including John Adams, Thomas Jefferson, and Benjamin Franklin, drew up the Declaration of Independence and condemned King George III for 'cutting off our trade with all parts of the world."

"Look—I don't need to give you a lot of quotes and philosophy," Sean said. "We needed to open the gates and let the people in during the infancy of this nation. Now that we have matured and have established laws, we need to enforce the laws. Without laws, you have chaos, more crime, and more drugs. If you come here, you should have a reasonable purpose, a job, or family to go to. I know some people in this world have it tough, living in poverty and dangerous dictatorships. That's unfortunate, but we can't solve all the world's problems. We have to protect our citizens from those who come here to commit crimes. What's wrong with checkpoints to at least try to filter out those who may be trying to get in to commit crimes, or worse yet, commit terrorist acts? Do you think we should allow someone in this country who has previously committed a crime? Yes or no?"

"Not a known felon, but we will never have a perfect system, just like we can't prevent all crime among our citizens. Why spend billions on a wall to stop a few bad guys? We have a lot of citizens committing crimes."

Jackson said, "One thing we can all agree on is that we need comprehensive immigration reform."

"We can all agree on needing the reform. I doubt we'll ever agree on the content," Rachel answered. "Not unless some of us are willing to bend a little—and I think that is possible."

"Not if you just want to let anybody come in at any time," Sean argued. "Look—I keep hearing the argument that we are a nation of immigrants, and somehow that equates to the need to let foreigners just flow in. The immigrants who are coming in today are not quite like those who passed through Ellis Island. Too many of those coming in today are coming for the wrong purpose. The people coming around 1900 had to get off a ship in New York to be documented. On arrival, many got down on their knees to kiss the ground. They pledged to obey our laws and support their new country. They sought a new life for their children and to assimilate into our culture. No free lunch or welfare. They had the skills to contribute and wanted to work to get ahead. Many joined our military to defend their new country. To many of the immigrants of today come to seek benefits and usually don't assimilate into our society. They often form gangs. Some want to take down our Statue of Liberty. Before you call me cynical, I assure you I realize many want to come here for the right purpose. We want those to come. The question is, how do we get those coming for the right purpose. We do it with a border-controlled immigration system and identification."

Rachel squirmed in her chair. "Sean, you have a very cynical and unsympathetic opinion of today's immigrants. We can never agree on immigration policy as long as we are so far apart on the character and quality of the people. Jackson, I would like to hear your opinion. Border walls are shameful. How do we just turn away from people who are desperate for better lives?"

"Okay, I'd like to get logical. I don't get it when I hear people say borders don't work. If you want to go from place A to place B, it's certainly more difficult to get there if you have a wall to cope with, and how many get by depends on how good of wall you build. Also, I can tell you, in my opinion, totally open borders, allowing drug dealers, previously convicted criminals, and potential terrorists come in is setting this country up for a lot of problems that will haunt our future. I can see the objection to a wall. It seems kind of cruel. Yet we have to protect our country from the bad guys. I realize we need immigrants. And, Sean, I think you underestimate the quality of those who want to come here. I agree that we are a nation of immigrants and always will be. Rachel, you have to have qualification requirements for teachers. Sean has quality control in his restaurants. I have quality control in this bar and provide an atmosphere of comfort for our lawmakers. Everything in life has a filter to screen the good from the bad. I keep thinking about the plan I have that I am not ready to talk about yet. I can tell you if it could ever get legislated and approved, it would save lives and money and solve many problems."

"Gee, I can't wait. A miracle plan?" Rachel smiled.

Sean looked at Jackson skeptically. "No countries have fully open and free borders, welcoming all comers. Let's look at what happens when you cross some borders around the world. If you cross the North Korean border illegally, you get twelve years hard labor. If you cross the Iranian border illegally, you are detained indefinitely. If you cross the Afghan border illegally, you get shot. If you cross the Saudi Arabian border illegally, you will be jailed. If you cross the Chinese border illegally, you may never be heard from again. If you cross the Venezuelan border illegally, you will be branded a spy—and your fate will be sealed. If you cross the Cuban border illegally, you will be thrown into political prison to rot. If you cross the US border illegally, you get a job, a driver's license, and a Social Security card."

"Okay, okay. I get the picture. That's an exaggeration."

"What do we have borders for if we don't control them?"

Rachel said, "Capital, big business, and the rich already have open borders. It's time to extend that to everyone."

"But, Rachel, wherever border policing is out of control, and practically all comers are welcome, big problems occur."

Rachel opened her mouth, but Sean softly held up his hand. "I'm almost done, I promise. I think you'll find this next part interesting. Most Americans don't realize that Democrats make money and power off illegal aliens being in their districts. This is why they create 'sanctuary' cities and states. By including them as part of the population in the census, they get millions of dollars from federal government-assistance programs from your tax dollars ... and for every 770,000 illegal aliens in their Democrat-controlled area, they get a seat added in the US House of Representatives subsequent to a new census.

"A while back, the topic of crime committed by illegal immigrants with criminal pasts hit the front-page news with the murder of two California law enforcement officers and a woman in San Francisco. A study released in 2011 by the Government Accounting Office reported on incarcerations, arrests, and costs of criminal immigrants. It estimated that the study population of these 249,000 criminals had actually been previously arrested around 1.5 million times." Looking at his cell, Sean added, "This involved a half-million drug-related offenses, 70,000 sexual offenses, 213,000 assaults, 125,000 arrests for larceny/theft, and 25,000 homicides. That report noted the number of criminal illegal immigrants in federal prisons in 2010 was about 55,000; the number incarcerated in state prison systems and local jails was approximately 296,000 for 2009. The makeup of those criminal immigrants incarcerated in federal prisons: 68 percent were citizens of Mexico, and almost 90 percent were from one of seven Latin American countries: Mexico, Colombia, Guatemala, Honduras, El Salvador, Cuba, and the Dominican Republic. I could come up with more. The numbers are stunning."

"I think we can agree that immigration reform is definitely needed," Jackson said. "We have duly elected legislators. They should get on it and work out the details. The broad guidelines should be within the framework that complete elimination of immigration or complete open borders is unrealistic. Obviously, the answer lies somewhere in between. Our legislators should create a plan to allow immigration of those who are not known to have criminal records and are seeking work in areas where we in America are in need of workers or in situations where they have an approved job. A study should be done to establish if and where border walls have been helpful. Those who have already been here for a reasonably stipulated time should be given a reasonable path to citizenship. Felons should be exported, and those with three or more misdemeanors should be identified as probationary immigrants and be required to maintain a clean record for three years, whereby more than one additional misdemeanor or a felony would require their deportation. Quite obviously, the only way this will work is with a meaningful identification system. All immigrants should be registered and carry verifiable identification. Any employer who hires an immigrant without an appropriate ID should be fined. All cities should be required to cooperate with the plan. All the fine details should be resolved by Congress. I know ... how will that ever happen?"

Rachel shook her head. "I was just going to say good luck with that."

"Tell me this, do you agree that if we could proceed like I have outlined, we would have improved our immigration system?"

"I have argued open borders to make a point and defend my positions with my liberal friends. In practice, I agree that completely open borders would be dangerous. I think your plan is too restrictive; it's too much in line with Sean's thinking."

Rachel patted Sean on the hand. "However, for the sake of your impressive efforts and depending on the final details, I could live with it until a more immigrant-welcoming plan arrived."

Sean, privately enjoying the affection from Rachel's hand—thinking he would like her to hold her hand on his a little longer—simply said, "I like it."

Rachel patted Sean's hand again. "Figured you would."

"Okay, trivia time again. I need to see a winner. One of our presidents appeared in *Playboy* magazine in an article that quoted him as saying 'I've looked on a lot of women with lust. I've committed adultery in my heart many times. This is something that God recognizes I will do—and I have done it—and God forgives me for it.' It was during a presidential campaign too, which made the outcry even more pronounced."

Rachel quickly answered, "Jimmy Carter."

"You got it—and go one up."

"Which man was born Leslie Lynch King, Jr. become president?"

"It was Gerald Ford from Michigan."

"That's it, Sean—even again."

UBER COMES

Sean looked at his phone. "Hey, my Uber is coming … nine minutes … now eight. Let me pay my tab."

"Sure enough," Jackson replied. "Can I get your emails? I'm counting on you guys meeting again. If you have to come in on a Sunday night, could you come in early, like in the early afternoon, so we can meet here? We don't open until five on Sundays so that we can have the place, uninterrupted. Sunday nights are slow, and we can go at it after five as well. Look—I know this is asking a lot from two patrons, one of whom I just met tonight, but I would really appreciate your help."

Sean placed his tab money in Jackson's hand, complete with a sizable tip. "Let's do it. This has been interesting."

Rachel stood up to pay her tab as well. "A little unusual, I have to say."

"Yes, I understand, and I really appreciate your help."

"Rachel, you're covered," Sean said, gesturing to her empty glass. "Let's head out. See you in a few weeks, Jackson."

The two left the bar, Sean placing his hand on the small of Rachel's back as he opened the door.

"Two minutes," Sean said once they were outside. "I think we got him."

Once the SUV pulled up, Rachel climbed into the back seat.

Sean opened and held the door, closed it, and then proceeded to the other side of the vehicle.

Rachel turned to look at Sean by her side. "This has been an interesting evening. Jackson is a unique character."

"He sure is. Unusual political positioning for an African American, and I didn't ask, but I assume he is in a union."

"Don't you think you're profiling him?"

"I didn't mean it as a criticism. I admire his independence."

Rachel chuckled. "Smart guy."

"How about you? I'm curious, where did your liberal views come from? Parents? Friends? College? Work?"

"I'm a logical thinker, and I care about the poverty in this world, the unfairness, the disparity between the privileged wealthy and the poor, many of whom just inherited their wealth."

"I understand your views. You developed that line of thought from someplace in your environment."

"Okay, I would consider my parents nonpolitical but very empathetic to others. My friends, including my associates at work, are pretty much all progressive."

"You seem to have the impression that conservatives are without compassion. The Republican Party also believes in extending welfare to as many people as possible. In fact, I think it was the Republican Congress Welfare Reform in 1996 that gave states greater flexibility in managing the Temporary Assistance for Needy Families Program. The thinking is that the states can do a better job than the federal government. According to the party, welfare should be taken as a step up to greater things, rather than a way of life, and that is what the Welfare Reform Act of 1996 aimed to do. Similarly, the Republican Party supports further reforms and legislation that move in this direction and allow welfare recipients to move into jobs and onward from their welfare rolls."

Sean turned more toward Rachel. "The focus is especially on single mothers and women who rely on welfare for long periods of time. We sympathize with the difficulty and fear women have to get into training or educational courses or find a job because of their commitment to children. We also support extending welfare benefits to promote healthy marriages and provide work assistance like transportation, training, and childcare. The party thinks Americans need the opportunity to earn an income so they can become proudly self-sufficient."

"That sounds impressive, Sean. I wish I could see more results. Now let me give my standard praise of what the Democrats stand for. Democrats, historically, have been more progressive on social programs and welfare, by far, than Republicans. FDR, for example, is responsible for the Social Security Trust Fund and Administration, aiding the blind, disabled, elderly, and children in low-income families. He also created the New Deal during the Great Depression, which gave eight million people jobs building public infrastructure, murals, and sculptures. They built the Golden Gate Bridge and the Triborough Bridge. Not to mention the Civilian Conservation Corps, which improved public lands. We have Medicare and Medicaid thanks to Lyndon B. Johnson, as well as PBS, the National Endowment for the Arts, and even drivers ed."

"I'm impressed. You've really got it down pat. We both want to help people in need. The difference is in how we go about it. I feel better about the Republican approach because they place more emphasis on management at the state level and placing more emphasis on creating jobs so that most people can earn their way, giving them the sense of pride in supporting their families. One more thing … you referred to many Republicans inheriting their money. Inheritance happens to Democrats as well. And I can tell you that I didn't inherit my company. I grew up poor and worked hard as a teen, and then for twenty years as an adult, working seventy to eighty hours a week. I took big risks and struggled through some tough times until it eventually paid off."

The driver was approaching the corner on Adams Street, and when the traffic light turned yellow, the driver accelerated to make a right-hand turn. Suddenly, the vehicle went into a spin, and Rachel tumbled into Sean's lap.

In the process of trying to keep his own balance, Sean unintentionally brushed his hand across Rachel's chest and immediately removed it.

Rachel pulled herself back upright and gave Sean a serious look—and then she saw the embarrassment on his face.

"Sorry, I assure you that wasn't intentional."

Rachel paused for a few seconds and smiled. "Of course, I take your word for it."

The driver straightened his vehicle and continued on.

Sean tapped the driver on the shoulder. "Take it easy, buddy. We're not in any rush. It's been a long night … beating a traffic light isn't necessary."

The driver, seemingly unconcerned, mumbled something that neither Sean nor Rachel could understand.

"Sean, I'm a Democrat because the Democrats are all about equality. It goes way back to Truman when he was a young man in his thirties when he supported the Nineteenth Amendment in 1920 that gave women the right to vote. He supported the Fair Deal that raised the minimum wage and prohibited hiring discrimination. Just think about that for a minute; before 1920, women weren't allowed to vote. That's not that long ago. Hard to believe my grandmother couldn't vote when she turned twenty-one."

"Giving to and supporting those in need is important and is an American tradition. We are the most generous country in the world, both Democrats and Republicans, but giving has its limits. I recall a quote, and I can't recall who said it: 'Any government can prosper until the citizens learn how to vote themselves access to the public treasury, then it's a descent into anarchy.'"

As the Uber pulled up to the entrance at the Marriott, Sean swiftly got out of the car and moved around to get the door for Rachel. Then, as they walked toward the entrance, he gently put his arm on her shoulder. "This has turned out to be a nice weather delay; the time went by fast."

Rachel smiled. "Yes, I enjoyed it."

As they entered the lobby, Rachel looked to her right. "Steven, what are you doing up this late?"

Rising from his chair, Steven embraced Rachel, and Sean stood by awkwardly.

"Steven, meet my new friend, Sean. We were stuck together at Filibusters. We had a long chat with the bartender. Solved all the world's problems."

Sean shook Steven's hand. "Good to meet you. It's been a long day. I'm going to my room."

"We'll share the elevator with you," Steven said.

They proceeded to the elevator, and Sean pushed the up button.

"So how about you, Steven?" Rachel inquired as they waited.

"Beat the storm, been here since three, just came down to get out of my room for a bit."

The elevator door opened, and all three entered. Rachel pushed the button for level 4, and Sean pushed 6.

"You would have enjoyed the conversation, Steven. Very political. We practically had the place to ourselves, and Jackson, the bartender, was a political issue fanatic. Very bright and knowledgeable."

"A progressive, I assume."

"Nope, he was right-wing compared to you."

The door opened to the fourth floor, and Rachel and Steven exited.

Rachel offered a handshake, and Sean accepted. "Have a good night's rest, Sean."

Arriving at room 407, Rachel flashed her door pass and entered, immediately plopping down on the one chair in the room. She pulled her iPhone out of her purse, located her friend Julie in favorites, and hit the call button.

"Rachel, are you all right?"

"Fine, actually great."

"Then why are you calling me at midnight?"

"Julie, I just spent the past four hours with a real hunk. He's tall, fit, handsome, intelligent, successful, and charming."

"Wow, but how was it, for you, I mean?"

"Oh no, no, not that. We happened to be stuck at Filibusters Pub near the White House—for four hours. The city was like in a lockdown, no cabs available, too cold and slippery to be outside very long, so I went into the first place I could find. This guy, Sean, and I were the only two at the bar."

"And?"

"He sat one stool down from me, and we talked for four, maybe five hours."

"Just the two of you?"

"No, Jackson, the bartender, another handsome but older man, was there. He was very bright and knowledgeable about DC and joined our conversation."

"So, you spend five hours getting to know this handsome guy, and then you each go back to your own rooms?"

"That's it, of course; I'm married."

"But you're not sleeping together."

"I know, we gotta go to counseling. The twins love their dad. We have to work things out."

"What about the guy you work with? Steven?"

"We're just business partners. I saw him at the hotel. The three of us rode the elevator together."

"You woke me up at this time, and all you have to tell me is that you rode the elevator with two studs."

"You're my best friend. Who else can I talk to?"

"You really spent five hours talking politics?"

"No, there's more. We're all going to meet again to help Jackson with his final paper for a poly sci class."

"You what? This is too much for me to comprehend at this hour."

"Okay, I'll fill you in tomorrow."

CHAPTER 15

SEAN AND BETH

"So, we're just not going to talk anymore?" Beth asked Sean as they sat on the couch.

"What would you like to talk about? How I'm gone all the time, or your favorite: when are we gonna get a life?"

"Those sound like pretty good questions. I'm at least pleased to find you have them memorized. How about we just skip the obvious and you tell me about your weekend?"

"Okay, I went to an NRA meeting, a rare one because we usually don't meet on weekends. This was the big annual dinner with awards and speeches. If you heard the weather reports in DC, you could imagine the rest of the weekend. All transportation was shut down, and I got stuck at Filibusters from around six until after midnight. It's a quaint little pub, been there for decades."

"Was it busy?"

"No, because of the storm stopping all traffic, the place was practically empty: me, a lady named Rachel, Jackson the bartender, and one other couple."

"You got her name ... how about her phone number?"

"Of course. I added it to my little book with all my other lady friends."

"Okay, this isn't going anyplace. Can you tell me what you and Rachel talked about for four or five hours?"

"As a matter of fact, we had a very interesting conversation. Rachel, me, and Jackson, the bartender. Jackson is an amazingly knowledgeable guy. He's about sixty to sixty-five years old. Like a walking computer with the number and name recall, knowledgeable about all past presidents. You would like Rachel. She's an off-the-wall, left-wing liberal. Anyway, we came up with solutions to all the world's problems. And I'm going back in three weeks for a Monday afternoon meeting, but I'm going early Sunday so that Rachel, Jackson, and I can meet again. Now, if that sounds kind of weird, it is. Not sure why I'm doing it, other than Jackson is writing a paper for his poly sci class. He asked, and I felt like being helpful."

"So, that's it. You're leaving a day early to spend time with Rachel, and oh, also Jackson. Okay, I've also made plans for a meeting, this Friday at two with Dr. Hanson, a marriage counselor. That was her only opening for the next month. She's highly recommended; I assumed you would be willing to come."

"Sure, I'll come," Sean responded quickly.

Beth, suspicious of his quick response, said, "Great, I will plan on it. Oh, but first, describe Rachel for me."

"She's very attractive, bright, pleasant smile, about five-foot-seven. Where are we going with this?"

"We're talking about our marriage." Beth pulled out a notepad. "Our marriage is in jeopardy. The top seven reasons for divorce are infidelity, substance abuse, lack of commitment, too much arguing, growing apart, financial problems, and getting married too young." Beth looked directly at Sean. "Which of those do you feel are problems for us?"

"That's not a complete list. Differences in ideology, trust, and ineffective communication are our biggest problems. Concern for children is also an important factor."

"Interesting. Of course, the children are an important consideration, but if we can't have a compatible marriage, we not doing the kids any favors by staying together. I guess we will let Dr. Hanson sort it out if she can. Good night."

Beth stood up abruptly and proceeded to the bedroom, and Sean changed the channel from CNN to Fox.

CHAPTER 16

RACHEL AND JAKE

"Is it safe for me to come in?" Rachel said in a cautious voice as she opened the door from the garage to the kitchen. All was quiet. No sign of Jake.

"Mom, Mom." Jason and Jamie both dashed in from the family room. "How was DC?" Jason asked. "Did you meet anyone important? I signed up for tennis." He and Jamie embraced her from both sides.

"So good to see you." Rachel gave them both a squeeze and roughed up their bushy heads of hair. "Did your dad tell you when he was getting home? How long have you been here alone?"

"He's right there." Jason pointed to the kitchen window out to the backyard. Jake and his friend Dean were playing catch with a football.

"Oh, why aren't you playing catch with them?"

"We've got homework to do."

"Well, that's a good idea. Where is it? Can I help you?"

Rachel helped the boys with their homework, prepared a large salad, and grilled four hamburgers and four bowls of mixed fruit. She declined the request for ice cream. "Only once a week with that stuff."

Jason whined, "Randy, in my class, says he has ice cream every night."

"Take your mom's advice," Jake said, now back inside. "You'll grow up bigger and stronger."

"Don't think so, Dad. I don't think you have ever seen Randy; he's bigger than Jamie and me put together."

Rachel and Jake took turns tucking the boys into bed in their separate rooms, and then Jake went to his office-bedroom, and Rachel went to the kitchen to do the dishes.

Fifteen minutes later, Jake and Rachel moved to the living room, coincidentally at the same time. Jake turned on a golf tournament replay.

"I would prefer CNN if you don't mind," Rachel said.

"I do mind, but I'll switch it."

Jake switched the channel, shook his head, and left the room.

PART II

CHAPTER 17

RETURN TO FILIBUSTERS

The motor sound from the refrigerator and an occasional drip from the sink accounted for the only sounds at Filibusters at eleven o'clock on a Sunday morning. Jackson had entered the building from the back kitchen entrance. He checked all kitchen and bar thermostats, organized and took approximate inventory of all essential food and bar items, checked every corner for cleanliness, walked to the bar area, and took a seat at a table in a space with adequate lighting for his meeting.

Would they both show? He had emailed Rachel and Sean five times each before getting a date and time agreement. Reviewing his notes from their first meeting, they had covered about a dozen topics; immigration had been the most time-consuming. They still needed to cover health care, guns, foreign policy, education, welfare, military, taxes, trade, more on Trump, the Green New Deal, and national security.

Jackson tried to decide what he would do if only one of them showed; that would be worse than having them both not come. With little concern, he decided that he was confident Sean, a longtime customer, would come. Rachel seemed like a sincere person and also appeared to enjoy their first marathon session three weeks prior.

The first knock on the back door came as Jackson instructed: at eleven thirty. Pleased to see Sean, Jackson served him some coffee, and they chatted while waiting for Rachel.

"What do you think of Rachel?" Jackson quizzed.

"She's a fox, Jackson. And a smart one at that, classy lady. If I were single, I would try to get to know her better—even though our ideologies are about as far apart as the earth and the sun."

Jackson smiled. "What I like is she can disagree and not get angry. You're the same. It's hard to find two people so far apart ideologically who can still have a civil conversation."

A knock on the back door. She was only five minutes late.

Jackson hustled to the back to open the door and greeted Rachel. "I am so pleased and appreciative that you are doing this for me."

Rachel looked around the kitchen as she followed Jackson, wondering if Sean had arrived.

Sean stood as they approached the table and gave Rachel a welcome hug.

Rachel turned to Jackson, gave him a hug, and said, "I feel we have known each other for a long time."

"We have; it's been three weeks and five hours," Jackson offered as he pulled a chair out from the table for Rachel.

Rachel and Sean made small talk about their flights and their delight at the much-improved weather conditions for about five minutes.

Jackson said, "How about some more trivia before we get started?"

"Great! I gotta catch up."

"Some of our past presidents were said to be of presidential material because they were related to past presidents. We have seven who fit that category. Who were they? A point for each one."

Sean said, "Roosevelt, Adams."

Rachel quickly added, "Harrison, Madison."

"Two each. Still even. You left out the easy one: the Bushes."

Rachel raised her hand. "I thought of one more: Donald Trump. He is related to the devil."

"Come on now. That's not nice."

"Just kidding."

"Let's move on."

CHAPTER 18

NATIONAL DEFENSE

After some brief chatting, Jackson said, "Can we start with national defense?"

Rachel said excitedly, "I'll start. I hear Republicans accuse Democrats of being soft on national defense. I think that is because Democratic presidents, three, in fact, have won the Nobel Peace Prize. President Wilson entered World War I and received a Nobel Peace Prize for brokering the Treaty of Versailles. President Roosevelt began gearing up for World War II even before Pearl Harbor. That doctrine shifted American foreign policy from isolationist to globalist. Truman was also active in Korean War decisions. President Jimmy Carter received the Nobel Prize for his efforts in 1978 with the Camp David Accord. The Salt II nuclear limitation treaty with Russia was also negotiated by Carter.

"JFK was responsible for the Bay of Pigs invasion in Cuba, and they blockaded Cuba, facing down Russia, to end a missile crisis. More recently, President Obama was awarded the Nobel Peace Prize for ending the Iraq War. And just look at the military spending of seven hundred to eight hundred billion per year for Obama compared to six hundred and fifty for George W. Bush. I think both parties agree that cybersecurity is the most dangerous threat to our national security, but Democrats don't believe the country is more secure under the Trump administration."

Sean rubbed his hands together, pleased at finally being able to debate Rachel again. "Republicans have warned that cyberattacks are now the biggest threat to the United States. We introduced Homeland Security fifteen years ago to prevent another 9/11. An attack of that magnitude is now more likely to reach us online than on an airplane."

"I think this is an issue both parties agree on," Jackson said with a smile.

"Our electronic grid could be in danger, and if it was disabled, that would cripple our country," Rachel said. "We know they are attacking our elections. What next? Cybersecurity is currently the most pressing national security issue. Democrats argue that some of President Trump's policies are making the country less secure. It makes us less safe when we have a president who is weakening our alliances. I don't agree with Trump's relationship with Putin in Russia. He seems to want to be friends with him. I think that puts us at risk. Putin can't be trusted. Trump thinks he is keeping the whole world safe because he has put ISIS on the run and is playing footsie with his newfound buddy in North Korea."

"Your view on national security portrays the typical liberal bias. You have left a few things out. Republicans have had to battle with Democrats year after year to obtain the funding to maintain a strong military. Republicans, going back to Reagan, are responsible for making the United States the world's most powerful military. Peace is gained through strength, not weakness. President Reagan proved that when he defeated Russia in the Cold War, establishing the United States as the world's number one military power with advocacy for world peace. President Bush signed Project BioShield, which helps us protect against attacks, including chemical and nuclear attacks. It put in place major new biodefense capabilities. Republicans want to see national security fought on multiple fronts, including stopping terrorists before they attack, eliminating their financing sources, and letting law enforcement and intelligence agents combat organized crime and drug trafficking.

"Before Trump came into office, ISIS was a huge problem. Obama claimed they were insignificant and left Trump with a big problem to deal with. He dealt with it and reduced ISIS to a periodic irritation. He has lowered troop levels in the Middle East and made the region less of a threat to the United States and Europe. He scrapped the Obama-Kerry Iran nuclear deal because it was worthless. It guaranteed Iran would have the nuclear capability within ten years—or sooner. North Korea was considered by many, including Obama, to be the most immediate threat to world peace when Trump came into office. Thanks to Trump, now we are talking about the possibility of denuclearization of the Korean Peninsula.

The Trump administration has been working with Venezuela to help get rid of a dictatorship. Most importantly, Trump has worked to strengthen our military from the deterioration that occurred during the Obama administration."

"Why I am not surprised at what both of you have to say?" Jackson said. "Personally, I think both parties are motivated to keep America safe. Over the past couple decades, Democrats have placed more emphasis on peacekeeping missions, and Republicans have placed more emphasis on a strong military. They both have the same objective. What they need to do is work together more. I see and hear too much in the way of accusations and not enough cooperative efforts. Political activists keep seeking ways to accuse the other party of misdeeds to the point of making accusations of disloyalty. Republicans questioned John Kerry's loyalty because he was the chief negotiator in the Iran deal, and his daughter was married to an Iranian with high-level connections to the Iranian government. Trump has been accused of conspiring with Russia for help in his election win over Hillary Clinton.

"I think both parties represent 100 percent loyalty to America. They just look for issues they can attack the other party on for political gain. The one area I am a strong believer in is maintaining the most powerful military in the world—while making every effort to find ways to seek peace. I've still got some good trivia questions. I want to see one of you break away. You're both good.

"Quite a few of our presidents had affairs while in office. One relationship was revealed when a series of love letters revealed that he had a relationship with his wife's best friend. This president had another relationship disclosed when a woman claimed her daughter's father was the president. The accusation was proved true by DNA testing in 2005."

Rachel and Sean both tried to focus on the answer.

"Can you give us a hint … like what century?" Rachel pleaded.

"Twentieth."

Sean said, "Yes, it wasn't Wilson or Hoover. I'm going to say Warren Harding."

"You got it—and go one up."

"You rat, I helped you find the answer again."

Jackson stood up and said, "Need to take a break. Be right back."

Sean looked at Rachel. "Got a busy week with Steven again?"

"He's not with me on this trip."

"Are you at the same hotel as last time?"

"Yup."

"So, we can Uber together again?"

"Sounds good," Rachel said with a smile.

CHAPTER 19

GUNS

Jackson returned and said, "I would like to talk about guns if you're both okay with that."

Rachel and Sean both nodded.

Sean said, "Jackson, what did you think about the shooting last month in that bar in Memphis? Twelve killed, including the bartender and a waitress. That had to get your attention."

"Getting to be old hat. It's gonna happen again and again."

"What would you do if a shooter came in here?" Rachel asked.

"I'm a sitting duck, and I can't have a gun behind the bar to protect myself and my customers. Either have laws to get the guns off the streets—or let me have a gun."

"I think you should be allowed to have a gun," Sean said.

"Tell ya what, my friend, if I have a gun that I can get to fast, and a dude comes in here with a gun, I would take him out."

"That's the answer. Bars and other store owners should have the right to have a gun on the premises. Word gets out that you have a gun, and these nutcases will drop off sharply."

Rachel shook her head. "You can't be serious. A Wild West shootout? So bartenders, teachers, retail stores all gotta holster up. The fastest on the draw and the best shooter wins? It will never work, and it will only cause more deaths. We have too many guns out there now. We sure don't need more. Law enforcement, security guards, and hunters with licenses are the only people who should be allowed to have guns. And they should have an identification permit."

"You're gonna repeal the Second Amendment?"

"That's the gun lovers' number one excuse. I don't believe the authors of the Second Amendment intended for guns to be as prevalent as they are today."

"Let me clarify my position," Jackson said. "Look at guns realistically. Having a gun would work for me because I'm an experienced gun handler. As for every teacher and store owner having a gun, I don't think it would work. That plan would involve millions of more guns out there. We definitely need to find a better way to lower the number of incidents. Think about it. I said lower the killings, not eliminate. We have to be realistic. We will never completely eliminate killings by the mentally ill or people without a conscience, but we can take measures to substantially reduce the number of incidents. Limiting gun ownership to establishments where security is a potential issue and having traceable permits would not be a total solution. It will though, with a national effort and some sacrifices and inconveniences for gun owners, save thousands of lives. The fact is, the more guns we have out there, the more deaths we have. Clearly, it is verifiable that, for the most part, countries with more access to guns have more gun deaths. That's an undeniable fact. Sensible gun control is a part of security I would like to see happen."

"And the plan is?" Sean asked.

"It will be challenging and complicated; unfortunately, it may be too complicated for our elected representatives to cope with. I'll tell you about it when I finish the plan I am proposing in my report. I call it 'A Security Plan to Make America Safe.'" Tell me, Sean, you want immigration control to protect Americans from the bad guys, criminals, and drug dealers, to save lives. Right?"

"And crime, and to save money, yes."

"Let me ask you and Rachel, why do you want gun control to save lives, but you don't want immigration control to save lives? Seems like you are both more tied to political allegiance than looking at the facts."

"If gun control worked, wouldn't Chicago be the safest place in America? If guns kill people, then pencils misspell words, cars make people drive drunk, and forks make people fat."

"Sorry to put it this way, but you're out of touch with reality," Rachel said. "Chicago is an exception and a poor example. Gun buyers can simply cross the state line to buy guns. The NRA and other gun advocates use selective and misleading data to defend gun proliferation. The facts are very clear, in the United States and worldwide, that the more guns we have out there, the more gun deaths. It's a simple, logical fact. I have a personal concern because my husband has a gun in our house, and I feel he is totally irresponsible with it. Yes, he may be an exception, and I'm sure most gun owners are responsible. Responsible gun owners are not the problem; the problem is the availability of guns to just about anyone who wants one. The Rand Corporation did an extensive study not too long ago and found that available information on the subject is not reliable. In their own study, they concluded the close to two hundred lives could be saved annually with an assault weapons ban, universal background checks could prevent more than a thousand homicides yearly, and raising the age limit for buying firearms could prevent more than fifteen hundred homicides and suicides."

"Let's let Sean respond," Jackson said.

"Most of the gun studies out there are unreliable. I think the Rand Study you refer to addressed that point. I have more confidence in the study done by the American Medical Association. They found no difference in homicide or firearm homicide rates to victims in thirty-two states subject to the Brady Act."

"That was a faulty, incomplete, and biased report," Rachel said. "According to Dan Gross, the president of the Brady Campaign to Prevent Gun Violence, it is clear that background checks, where they have been enforced, have saved lives. The law needs to be expanded and more uniformly enforced."

"I don't want to question your research skills, but I have found so many studies on the impact of guns to be flawed that I have to question the study and the motive of the researchers. The mass shootings in schools are a terrible thing, and I am all for a solution. The solution is to have armed guards in schools."

"I was afraid you were going to give me that idea next. Guns in schools? I find it scary. Stricter gun laws in California in the early nineties brought about a 50 percent decline in the firearm mortality rate. Per an NPR survey, something like 90 percent of Democrats, along with more than 75 percent of independents—and even a majority of Republicans—said they are for banning assault-style weapons. Another report, not sure who it came from, indicated that a majority of Americans now say gun control laws should be made stricter. The vast majority of Americans support background checks for gun ownership." Rachel flipped her hands in the air. "Why in God's name would anyone oppose background checks?

"Correct me if I'm wrong on this, but I think a majority of

NRA members support requiring background checks for all gun sales. American voters, as a whole, support stricter gun laws. The obstacle is the NRA. Their only interest is in gun sales for the manufacturers they represent."

"The NRA people are my best customers," Jackson said. "It's not that they drink more than anyone else, but they do seem to pick up a lot of tabs for people who oppose new gun laws."

"Of course, they do. The NRA owns the Republicans."

"Come on. Lobbying is a part of Washington for Democrats and Republicans."

"I'll buy that, but the NRA's control of the Republican vote on gun issues is so powerful that anyone running for office as a Republican has to be all in with the NRA—or else they might as well forget about being a candidate."

"Okay, what about unions and the Democrats. You can't run for office as a Democrat unless you support unions."

"Can we stick with guns?" Jackson asked. "You've talked a lot about the founding fathers and their intentions for this country. How do you think they would address today's gun controversy?"

"Okay, let's move on to the right to bear arms, which shouldn't take long," Sean said. "That is, unless you have no regard for the Second Amendment to the United States Constitution."

Rachel sighed. "Okay, we're on guns. Tell me, do you believe in finding a way to save thousands of American lives?"

"Are you referring to the use of guns to save lives?"

"That's a typical right-wing response."

"No, it's a simple question. Do you believe in saving American lives? Never mind the rhetoric, just answer the question. I'm sure you do."

"Of course, but the question is—"

"It's not a question," Rachel interrupted. "Let me give you some facts. It's so obvious. Take four other countries: Japan, China, the United Kingdom, and Germany, that I can think of offhand, and compare gun deaths per hundred thousand people. The United States has far more than all those countries put together. As for the crime, immigrants don't commit any more, proportionately, than native-born Americans do. It's simple; we have no significant limitations on gun access. The founding fathers you conservatives refer to didn't intend for this to happen. As for the Second Amendment, it says, "A well-regulated militia being necessary to the security of a free state, the right of the people to keep and bear arms, shall not be infringed.' The militia, the militia!" Rachel raised her voice and threw up her hands.

Sean quickly responded. "Sorry, wrong, wrong, wrong. The United States Supreme Court reached a decision about ten or twelve years ago. I forget the exact date. They concluded that the Second Amendment to the United States Constitution confers an individual right to possess a firearm for traditionally lawful purposes such as self-defense. It also ruled that two District of Columbia provisions, one that banned handguns and one that required lawful firearms in the home to be disassembled or trigger-locked, violate this right.

"Furthermore, the stats you refer to are selective. Look at mass shootings in the United States compared to other countries. A study by the Crime Research Center shows the United States doesn't make the top ten for mass shooting deaths. Countries like Norway, Serbia, France, Macedonia, Finland, and Belgium all exceed the United States."

"Come on, come on. You have selected one category in selected countries. Where did you get those numbers, from the NRA?"

"Those are verifiable numbers."

"The NRA is pathetic. Purely a sales advocate for the gun manufacturers. And I will grant you they are very good at their job. Probably the most effective lobby organization in the country. Let me ask Jackson a question. Have you ever heard of or seen an elected Republican congressman who favored gun control and was not backed by the NRA? Anyone who runs as a Republican for office in the United States has to support the NRA to have a chance of getting elected. Jackson, would you agree?"

"Remember, I'm neutral here, but that's likely a statistical fact."

"Look, Rachel." Sean put his hand on hers on the bar in an arrogant gesture of authority.

Rachel paused for a few seconds and then pulled her hand away.

Sean pulled his hand back almost simultaneously. "The NRA was formed more than a hundred years ago and is not financed by the manufacturers. The organization is entirely financed by the dues and small contributions of its 3.2 million members—not by money from the gun manufacturers."

"That's a joke. Clever maneuvering by the NRA. The five

million members are happy to pay because they get big benefits from the manufacturers that put on shows."

Jackson said, "Not ready to offer my idea yet, but it will be very helpful for a compromise position."

"I can't wait, Jackson," Sean said. "Look—hostility toward the NRA is about liberal media hostility. They continuously report distorted statistics. The fact is, a Luntz–Weber poll found most Americans don't think gun control will reduce crime or violence. When they held a news conference to make the report, the media didn't even show up. When Handgun Control Inc. gave a report, the room was packed with media."

"The Second Amendment is very clear. It reads: 'A well-regulated militia, being necessary to the security of a free state, the right of the people to keep and bear arms, shall not be infringed.'"

"Not surprising that you would have those words down pat," Rachel said. "And I am glad you made it so clear that they said, 'A well-regulated militia.' They didn't say all the people."

"Oh, but we have to examine what the framers of the amendment meant by the well-regulated militia. The words 'well-regulated' had a far different meaning at the time the Second Amendment was drafted than today. In today's English, the term 'well-regulated' can be determined to mean heavy and intense government regulation. That was not the intent of the framers. In determining the meaning of the Constitution, we need to start with the actual words of the Constitution. You have to look at the purpose of the Second Amendment. The primary purpose was to guarantee the right of the people, as individuals, to keep and bear arms."

"How about the quote by Noah Webster in a pamphlet urging ratification of the Constitution? 'Before a standing army can rule, the people must be disarmed; as they are in almost every kingdom in Europe.'"

"Ah, Noah Webster, a liberal. I give more validity to George Mason, who remarked to his Virginia delegates regarding the colonies' experience with Britain, in which the monarchy's goal had been to disarm the people, that it was the best and most effectual way to enslave them. The founders specifically intended the concept of the people's self-regulation as nongovernmental regulation. This was in line with the limited grant of power to Congress 'for calling forth' the militia for only certain, limited purposes. They never intended limitations on their rights as individuals to bear arms.

"In all of these references to the intent of the founders, I still don't see a clear representation of the founders' intent to allow all the people to be carrying guns."

"We can't just look at the lawbreakers. We need to consider the law-abiding, armed citizens who pose no threat to other law-abiding citizens. The framers' writings show they also believed that the 'well-regulated' militias would be ready to form militias that would be well trained, self-regulated, and disciplined and would pose no threat to their fellow citizens. Their purpose would be to protect themselves and their families."

"That's a distorted interpretation. The framers intended the Second Amendment to protect the 'collective' right of the states to maintain militias rather than the rights of individuals to keep and bear arms."

"Okay, all very interesting and complicated," Jackson said. "To me, both of your points are well presented. Just what I expected, and it doesn't settle anything. The founders were dealing with a whole different environment than what we have today. Big changes have taken place. We have … well, far more crowded conditions, far more options for guns, and far more mentally disabled people."

"Which means a far greater need to protect yourself," Sean said.

"And far more need to have limitations on the mentally disabled obtaining guns," Rachel countered.

Jackson shook his head. "Debating what the founders intended won't get you anywhere. The question is, do we need more regulations or not? Every time we have a mass shooting, the issue of gun regulation becomes a national debate. That lasts about two to three weeks, and then the gun control issue fades away."

"Yes," Rachel said. "It becomes the press versus the National Rifle Association. The NRA is one of the most powerful, if not the most powerful, Washington lobbyists. Their objective is to sell guns. They are indirectly owned by gun manufacturers whose sole objective is to sell guns."

"You're wrong," Sean said. "The NRA doesn't receive any money from the manufacturers. All income to support their cause to protect the Second Amendment rights of citizens comes from membership dues and not from the manufacturers of guns."

"I will say it again: the NRA is *indirectly* owned by the manufacturers. Without the support of the manufacturers, it could not exist. The support comes by way of the back door."

"What's that supposed to mean?"

"It means members pay dues, which entitle them to numerous benefits. Join the NRA for about forty bucks and save hundreds of dollars in discounts from manufacturers. So, who bears the cost? The manufacturers of guns. I have studied the gun industry because I feel so much could be done to save thousands of lives every year. I know the facts, and the numbers cannot be denied.

"The American gun industry manufactures around ten to eleven million firearms for domestic consumption yearly. The NRA represents more than five million members from all fifty states. The majority financial support of the NRA comes in the form of contributions, grants, royalty income, and advertising. Most of it originates from gun industry sources. This is all beneficial to the manufacturers. They favor anything that sells more guns. To see it any other way is being naïve or insincere. The gun industry and its corporate allies raise fifty million dollars or more through the NRA Ring of Freedom sponsor program. Some of the supporters are firearm companies like MidwayUSA, Pierce Bullet Seal Target Systems, and Beretta USA Corporation."

"Let's hear what Sean's response is to your research."

"Let me just make one more point, Jackson."

"Okay, but I think you should make it brief. I wanna hear what Sean has to say."

"An author by the name of Blanchard—I think Ken is his first name—wrote a book that he titled something like *Responsible Gun Ownership for African-Americans*. He describes how his great-grandmother, a slave, said to save her sons, she made sure they would not touch, look at, or think about owning a gun because it would mean certain death. And then there was Martin Luther King Jr. His home was firebombed in 1956, after which he applied for a concealed carry permit for self-defense in the state of Alabama. King's application was denied, even though his life was threatened routinely, and of course, we all know he wound up getting assassinated. I don't recall the NRA ever helping Dr. King.

"A couple more points: The NRA rarely, if ever, supports gun limitations. Yet, in 1967, a group of Black Panthers openly carried guns into California's state capitol. Soon after, Governor Reagan signed a law that made it illegal to openly carry firearms in the state. The law was backed by the NRA, a rare instance of the NRA supporting a gun limitation."

"I have to admit being skeptical about the NRA," Jackson said. "The NRA was formed in 1871 with the purpose of protecting the rights of people to bear arms. They apparently didn't mean all the people because nearly fifty years later, black people still aren't protected by gun laws that shield white Americans. I might sound like I'm taking sides, but those are just facts that I happen to be aware of."

"Okay, Sean, you're on."

"What the media pundits don't talk about much is how often guns in the right hands have saved lives. Let me recall some actual cases: I don't recall the exact dates. In Texas, Robert Rodriguez and his wife woke to an intruder in their house. Rodriguez had a gun handy and held the intruder at gunpoint until the police came. I know of several cases where small store owners shot and wounded would-be robbers. In March 2016, a twenty-two-year-old woman pulled a gun on two men who were following her to her car, demanding her belongings. They ran away. I could go and on with similar situations. The fact is, guns save lives. If you want to talk numbers, yes, the number of firearms has increased every year since 1990. At the same time, we've have had a very notable decrease in violent crime and gun crime in the United States. You just can't show a correlation to the number of firearms in private hands to the amount of gun crime. Every time a single incident occurs, the media promotes the perception that gun crimes are getting worse. That's simply not true."

Rachel answered, "Making a case with numbers to defend the proliferation of guns is just not credible. Just take a look around the world. The United States is the gun ownership capital of the world and the gun death capital of the world. In the United States, guns are a $12 billion industry, employing thirty-five thousand people—another huge cost against eliminating guns. The NRA and its members spend about 1.5 billion a year lobbying and supporting candidates for election. The price we pay for that is more than twelve thousand gun deaths each year—and about three thousand of those victims are under the age of fourteen."

"You want gun control? I have a suggestion for you. Move to Chicago. They have the toughest gun laws in the country. Before you make a move, though, you may want to check on what those strict regulations have done for them. They have the highest murder rate in the United States."

"That's a bad example. Gun laws on a local or state level are, for the most part, ineffectual. A simple drive across state lines provides access to guns and boosts the sales of guns in neighboring states. Gun control laws have to be national to be effective."

"Let me offer my two cents," Jackson said. "My life and my ancestor's lives have been all impacted by guns. I was born in Mississippi in 1955, my father in 1920, grandfather in 1890, and a great-grandfather in 1860, around the time of the Civil War. Lincoln emancipated slavery, but for all practical purposes, slavery continued for decades, especially in the South. In fact, not until the sixties and seventies did black people begin to get anything close to equal rights. I realize things are better today. In fact, I feel my family and I have every right you do. Though I can't say that is so everywhere in this country.

"I don't want to take sides, but people just have to look at this logically. What's more important: protecting gun lovers' privilege to own guns and what our country's founders wrote two hundred years ago, whatever they intended, or saving lives. I know you, Sean, don't see controls saving lives, but I listened to both of you and read those numbers before. The numbers, especially comparing us with other civilized countries, obviously favor the need for more controls. I see it's a sacrifice and an inconvenience for gun owners. I get that, but what's more important than the lives of men, women, and children? We can't and shouldn't expect to eliminate guns—just add more responsibility to owning guns. Gradually phase in some restrictions. Guns are too easy for dangerous people to get a hold of. A gun buyer should be willing to prove he or she is a stable and law-abiding citizen. Why not, for heaven's sakes? A gun owner who is irresponsible enough to leave their gun where it is accessible to another person who uses the gun to commit a crime should be fined and lose their right to own a gun. Assault weapons shouldn't be sold to the public. Why do people need to own assault weapons? You don't go hunting with an assault weapon. Because they like the feeling of power the gun gives them. It's a sporting pride. That's all nice, and I can sympathize with that desire, but having them out there, easy to buy, creates the danger of putting those powerful killing machines in the hands of the bad guys or the mentally unstable. Sorry, gun lovers, I know you're mostly responsible, but we have a lot of mental sickness in this country. You need to give up a little something to save lives."

Sean shook his head. "You have been listening to too many Democrats. If I thought controls could save lives, I would support controls. The numbers you allude to are just not valid, and we can't start disregarding the guidelines our founding fathers provided us. If we cast aside one amendment, what will come next? The United States is the most successful nation in the history of this planet—all because of the foundation established by our founders and because we have adhered to the principles they provided us. We just can't mess with the rights they gave us."

Jackson said, "If Jefferson, Washington, Hamilton, and the others looked at what was happening today, I believe they would favor some adjustment."

"Come on, Jackson. You support the Constitution. I've heard you praise the founding of this country. You have friends who have guns. Do you want them taken away? They play a lot of games with those stats to show the results they want to hear."

"It's not a game. I can show you facts that more than three hundred people will die from gun-related deaths today, probably twenty while we're talking about this."

"So, you think new laws are going to change those numbers? Not likely. And more people would get killed because they couldn't protect themselves."

"There was a new law passed in Colorado this year," Rachel said, looking at her phone. "Here's the report from the *US News*: 'Polis signed into law a bill that will give judges the power to take firearms from people they believe are at a high risk of harming themselves or others, making Colorado the fifteenth state to adopt a "red flag" law. The measure was fiercely debated in the Colorado legislature and passed the state Senate by just one vote.' That is hardly an impactful law, but every little bit helps.

"Look at the numbers." Rachel looked at her phone again. "The best example is comparing the United States to the United Kingdom. For homicides (murders of all types) the UK has five hundred and fifty (fifty-eight by a gun), and the United States has fourteen thousand homicides (twelve thousand by gun). This is per the UK News and Homeland Security in the United States. American gun deaths are twenty times higher than in other high-income, civilized nations. What I'm saying would be a huge cost and sacrifice, but based on what happens in other countries, we could save at least five thousand lives—more lives and lower cost than the war in Iraq. Cost shouldn't be an issue when saving lives comes into play. We have, amazingly, twenty-five thousand to thirty thousand guns deaths per year in the United States, about half by accident and half intentional. Gun control couldn't save all those lives, but what if we enacted some controls that reduced those deaths by 10 percent? That's two to three thousand lives. How much is that worth? The medical costs for deaths and injuries in the United States is five billion."

"What about the cost of changing?" Sean argued. "You would have huge costs enforcing those new laws."

"There is no cost greater than the loss of lives. Let's look at the numbers. They are totally compelling. The six countries with the strictest gun laws are the United Kingdom, Japan, Sweden, Singapore, Malaysia, and Germany. The United States has more gun deaths in one month than all six of those countries do in a year. The World Health Organization did a study comparing the top twenty-two high-income nations. There were more gun deaths in the United States than in the other twenty-two countries combined. Wikipedia lists the number of murders per hundred thousand by country: United States, 4.2; U.K., negligible; France, 1.1; Japan, 0.3; Singapore, 0.3; Germany, 1.1; Greece, 1.5; China, 1, India, 3.4. That's my case: get out your guns and start shooting. To me, it seems so logical. It's absurd to argue against the position that more guns mean more deaths. It only seems to become a reality when the violence hits home."

Jackson whistled. "Sean, you can't win the battle of stats. It's too overwhelming."

"We just can't start changing our Constitution because we have some reckless characters on the streets. James Madison wrote that Second Amendment in 1789, and we should honor it."

Rachel said, "But you need to think about what Madison's good friend Thomas Jefferson has to say. Something to the effect that every constitution, and every law, naturally expires. And he gave a number of years. I think it was twenty. If enforced longer, he said, it is an act of force and not a right."

"This probably sounds like a crazy idea to NRA people," Jackson said, "but I have often wondered why we can't do more with Taser guns replacing real guns."

"Sorry, but that is a crazy idea," Sean argued. "A fake gun is like fake news. I hear the panic every time we have a shooting. And of course, it is disturbing. Yet the fact is, according to an article I read, I think in the *Washington Post*, the current rate of firearm violence is less now than in 1993, when the rate was around six deaths per hundred thousand people, compared with three to four today. There is just no research indicating that background check laws as they currently exist save lives."

"But three or four per hundred thousand is a big number in a population of more than 325 million. I hear a lot of demand for extending background checks to private sales."

"That's the problem," Rachel said. "The content of the Federal Brady Law mandates background checks for firearm sales, but it exempts sales by private parties."

Sean, with an exasperated tone, answered, "There is no compelling, peer-reviewed research on the effectiveness of extending background check requirements to private sales."

"There would be if those requirements were paired with a permitting or licensing system for purchasers," Jackson said.

Rachel nodded. "All reports I have read show that state laws requiring checks by way of permitting requirements reduce the use of guns for criminal use."

"I have a hard time believing that diagnosis."

"What about mental illness and guns?" Jackson asked.

"Opinion polls show that the majority of Americans believe that mental illness—and the failure of the mental-health system to identify those at risk of dangerous behavior—is an important cause of gun violence."

"It's certainly a factor," Rachel said, "but it's not the major cause. A *New York Times* analysis of more than two hundred mass killings came up with less than 25 percent of the perpetrators being mentally ill. When the right-to-carry law was adopted, whatever year that was, violent crimes increased every year after. I think the number was 10 to 15 percent higher. It's just logical. Guns can kill, so when you have more guns, you get more deaths. You seem to like the idea of armed citizens carrying guns to save lives at mass shootings. Louis Klarevas did a study that showed zero of more than one hundred gun massacres didn't show any citizens stopping mass shootings. We have to look at this internationally. In 2016, the largest worldwide study on guns ever conducted found a clear link between gun regulations and fewer deaths. The study proved to be far more meaningful than studies within one country. The results demonstrated an obvious conclusion that gun restrictions equate to fewer deaths. The study, I think I recall, was done by Columbia University. The study involved about ten to twelve countries and covered a period of more than fifty years."

Jackson said, "You, Sean, mentioned Chicago as an example of gun restrictions not working. Do either of you have other examples?"

"Yes," Rachel answered. "The last time I checked, the states with the strictest gun laws were Connecticut, Massachusetts, Hawaii, New Jersey, Rhode Island, and New York. Gun deaths were around three per hundred thousand people. Those with the least strict laws were Alaska, Arizona, Nevada, New Mexico, Idaho, and Colorado. The gun deaths there were at about twelve per hundred thousand. I'm not up to date on all the gun death numbers. I just understand it's frightening. I recall reading about one incident where a killer's mother had, in her house, some kind of Bushmaster automatic capable of twenty-five—or maybe even more—rounds of rapid-fire killing. What does the salesman say to the lady? 'This gun will enable your son to kill twenty-five people quickly.' What other purpose does the gun have? I just don't get it.

"A few years ago, Connecticut's legislature proposed a law banning one of those killing machines. I think it was the AR-15. The legislatures were bombarded by the NRA and its members, essentially telling them they couldn't pass such a law—so they didn't. Those trying to legislate laws for gun control against the influence of the NRA find it is an impossible task. I know of an advocate group from Washington state and Colorado that spent millions of dollars over three years on passing laws requiring criminal background checks on every gun sale. The end result, after three years, was that the laws had a little measurable effect, primarily because citizens simply decided not to comply—and there was a lack of enforcement by authorities."

"I have to look at the facts," Jackson said. "From all the conversations I have heard on guns and control of guns, the NRA supporters are in denial. I have friends who have guns. They are careful with their guns. They take pride in them. These guys are not threats, but they refuse to look at the facts. The facts are overwhelming. I studied because, well, let me give you some numbers that I researched a while back. I know them well, so they will be accurately close, but not exact.

"I looked at four countries—Japan, Germany, Italy, and the United Kingdom—with an approximate population of the United States, around three hundred twenty million. Those four countries all have far stricter gun controls than the United States does. They still have about eight thousand gun-related deaths per year. Eight thousand! That's a lot of deaths in one year. How many do you think the United States has? Same total population as those four countries. Four times as many, about thirty-two thousand—and that's not counting another fifty thousand or more serious injuries.

"Now, just think for a minute about the terrible wars this county has been in more than the past fifty or sixty years—Korea, Vietnam, and Iraq—those horrible wars that we have all read about. If you add up just the last three or four years of modern-day gun-related deaths in the United States, the number is similar to all the American deaths in those three wars. It's not realistic to say we could get the gun deaths down to the level of those countries. The question I have is how many lives we want to save. What if one of your family members died from gun violence? Would that make you feel differently, Sean? What if we just had a record of who owns guns and didn't sell them to people without proper identification? And maybe we could find a way to trace the ownership of the guns used in killings. And what if we made gun owners responsible for keeping their guns out of the hands of mentally challenged, underage, and violent people. If I have a gun in my closet that is easily accessible to a child or an irresponsible acquaintance, I should lose my right to own a gun and have to pay a fine.

"When looking at gun possession and gun deaths, the United States is downright weird compared to civilized Western Europe or Australia." Jackson looked at his phone. "Per the website CommonDreams, annually, there are twenty-six gun murders in England, versus 11,004 in the United States, all while taking into account the population difference. Of the more than one billion firearms in the world, American citizens hold about four hundred million—for a population of roughly three hundred twenty-five million. According to the report, that is gun ownership of one hundred twenty firearms per hundred civilians. The next highest rates are in Yemen, Montenegro, Serbia, and Canada. And the total of those countries combined is less than in the United States. How many ways can you look at and not see the obvious? We have more guns and more deaths.

"My own view is that the Brady Act was a useful—but modest—first step in reducing the availability of guns to high-risk groups such as teens and convicted felons. If I can sum it up, I am a strong believer in our Constitution and can clearly understand those who feel that the Second Amendment protects our right to own a gun, as I do personally. Having said that, I also have compassion for the government to do whatever is possible to save lives. Facts are facts. I just don't see how you can deny the obvious: that the stricter the gun laws we have, the more lives we would save. Sure, tougher gun laws would be an inconvenience to gun owners, but we are talking about human lives. I realize that my friends in the NRA—the enthusiastic NRA supporters—will deny what I am saying here no matter how many facts I present. The NRA offers misrepresented numbers to support their position. In my opinion, the NRA places first priority on whatever will sell more guns for the manufacturers.

"I would like to see required registration with a permanent serial number traceable to the owner combined with a substantial fine if the gun is used in a violent situation. In other words, gun owners would be responsible for the safekeeping of their guns. It is meaningless to have gun registration if the gun can be accessible to another person. I will get into the ID system later because registration is only beneficial to the extent we have an effective ID system. Inconvenient and costly, yes, but how much is a life worth?

"Let's do a little more trivia and then go to drugs. Which one of our presidents, under serious stress, had several strokes while in office and became partially paralyzed and almost blind but continued in office for two years to the end of his term?"

"I know. I know," Sean answered. "Woodrow Wilson."

"You're in trouble, Miss Rachel. Sean just went two up."

"Not over 'til it's over," Rachel replied.

CHAPTER 20

ALCOHOL

As usual, Jackson started off the discussion. "As we talk drugs, let me ask you what class of drugs kills the most people in America?"

"Opioids," Rachel answered.

"Actually, it might be alcohol," Sean said.

Jackson nodded. "You're right."

"Does that count as trivia?"

"The drastic rise in alcohol-related deaths generally has been overshadowed by the opioid epidemic. More American residents die from alcohol than from opioids each year. Alcohol kills around eighty thousand people each year, which is about fifteen thousand more than opioids. It's also at least three times more expensive to treat alcohol. I've studied this. The World Health Organization estimates that there are more than three million deaths worldwide per year due to harmful use of alcohol. Therefore, alcohol-related deaths make up nearly 6 percent of all global deaths per year."

"The obvious reason is that alcohol, in moderation, is socially acceptable," Rachel said. "College kids party hearty with booze, teenagers often snitch some beer, and businesspeople make a common practice of meeting for a beer. In moderation, it's not a problem, but some people—many people, in fact—are genetically predisposed to becoming addicted.

"Some researchers refer to deaths from drugs, alcohol, and suicide as 'despair deaths.' And depression, along with stress, are major causes behind the increase in alcohol-related deaths, especially among women. According to reports I have read, the number of alcohol-related deaths in the United States rose by 35 percent over the past ten or fifteen years."

"I bet we all have friends or family members who are on the path or already have an alcohol problem," Sean said.

Rachel said, "I know several."

"And I see them come here," Jackson said. "I can tell when it's happening. I sometimes lose customers because I tell them I can't serve them another drink. It's difficult … like I'm insulting a friend. I've had some come back later, order a coke, and thank me for helping them recognize they had a problem. With the majority who come to my bar, it's not a problem. Like you guys, you're drinking slowly and sensibly. I found it surprising that a rise in alcohol-related deaths is especially troublesome among women. The increase in the past decade has been twice as much among women as men. Also, and this is good news, alcohol-related deaths among teenagers have decreased by 10 or 15 percent. On the negative side of the trends, deaths among people ages forty-five to sixty-four rose by about 25 percent.

"One big problem is that excessive drinking of alcohol can lead to a variety of illnesses that can result in death, including a number of different cancers along the digestive tract and breast cancer. Also, toxicity can damage individuals' nervous systems. Alcohol is not only harmful to individuals; it is also harmful to society as a whole. Its negative effects include injuries, car accidents, violence, and sexual assault. Past reports have shown that alcohol is rated the most harmful drug overall and almost three times as harmful as cocaine or tobacco. Ecstasy, for example, is only one-eighth as harmful as alcohol. This has encouraged scientists to say that aggressively targeting the harms of alcohol is an essential public health strategy. They also mentioned that the current drug classifications had little to do with the relationship to the evidence of harm. Even though cocaine and heroin are illegal, it doesn't make them more dangerous. The World Health Organization estimates risks linked to alcohol as causing more deaths worldwide each year than from heart and liver disease, road accidents, suicides, and cancer."

Jackson said, "We all agree on the alcohol problem, but let's not pass up prescription drugs. The opioid drugs that have been a great comfort for a lot of human pain may be the most deadly prescription drugs to ever hit the market. The United States and many other countries around the world struggle with an epidemic of opioid addiction and abuse. The death toll is frightening: more than seventy thousand per year, which is at a pace similar to the annual deaths in World War I, the Vietnam War, the Korean War, and more than the Iraq War. It's also higher than HIV, car crashes, and gun violence. The economic toll is beyond staggering. The yearly annual economic impact from the misuse of prescription drugs, illicit drugs, and alcohol is more than four hundred billion dollars. Think about that number for a second. That is so destructive to our economy and human life. And get this, while the problem is taking root everywhere, we in the United States are the world leaders.

"And as for which segment of our population has the biggest problem, there is a long-standing belief that drug addiction and poverty go hand in hand. It is hard to believe that someone who doesn't have a job or has little income can afford the expense of addiction. However, addiction causes poverty rather than the other way around. Those who live in poverty and are addicted to drugs have less access to rehabilitation centers and treatment for their condition, which creates serious problems for communities all over the United States. Do you think addiction problems are more prevalent among men or women?"

"I say men," Sean answered.

"Women," Rachel said.

"Women is correct. I'm not sure why that is."

Rachel answered, "Increased pressure in the job market, combined with being a mother, and women not being as accepted in the workplace, especially as they get older—too much pressure. I became motivated to do some extensive research on drug addiction when my brother's wife's family developed a huge problem. Jane, my sister-in-law, had a high-pressure job. I don't know how it started with her, but she became addicted to opioids. She and my brother both keep a busy schedule, and their two sons, Denny and David, somehow got into it too. When Jane started questioning her supply, the boys looked for ways to buy their drugs elsewhere. When I got wind of the problem, I started to research and got guidance from a customer. I eventually directed them to treatment. Unfortunately, even though they got temporary relief, they are still having problems. The only answer, in my opinion, is more treatment. The obstacle there is cost."

Sean asked, "How are they doing today?"

"It's a work in progress—for me and the rest of the world. We, in America, are the world's drug-use leaders. Americans consume the majority of the opioid drugs in the world, both prescription drugs like hydrocodone and illicit drugs like heroin. What is the root of the issue? Why are ninety people dying every from addiction to crap when we have so much to live for: our families, food, and social activities? Maybe development can be pointed to as the cause of this huge problem. Opioid medications are critical to some medical treatments, yet many of these drugs have become vehicles of abuse, and then many more substances have been diverted or developed, leading to overdoses in recent years. Some opioids are more dangerous than others, although the vast majority of them carry some associated risk. I know, from my research, the names of some these killers.

"Grey death is probably the deadliest opioid. It is a dangerous mixture opioid, including fentanyl and carfentanil. Since the substance is essentially scraps from other opioids, it's unpredictable in potency and nearly impossible to consume without overdosing. Carfentanil is probably most powerful synthetic opioid available. Even though it was designed to be a medication, it wasn't supposed to be used by humans. It is used only rarely in veterinary medicine to tranquilize large animals like elephants. Carfentanil is thousands of times more potent than morphine. Even vets have specific safety procedures to properly dose the drug to animals because it can cause immediate death with a slight overdose. Many people are hearing about fentanyl addiction lately. It was originally designed for cancer patients, but it's become a new opioid in the epidemic. Heroin, of course, has been around for a long time. Especially when taken intravenously, it hits hard, but it doesn't last long, which makes the withdrawals that much faster. Methadone is a little different. Doctors prescribe it to help with withdrawals for people who have long-lasting opioid addictions. But it too can be dangerous, if not taken to taper off addiction. OxyContin is often blamed for creating the opioid abuse epidemic. Doctors prescribed it back in the nineties for pain relief, but it was used widely due to aggressive marketing from pharmaceutical company. Okay, let's get into foreign policy."

CHAPTER 21

FOREIGN POLICY

"I doubt that any of us are foreign policy experts," Jackson began. "I think foreign policy decisions should be evaluated by those who are knowledgeable in international affairs."

"You mean, like Donald Trump," Rachel huffed.

"I was expecting that. I'm not saying presidents should be required to be experts in international affairs. They should, however, have fundamental knowledge, consult with and give proper weight to military and foreign affairs experts, and not try to be experts on their own.

"The progressive view on foreign policy is, as Elizabeth Warren says, not all about tanks and troops. I hear this continuous debate about how many troops we need in Afghanistan. Bring them all home. We have wasted too much money and lost too many American lives in that everlasting war. We need to cut the wasteful Pentagon budget. I think it's absurd that defense contractors are intricately involved in the defense budget. Liz Warren wants to tackle Wall Street corruption by taking on the defense contractors. I think that's a great idea. Priority one in foreign policy should be a world free of nuclear weapons."

"That all sounds wonderful," Sean said. "I wish it was viable. The fact is that it's a recipe for disaster. A sound foreign policy starts with a respect for history and the historic predictableness of human behavior. Survival of the fittest, in a military sense, is survival of the most powerful. We can and should certainly seek a nuke-free world. What we can't do is become vulnerable by not maintaining the strongest military on the planet. Conceive for a moment Russia or China with a clear military lead. Do you think they would have any interest, whatsoever, in creating a nuclear-free world? I don't think so. Our planet has forever been a planet of wars. Seeking power and territory has always the objective, going back thousands of years, for countries around the planet. The United States is in the historically unique position of not seeking more territory and only wanting peace. If we give up our position of power, we are putting the rest of the world in danger. Of course, we want and must seek a safe and peaceful world. No one who knows anything about devastation and suffering of wars ever wants a war."

"I'm impressed with your knowledge on the basics of foreign policy," Jackson said. "You both try to deal with the core issues, peace through strength or diplomacy and reason, intervention or nonintervention. You also allude to the importance of measuring the emphasis on national or international affairs. It becomes a question of the idealist or realist interpretation of the world. I like and want to believe a less aggressive approach—and a policy of not encouraging an arms buildup—would encourage other powerful nations to do the same. I then think about the danger that places us in. Look at the results over time for nonmilitary or weak-military nations versus those with powerful militaries. You know who has survived … I'm just being realistic. You have to consider it.

"I would like to see a new world peace council. I realize it would be perceived by most as useless because that has pretty much been the historical result of international efforts to denuclearize. In life, big goals are mostly achieved by those who have dreams and never give up trying. I would love to see the American government make huge cuts in the military budget and use the savings to help the poor. The problem is when I become realistic in my thinking and look at history, allowing Russia, North Korea, and China to have the superior military power to the United States, the thought of it for the future of my sons and my grandchildren scares me. As far as military intervention in other countries like Iraq and Afghanistan, I'm opposed to it in concept. Having made that declaration, we always have to consider there will be exceptions. In some cases, intervention is necessary to save lives. Those exceptions have to be weighed carefully. If we can't feel confident of a quick and decisive intervention, we are better off staying out. The military experts, those who spent their careers in military assessment and strategy, should assess the potential results of any intervention. As I envision it, military experts in conjunction with civilian leaders would develop an outline for a plan for world peace, seek out leaders from all countries that we perceive as being favorable to the idea, and then keep expanding until they had all nations on board to seek a peaceful world. The latter would be next to impossible to achieve. It doesn't seem like it should be that difficult when you recognize what that would mean for the health and survival of all who reside on this planet. All of a nation's resources could go toward making a better life for everyone. Pipe dream? Probably, but it's better than any alternative. The obstacle is the lust for power by individuals and groups within each nation. Wars and the threat of wars keep dictators in power. A peaceful democratic nation is not an environment for long-term leadership. The dictators need not be concerned about losing their power as long as they don't have elections. What do you think of my idea for a world peace council?"

"I think it's great," Sean said. "The problem is that it would never work. Just look at history."

"I think it would be great, and the way to show off our leadership would be by cutting our military spending to set an example," Rachel said.

Jackson said, "The sticking point is similar to where you have two people pointing a gun at each other and seeking to have one lay down their gun. Not being able to solve that dilemma will keep the world in danger until some nutcase dictator pushes the button. The very long-shot possibility of a successful world peace council is our only hope. I think we are close to an agreement between the three of us—if Rachel is not going to have us lay down our arms and pray."

"I'm not suggesting just laying down our arms. We would need to develop internationally supervised disarmament—one in which we take the lead."

"Let's just dream we can make that work. Do you think Trump's efforts in North Korea were meaningful?"

Sean answered, "North Korea has been considered by many to be, prior to Trump, the major threat to world peace. President Barack Obama conveyed his opinion to that effect to Trump just before leaving office in 2017. No previous president has even talked to Kim. You gotta give Trump credit. He did something that no other past president could do. I don't think Obama ever made a realistic effort to deal with North Korea."

"Come on, Sean," Rachel countered. "He goes over there, what, two or three times? They fall in love but never get anything done. A lot of smoke. My question is, what has really changed."

"Personally, I question if Kim has control of what North Korea does," Jackson said. "I think the military is in control, and Kim just inherited the symbol from his father and is the pipeline for the bull crap that the real power feeds the people. I have thought of the possibility that Kim played Trump like a fiddle and attained world recognition beyond what North Korea ever had before. I wonder if the real power in North Korea, which is likely the military leaders, just moved some weapons around and enjoyed the recognition. I can't say though that it was wrong to talk to him—just like I don't think it was wrong for the Obama administration to talk to Iran. In the end, that didn't accomplish anything either. I think we can agree that talking to the leader of another nation is better than not talking to them, especially when they are testing and showing off weapons that can kill millions of people. Are we in basic agreement?"

"I'm with you," Sean said.

"Okay," Rachel said, "with some reservations and not conceding that Trump accomplished anything."

"So, we agree on the basic premise that talking to Kim was worth the try." Before Rachel could express any further disagreement, Jackson said, "Let's do some more trivia. What president was elected and served a four-year term between the elected terms of another president?"

Rachel answered, "Benjamin Harrison—between the terms of Grover Cleveland."

"You beat me to it," Sean said. "You're only one down now."

"Good answer," Jackson said. "I'm going to have to think of a tougher question. I would like to hear what you guys have to say about the Saudis."

"I think Republican presidents have been too soft on the Saudis' actions," Rachel said. "They certainly are not loyal friends of the United States. They get away with murder because of their influence on oil prices. They also murdered journalist Jamal Khashoggi, who was an employee of the *Washington Post*—and we did nothing about it. Furthermore, the Saudis have played a role in the Yemen Civil War, where thousands have died."

"What do you propose we do?" Sean asked. "You have expressed opposition to our getting involved in foreign wars."

"I'm not talking war or sending troops. I'm talking sanctions."

"First off, Khashoggi was not an American citizen. He just did some work for the *Washington Post*. He was also editor of the *Al-Arab* news channel. I don't think we should jeopardize our relationship with the Saudis for Jamal Khashoggi. What the Saudis did to Khashoggi was wrong, and we need to and did let our disapproval be known."

"I don't think we are too far apart on this one. A collapsed or enemy Saudi Arabia would be much more damaging to American interests, and it would not make any significant change in their behavior. It's a dilemma. I agree with Rachel that we need to show that we are willing to use sanctions if they go too far. Again though, we have mutually beneficial interests. Both sides still agree that opposing Iranian regional influence and countering terrorism are priorities. Our relationship with the Saudis needs to be a carefully managed balancing act."

Sean asked, "Rachel, don't you agree that our top priority is to avoid war? Our priority is to keep America safe?"

"Of course."

"But, if we push sanctions too far, we will lose an ally and bring us closer to war."

"I think you and I could agree on a measured response. We just have to be careful not to perceive the Saudis as true friends."

Jackson smiled. "I continue to like the way you two have basic knowledge about these issues from a liberal and conservative perspective and can still find some common ground. I think we are doing great for amateurs. I continue to be excited about what I am putting together here for my paper. As long as we are on a roll, let's talk about Iran."

"Yes, Iran," Rachel said, "where a major effort and a successful one by John Kerry in the Obama administration brought about a nuclear agreement easing international sanctions while allowing UN inspectors into the country."

"All liberal idealism," Sean countered. "The specifics of the deal are inadequate. It was a terrible deal, a deal that helped Iran and did nothing for us."

"So, we are a long way apart on Iran," Jackson said. "Going back to 1979, we have certainly had a poorly managed relationship with Iran, the highlight of which was the Iranian Hostage Crisis, where fifty-two American embassy workers were held hostage by Iranian revolutionaries for four hundred and forty-four days. In the years leading up to the crisis, the United States controlled the Iranian government by installing and supporting the oppressive dictator, Shah Pahlavi, who then turned the politically moderate nation into a dictatorship. In the ensuing years, the friction between the United States and Iran has been centered on the subject of covert Iranian nuclear weapons projects, which if successful could pose a threat to American allies and escalate into a global crisis. As a result, the Obama administration decided that the best solution to Iranian nuclear armament was a deal that eased international sanctions while allowing UN inspectors into the country. The big question today is, was it a good deal for America and the West. What are your thoughts, Sean?"

"First of all, I think John Kerry was the wrong guy to be negotiating a deal with the country where his son-in-law is a loyal Iranian. I'm not questioning Kerry's loyalty to the country he has served in many capacities for a lifetime. I just see it as a potentially inadvertent conflict of interest. I don't like the fact that Kerry was not open about that relationship."

"I can conceive that Kerry thought the relationship would be a benefit," Rachel said.

"A benefit for Iran. The son-in-law is not just an ordinary Iranian. He has some connections to the Iranian government."

"Come on, Sean. You're being cynical."

"I'm just stating the facts. I don't find it surprising that the liberal *New York Times* announced the marriage but didn't reveal the connection. I have studied the ramifications of this deal more than any other topic we have discussed. I see the agreement as a very bad deal. The deal falls short of addressing Iran's regional behavior or its missile program. The sunset provisions in the deal mean restrictions on Iran's uranium enrichment and plutonium reprocessing go away in ten to fifteen years. They can rapidly expand their nuclear program at that time to an industrial scale. They can then produce enough weapons-grade uranium for a nuclear weapon in a matter of weeks, if not days. And those were the words of President Obama. The international community doesn't have a complete picture of Iran's nuclear program, making it impossible to establish a baseline to guide future inspections and verification.

"Additionally, the deal gives Iran twenty-four hours' notice before an inspection can take place. That would give them more than enough time to move and conceal any weapons in development. After ten years, when the deal expires, Iran will be much further along in its aim to develop nuclear weapons and will pose a threat to Israel. Clearly the long-stated objective of Iran has been to destroy Israel. The UN sanctions on Iran's ballistic-missile program expire eight years after January 2024, and restrictions on the transfer of conventional weapons to or from Iran terminate after five years. I don't see how you have a deal with all those loopholes. The deal just kicks the can down the road for our kids to deal with.

"The windfall of sanctions relief has freed up tens of billions of dollars to finance Tehran's many destabilizing activities. Iran has increased its military budget 145 percent. They continue to be the world's leading state sponsor of terrorism, backing the terrorist organizations Hezbollah and Hamas. If Iran has the ability to enrich uranium to whatever level, it's not just Saudi Arabia that's going to ask for that. The whole world will be an open the door to go that route without any inhibition. Thus, the chance of destabilizing regional competition and conflict has increased."

Jackson answered, "The problem we have, Sean, is that Europe is still supportive of the deal. Seems like that puts the United States out on a limb. I don't see what we gain by pulling out of it while all the European countries still support it. I agree that the deal has a lot of limitations. So, what are our options now? I think we have to keep our sanctions on and keep trying to come to an agreement with the other countries."

"Anything that keeps down nuclear weapons development," Rachel said.

"I would not have voted for the deal, but since it is now a done deal and Iran, as best we can determine, is complying with the deal, all we can do is continue monitor and encourage Europe to do the same. What about Russia? Where do they come into play here?"

"I would say Russia is our most dangerous adversary at this time," Rachel said. "They have the most dangerous weapons systems."

"Russia now, China later," Sean added. "I've read a lot about both. The only way to deal with Russia is to not trust anything they say and deal with them from a position of strength. President Reagan proved that strategy to be successful in winning the Cold War. You can't believe Russia or anything they say. To them, distorting the facts and outright lies are the norm. Putin says and does whatever it takes to achieve his objective. When you negotiate with a country, typically you need to know their thinking process and the objectives of the governing leaders and whether or not public opinion comes into play. With Russia, it's just Putin. You have to know his position on anything you wish to talk about. Putin first served as president of Russia from 2000 until 2008. The Russian economy grew every year during those eight years. Then he returned at some point around 2011 or 2012. Between the two times he served as president, he served as prime minister, under Med—something. I can't recall the name. If he had been significant, I would remember his name."

"So, what's your point with Russia?" Rachel asked.

"My point is to think of meaningful collusion between Trump and Russia—or anyone and Russia—reflects a lack of understanding of Putin. He would never operate that way with anyone at Trump's level. I could see Trump doing a business deal. And what's wrong with that if he wasn't president at the time?"

"Trump looks out for Trump. He didn't really expect to win in 2016, but he is all about expanding his profile, his brand. He wants Trump to be the most recognized name on the planet."

"We all know he is overly loaded with self-confidence and is not shy about telling everyone."

"I have another word to describe his behavior: narcissism."

Jackson gently out put his hand. "I don't think we will make much progress by debating or slamming Trump's character. I pointed out my observations about him earlier. As far as Russia is concerned, we need to get as close to them as we can. The goal should be to monitor their every move and use sanctions wherever we need to keep them from acquiring territory. Let's face it—they want territorial expansion. We need to work closely with our allies to monitor them in a joint effort. They only understand power, and that is why I agree with Sean on the necessity of giving a high priority to keeping our military as powerful as possible. Putin doesn't understand weakness, only power."

"You just want to accept that we will never achieve peace with Russia," Rachel said.

"Not accept, cope with, and try to maintain a military advantage while we try to seek peace."

"I believe in lowering the defense budget when the economic situation calls for it," Rachel said. "Republicans overspend on military causes, and much of this spending is outdated. My views on the military also involve ending nuclear weapon development and safeguarding all nuclear materials around the world. The militaries of the major powers—the United States, Russia, China, and North Korea—are all so powerful that war is not practical. The war would mean self-destruction. I'm not saying eliminate the military—just give less priority to helping the poor people in this country, especially with health care."

CHAPTER 22

ISRAEL

"I don't think we made much progress on Russia. Let's move to Israel. I have in my note folder here, a copy of a letter published in the *Times of Israel,* credited to Mindy Weissenberg, after the Hague and apparently the international community criticized Israel for a ground offensive in Gaza."

Dear Mr. Hague,
You have stated that if Israel tries to defend its population through a ground offensive in Gaza 'it risks losing the sympathy of the international community.'

Let me tell you something about the sympathy of the international community, Mr. Hague. My father was liberated from Buchenwald Concentration Camp in 1945, having lost his entire family but gaining the sympathy of the international community at the time. After 6 million Jews had been annihilated at the hands of the Nazi regime, the international community had plenty of sympathy for the Jewish people. There is always plenty of sympathy for victims.

Israel doesn't need the sympathy of the international community.

What it needs is to defend its citizens.

When as a tiny country it gained its independence in 1948 it had to absorb 800,000 Jews who were thrown out of Arab lands in the Middle East, and it did so without fuss and with dignity giving them shelter and a place of security in which their children could grow up to become productive citizens. When Jordan, Egypt, Lebanon, and Syria tried to destroy Israel in 1948, and again in 1967 they took in hundreds of thousands of Palestinian Arabs but did they give them dignity or shelter? No, they left them to rot in refugee camps in order to maintain a symbol of grievance against Israel and use them as a political tool against the Jewish state. What has arisen in those camps is a complicated situation, but it is what has led to Gaza today.

So don't lecture Israel on international sympathy Mr. Hague. Not when Israel has just sent in 120 truckloads of food into Gaza to feed the Palestinian people there, because their own leadership is more interested in using its population as human shields, launching rockets against Israel from within major civilian centers.

Don't lecture Israel on international sympathy, Mr. Hague. Not when Israel targets with as much military precision as it can, only terrorists and their bases, trying its utmost to prevent civilian casualties.

Don't lecture Israel on international sympathy, Mr. Hague. Not when the Palestinian media deliberately uses images of victims of the Syrian civil war and presents them as casualties in Gaza to gain international sympathy.

Go read your history books, Mr. Hague, go see that since the beginning of the twentieth century all the Arabs wanted to do was destroy Israel. Go look at the country of Israel now since the Jews have established a state there. Go read what advances in science, medicine, biotechnology, agriculture, and high tech Israel has developed and dedicated that knowledge to making the world a better place for humanity. Can you imagine any other country that after 60 years of continuously being under attack could have achieved so much?

So Mr. Hague don't lecture Israel on international sympathy. Israel will do whatever it takes to defend itself from the outright attack on its citizens, whether it be from Hamas, Hezbollah, Iran or any other country or terrorist group that attacks it.

And if it loses the sympathy of the international community, so be it. We don't need the international community's sympathy. We don't need another 6 million victims.

Yours sincerely,
Mindy Wiesenberg

"Israelis have been the most persecuted people on the planet. I have never really understood why, other than the fact that they are self-sufficient and very ambitious. Hitler feared their ambition and potential for power, so he persecuted them. You don't hear Israelis complaining about equal opportunity. They create opportunity with ambition, hard work, and entrepreneurship. Furthermore, they have been our most valued ally in the Middle East. The unsolvable obstacle to peace in the Middle East is that Israel's neighbors seek total extinction of the Jewish people."

"Yes," Sean said, "and President Trump's move to recognize the Golan Heights in March of 2019 as part of Israel was long past due and overlooked by past American presidents. In past invasions and wars by Syria on Israel, the Golan Heights has been of strategic advantage to Syria. In its effort to protect the safety of its people, during the war more than fifty years ago, Israel gained control of the territory and has occupied it since.

"I have never been able to understand why approximately two-thirds of the American Jewish population votes for Democrats when year after year, Republicans are more supportive of policies that stand behind Israel. I must be missing something. The Iranians and most of the Middle East have made it clear that their objective is complete annihilation of the Jewish people. Six million Jews were annihilated by Hitler and Germany, and now Israel's neighbors seem to have a desire to do the same. Why would a Jewish person be against Israel? I don't get it. Israel, such a little nation, should be commended for standing up to and surviving while being surrounded by neighbors that want to destroy them. Why would a Jewish American accept that positioning?"

"Values, my friend, it's all about values," Rachel answered. "Repairing the world has been a Jewish value for many centuries. They identify with the liberal philosophy. Clearly the Democratic Party is more in line with liberal thinking. Actually, progressive is the term being more recognized today than liberal. Either, to me, means a government to protect individuals from harm and give equal opportunity. It's intelligent voting. They base their preference on governing and policy, especially on taxing for a more level playing field. They see Democratic policies as more helpful in providing economic opportunity for the middle class and small businesses."

"I read a survey done by *New York News and Politics* that I found interesting," Jackson said. "The survey showed that my people vote more with the Jewish people, yet surveys show that my people don't trust the Jewish people. More than 50 percent of black people say that given a choice between money and people, Jews will choose money. While the majority of Americans feel otherwise, a plurality of black people believe that Jews are more loyal to Israel than to America. Also, while a majority of the public denies the charge that Jewish businessmen will usually try to pull a shady deal on a customer, a narrow plurality of black people tend to believe it. For their part, Jews are more resistant to integrated neighborhoods than other Americans and are generally less willing than whites to send their children to schools with black people. I think much of this thinking comes from Jewish apartment building ownership. Let's move on. We have more to cover before we run out of time. We have had a lot of controversy regarding the Muslim population in America, especially since 9/11. Many are concerned with things like their historical treatment of women and involvement in terrorist attacks. Do you think we should be concerned?"

"Maybe the United States should look at Australia's prime minister, Julia Gillard, and her approach to dealing with Sharia law. She says Muslims who want to live under Islamic Sharia law were told to get out of Australia as the government targeted radicals in a bid to head off potential terror attacks. She says immigrants, not Australians, must adapt. Take it or leave it. I am tired of this nation worrying about whether we are offending some individual or their culture. We speak mainly English, not Spanish, Lebanese, Arabic, Chinese, Japanese, Russian, or any other language. Therefore, if you wish to become part of our society, learn the language!

"Most Australians believe in God. This is not some Christian, right-wing, political push, but a fact because Christian men and women, on Christian principles, founded this nation, and this is clearly documented. It is certainly appropriate to display it on the walls of our schools. If God offends you, then I suggest you consider another part of the world as your new home because God is part of our culture. We will accept your beliefs and will not question why. All we ask is that you accept ours and live in harmony and peaceful enjoyment with us."

"This is our country, our land and our lifestyle, and we will allow you every opportunity to enjoy all this. But once you are done complaining, whining, and griping about our flag, our pledge, our Christian beliefs, or our way of life, I highly encourage you to take advantage of one other great Australian freedom: the right to leave.

"If you aren't happy here, then leave. We didn't force you to come here. You asked to be here. So, accept the country that accepted you."

Rachel said, "That's a racist attitude. Whatever issues they have should be dealt with in an amicable manner—and not with threats and prejudice."

Jackson shook his head, "Maybe we better stick to the with United States. We have enough problems to deal with here without digging into Australia."

"I buy that," Rachel added.

"Let's do education. First, a little story."

☆　　☆　　☆

An older, white-haired man walked into a jewelry store one Friday evening with a beautiful young gal at his side.

He told the jeweler he was looking for a special ring for his girlfriend.

The jeweler looked through his stock and brought out a five thousand-dollar ring.

The old man said, "No, I'd like to see something more special."

At that statement, the jeweler went to his special stock and brought over another ring. "Here's a stunning ring at only forty thousand," the jeweler said.

The young lady's eyes sparkled, and her whole body trembled with excitement.

The old man, seeing this, said, "We'll take it."

The jeweler asked how payment would be made, and the old man stated, "By check. I know you need to make sure my check is good, so I'll write it now. You can call the bank on Monday to verify the funds, and I'll pick the ring up Monday afternoon."

On Monday morning, the jeweler phoned the older man and said, "There's no money in that account."

"I know," said the old man. "But let me tell you about my weekend!"

Sean and Rachel laughed.

"Rachel, let's see if I can think of a question that gets you back to even with Sean. One of our presidents had false teeth made of hippopotamus, ivory, bone, animal teeth, lead, brass screws, and gold wire."

"George Washington."

"You got it."

"All even—now you can pull away from him."

"Here's a double. These two presidents hated each other. One called the other a 'mean-spirited, low-life fellow, the son of a half-breed Indian squaw, sired by a Virginia mulatto father.' Quite coincidently, they died some years later on the same Fourth of July day only hours apart. Name both for two points."

"Thomas Jefferson," Rachel said quickly.

"And John Adams," Sean said.

"You each got one—still all even."

CHAPTER 23

EDUCATION

Jackson said, "I think it was in a Pew Research Survey I read where black people and Jewish people typically have favorable views of each other. However, Hispanics are less likely to say the two groups get along, and black people are more likely than Hispanics to say they are often victims of racial discrimination."

"It's all about education," Rachel explained. "People of different races are naturally going to have some mixed feelings about each other. It's up to our education system to teach that we are all created equal."

"I agree with what you are saying," Sean said. "However, our education system shouldn't promote political philosophy in a biased way. By a wide margin, I've read as much as 90 percent of our educators are liberal and frequently take advantage of their teaching positions to promote liberal views."

"Teaching political differences is a part of education."

"Yes, teach the fundamental differences," Jackson said, "but don't try to show political party preferences. We should be teaching critical thinking and empathy about marginalized groups. We can teach about racism and privilege in ways that support the system."

Sean said, "I read an article a year or so ago where schools in Minneapolis were promoting a left-wing agenda and bullying conservative students rather than teaching the subjects they were paid to teach. One school did an editorial implying that unity will exist only when all conservatives have been banished from the stage. This is wrong, and I think against what education for our kids is about. Universities across the country have liberal biases in their teaching. That's flat-out wrong. I have a problem with that in my own home. My wife is a left-wing, almost socialist teacher. I have asked her, many times, not to promote her liberal bias exclusively."

"Come on, Sean," Rachel argued. "You're saying we shouldn't inform our kids about our political views?"

"I'm not saying that. I'm just saying they should be taught to think for themselves. My kids are confused because I am conservative and my wife is liberal. They get confused that taking one side or the other means they like one of us better than the other."

"Do you both agree that we should advocate educational institutions to not promote extremes in political philosophy?" Jackson asked.

Rachel nodded. "I can agree with that, with the understanding that it's difficult for a liberal or conservative person to spend hours with kids and not exhibit a preference."

"Okay," Jackson said. "Let's move on to some specifics in education—other than politics. Well, this is somewhat related. I'm referring to religion and evolution."

Sean whistled. "That's a tough one."

"Shouldn't be—just teach the facts," Rachel countered. "Our genetics sequence, as humans, is with chimpanzees, which strongly suggests we share a common ancestor. This has been scientifically proven. There are thousands of fossils documenting progressively more humanlike species in the evolution of our lineage after it split from the other great apes and later from chimps. Biologists have actually observed evolution happening in other species. And animal breeders make evolution happen all the time. We have varieties of dog breeds that have been created from wolves."

"This becomes a problem if you think the Bible has to be interpreted literally," Jackson said. "Evolution contradicts the Genesis story that God created all organisms in their present form. But you can believe in God without believing that the Bible is literally true."

"I believe in God as the Creator of the Universe and that God sent Jesus Christ to planet earth to deliver a message," Sean said. "The message has been interpreted differently by various church organizations, and that is okay. Religion and churches have been an important and beneficial institution."

"Religion has been one of the top three reasons for war in the history of our planet," Rachel said. "The other two are territorial gain and economic gain. Jackson, you like to look at things logically. Looking at it from the standpoint of the proven science of evolution and wars, the logic just isn't there. I don't promote it, but to us boys and girls here, I have to be honest and call myself an atheist."

"I attend our church most every Sunday," Jackson said. "Churches and religious followings have been good for this country. They are supporters of many beneficial programs, such as helping the poor and creating good values. I think we can agree religion is compatible with a peaceful and beneficial lifestyle."

"I'm okay with that," Rachel said.

"I would go a little further than that," Sean said, "but what you say is certainly true."

CHAPTER 24

HEALTH CARE

Rachel looked at Jackson. "I think we should talk about health care, an ongoing disaster that's only going to get worse."

"Good choice. Good choice, let me start it off with a little story."

"Great. I love your stories."

A man comes into a hospital emergency and ends up having had heart surgery. After he survives the operation, he finds himself in the care of nuns at a Catholic hospital.

One of the nuns asks him what health insurance he has.

He says I don't have any.

The nun then asks him how he intends to pay the hospital.

He says he doesn't know.

She then asks if he has a relative who can help.

He says, "I have a spinster sister who is a nun."

The nun becomes agitated and lectures the man than nuns are not spinsters—they are married to God.

The patient replies, "Then send the bill to my brother-in-law."

Sean and Rachel both get a good chuckle

"Okay, my thoughts? My guess is that the idea has been proposed, but it never got very far. Our legislator is too busy with hearings and investigations. I think a good way to save a substantial amount of money on health care is to develop a standardized health rating for everyone over the age of eighteen—maybe even younger. The US Department of Health could develop standards based on physicals and the person having appropriate weight and abstinence from excessive use of drugs and alcohol. Insurance providers would be encouraged to provide discounts for high standards of health. Our auto insurance rates are based on safe driving records. Why not do the same with health care?"

"You're going to penalize people for not being slim and trim?" Rachel asked.

"No, I want to reward people for taking care of their health."

"What about genes? You can't help what you're born with."

"No, the evaluation would only be for what is controllable."

"I don't think so. Some doctors would fudge the reports for their patients."

"I didn't say it would be perfect—only that it would help some. It will take a combination of things to get costs down. Tort reform would be another help. Sean, what do you think?"

"I don't see any way this country can afford to provide free health care for everyone."

"Employers should pay it," Rachel said.

"Now you're just gonna eliminate a lot of small businesses. Furthermore, the cost of free health care would run up the national debt; it's now twenty-four trillion."

"Raise taxes on the wealthy."

"And see companies invest less and consumer sales decline, resulting in loss of jobs? It's the domino effect."

"I don't see how you can require people to maintain a specific diet. I agree that health care cost is our most pressing domestic problem. The cost of getting coverage for the average consumer is getting out of hand. Democrats have been proactive on the issue. Republicans' only concern seems to be keeping down the cost to employers."

"That's not an accurate statement. I think most employers are willing to share the cost. Shared costs promote positive behavior. If health care becomes free, the total cost will go up substantially. When people have to pay some of the cost, they are more cautious about rushing to a doctor every time they sneeze."

"If not totally provided, the next best alternative, I believe, is for the government to make health care affordable. Hillary Clinton proposed the Health Security Act of 1993. 'Hillarycare' was a managed competition strategy. The federal government would control doctor bills and insurance premiums."

"And it didn't fly. The government has a poor record of program management."

"You're right … because the Republicans, backed by the insurance companies, shot it down in Congress. Let me remind you that the Clintons achieved two other health care reform measures. The Health Insurance Portability and Accountability Act of 1996 was one. The program allows employees to keep their company-sponsored health insurance plan for eighteen months after they lost their jobs. The Children's Health Insurance Program was the other. It provides subsidized health insurance for children in families that earn too much to qualify for Medicaid. Also, we need to consider preventive health care. Obama's 2010 Patient Protection and Affordable Care Act seeks to lower the cost of health care. It requires everyone to have insurance or pay the penalty, providing health insurance companies with revenue to cover those with preexisting conditions. Preventive care reduces expensive emergency room visits."

"How's that worked out? Not very well, as I recall."

"Most of the problems Obamacare faced resulted from Republican-created obstacles, especially Trump trying to keep his campaign promise to dump Obamacare."

Jackson said, "As I see it, a single-player plan should save money—that is if properly managed. With private plans, the built-in cost is there. The insurance companies and their salespeople have to make money. With a single-payer plan, managed by Medicare, less cost may be involved. Ideally, we should have single-payer with supplemental coverage available through private companies. I do share, though, the concern Sean has, that the government management record of inefficiency, along with reckless use of the system, is a significant potential problem."

"With private, the affluent get better coverage because they can afford it, while the little guy has to live with the government program and its limitations," Rachel said.

"I have thought about that a lot, and I realize that people with wealth tend to get better health care. The best doctors are more expensive, and the wealthy can afford to pay the premium. Also, hospital donors, although it's not supposed to happen, tend to get preferential treatment. My wife had a serious problem last year, and we couldn't get her an appointment for the doctor that my friends highly recommended, so I asked for advice from a guy I know. I won't mention his name because I don't want to embarrass him, but he got us an appointment within three days. And it all turned out well, by the way. I have to say; I feel that was unfair to whoever got pushed back to make room for my wife. Actually though, I only considered what was best for my wife. I think what we did is very common."

"Yes, it is common and not fair," Rachel said. "The same old, same old: the rich get favoritism. It's free enterprise, capitalism at work."

"I won't disagree with you on that point," Sean said. "The point you are leaving out is that free enterprise capitalism has been the foundation of this country. It has made us the most successful nation in the history of the planet. It's not a perfect system, but it's the best among so many, like socialism, communism, and dictatorships that have all failed."

"I agree the rich get richer and have all the goodies. The fancy cars and … I bet you drive a Mercedes."

"You guessed it. And I earned it. I worked long hours and took risks to attain what I have. I have a Mercedes SUV, by the way. Let me make my point. If you overtax those who are successful, you take away the motive to grow, expand, create jobs, and give to charity. It does seem a little unfair, especially when you see children of the rich who haven't had to work and get all the goodies. That's a little flaw we have to live with that comes with an incentive-based system. I might add that my kids will not be spoiled; I do and will continue to give them the responsibility to earn what they get."

"Let me offer the compromise on this one," Rachel said. "I'm talking about national health insurance. The health care delivery system remains private. As opposed to a national health service, where the government employs doctors, in a national health insurance system, the government is billed, but doctors remain in private practice. It could save more than a hundred billion in paperwork alone. Our current system is so complex with administrative complexities that 25 percent of every health care dollar goes to marketing, billing, utilization review, and other forms of waste. A single-payer system could greatly reduce administrative costs. Businesses would save money. A single-payer system is more efficient than our current system; health care costs are less."

"And with the national health insurance I'm talking about, your insurance doesn't depend on your job. Regardless of your role in life, you're provided with care. This leads to a healthier population, but it's also beneficial from an economic standpoint. Workers are less tied to their employers, and those who dislike their current positions can find new work and not have their insurance impacted."

"You seem to have studied this, and I have as well. Countries with a national health system have long waits for elective procedures."

"Do you realize that Medicare, the government program for the elderly, has the overhead of approximately 3 percent, while in private insurance companies, overhead and profits add up to 15 to 25 percent?"

"Let me just summarize," Jackson said. "I can't recall any successful efforts to solve health issues. Reforms have often been proposed, but they have rarely proven successful. Politicians who have made attempts, like Hillary Clinton and Barack Obama, have not succeeded. It's an unsolvable problem and will continue to be because people are living longer, and new, helpful but expensive procedures are being added to the system year after year. I visited my cousin in the hospital, and as I walked down the hallways, I couldn't help noticing every room was full of elderly patients. It's great we can prolong life, but it increases the cost to the system."

"We need to find ways to cut costs without downgrading care," Jackson continued. "I know of a company, Marathon Health, that establishes facilities on the property of large companies and large cities. They provide in-house care, saving the cost of work time loss as well as treatment cost. The facility is managed by well-trained nurses who are capable of treating most health issues. This process is far less costly than having them miss work to go to a hospital or a doctor's office. I realize this will not solve all the problems. The idea I mentioned earlier, coverage discounts for those who maintain good health, and doing a better job of monitoring the legitimacy of doctor fees, will all help. As far as private or government management, we need both. Private enterprise has, historically, proven to be more efficient. They do, however, need monitoring to avoid mismanagement or greed. We keep debating this issue. It's time to get something done. I say a congressional committee should be established to work with a cross representation of health care industry experts to develop a plan to recommend to Congress. I want to go to the AOC thing called the Green New Deal. One more trivia question first. This president snacked on a bunch of cherries and washed it all down with iced milk. Bacteria was present in either the cherries or the milk, leading to his death a few days later."

Sean was quick with the answer: "Zachary Taylor."

"Sean's one up."

CHAPTER 25

GREEN NEW DEAL

Jackson made eye contact with both Sean and Rachel. "As I continue talking about these topics, I want to tell you about the ghost in the room. I will explain that comment later. I'm anxious to hear your views on the Green New Deal. As I am sure you are aware, the plan addresses both climate change and economic inequality. Use of the term New Deal is a take on Franklin Roosevelt's response to the Great Depression when he addressed social and economic reforms with public works projects. The Green New Deal combines Roosevelt's economic approach with modern ideas such as renewable energy and resource efficiency. Some have labeled it the 'Bad New Deal.'"

"Freshman Congresswoman Alexandria Ocasio-Cortez, commonly referred to as AOC, introduced her Green New Deal in the House. Cortez, only twenty years old, has done an amazing job in developing national recognition for herself. I like the concept. I just don't know if we can make it work financially. Dr. Martin Capages has written an excellent book: *Why the Green New Deal is a Bad Deal for America.* He points out that environmental experts have been debating the global warming issue for a long time. Some deny the projections, and others see it as a vital concern for the future of the planet. As I see it, we will only green the world when we change the very nature of the electricity grid—moving it away from dirty coal or oil to clean coal and renewables. And that is a huge industrial project. From what I am hearing, it would be much bigger than anyone has contemplated. If we can afford it—and it works, like the New Deal—it has the potential to create a whole new clean power industry to spur our economy into the twenty-first century.

"The campaign for the Green New deal is attempting to get Congress to approve a nonbinding resolution—not legislation. It lays out a broad vision for how the country might tackle climate change over the next decade while creating high-paying jobs and protecting vulnerable communities. Separate legislation would have to be introduced to make any of the resolution's goals a reality."

Rachel said, "Consider this. As temperatures rise, it could mean many of the biggest cities in the Middle East and South Asia will become lethally hot in summer, perhaps as soon as 2050. There would be ice-free summers in the Arctic and the unstoppable disintegration of the West Antarctic's ice sheet. Coral reefs would be lost. We would have tens of millions of climate refugees fleeing droughts, flooding, and extreme heat. In addition, we could have multiple climate-driven natural disasters striking simultaneously. The Green New Deal is all about saving our planet for future generations."

Sean shook his head, "I also refer to it as the Bad New Deal. It's ridiculed. The plan is like a manifesto that would be doomed to fail. The plan collects several otherwise disconnected social, political, environmental, and economic ideas of policymakers who mistakenly believe that a command-and-control economy is superior to a free marketplace. They want to impose their social and political preferences on others. The plan's authors have provided no explicit plan to achieve these goals—other than to claim that they are achievable because of the enormous expansion of government that occurred during World War II. But there is no realistic comparison that can be made with the 1940s wartime economy. That economy involved shifting resources from producing cars into producing tanks with existing technologies versus achieving zero carbon emissions. We don't have the technological know-how to make that concept realistic.

"Other environmental goals of the GND show that the authors do not understand basic cost-benefit analysis, which should be the foundation of every government program. They believe that the economic experience of World War II shows that we can spend as much today as is needed in order to implement a carbon-free economy. Many of the GND's environmental goals are not feasible. We just can't achieve 'net zero greenhouse gas emissions in ten years' and 'meet all of our power demand with renewables.'

"The idea of upgrading all existing buildings to maximum energy efficiency does not make economic sense. The costs of such remediation would significantly exceed the benefits for recently constructed buildings. The plan is just not practical. Furthermore, there are not nearly enough skilled heating, ventilation, and air conditioning—HVAC—workers to do the work in every building in the country along with building new housing. We would also have to consider the costs of insulation materials and HVAC systems. Building supplies would go through the roof, which in turn would raise costs and create a housing crisis.

"It is also my understanding that the production of building supplies, insulation, and new HVAC systems burn carbon-emitting fossil fuels. We would also have to consider other aspects of the GND, such as its pro-union provisions, which occurred during the New Deal of the 1930s, when many manufacturing industries agreed to substantially raise wages.

"I understand that this aspect of the Roosevelt New Deal de-layed the recovery from the Great Depression by seven years. Raising wages above worker productivity is an even more shortsighted idea today when many more jobs can be easily off-shored, outsourced, or automated.

"Many other aspects of the GND are just not logical. It's too vague to promise a living wage to everyone. What does a living wage equate to? Does this mean young and inexperienced workers would be paid the same as seasoned workers? How can beginners justify requiring the same wages as skilled workers?

"What if the guarantee of a 'living wage' leads some workers to put forth less effort than called upon? And should we impose such a substantial cost on employers when most minimum-wage earners are very young and/or part-time employees, and when only a small fraction of household heads earn the minimum wage?

"The GND would be extremely expensive, though it is hard to know just how much because much of it is vague. Experts estimate the cost to be close to a hundred trillion, which is already roughly five years of our GDP. And is often the case with many large-scale government projects, the cost of projects' completions are often double or triple the initial cost estimates.

"The authors of the GND don't worry about the cost because they believe that the government can just print new currency to buy whatever is needed. This idea is known in some circles as 'modern monetary theory.' In reality, it's a pitch of dream results without a comprehensive analysis of the cost.

"The GND represents the deficient economic thinking of a

new generation of the new socialist dreaming. There are much more cost-effective ways of dealing with greenhouse gases, including taxing carbon emissions and dealing with the growing pollution problems in rapidly developing countries such as China and India. China produces nearly one-third of global carbon emissions. Therefore, reducing carbon emissions must include China and other major carbon-emitting countries. But the GND is just for the United States. If the United States completely eliminated carbon emissions, it would reduce global carbon emissions by about 13 percent.

"More broadly, the command-and-control implementation of the GND, in which more than 50 percent of the economy would pass through the hands of the government, would be a major move toward a socialistic economy—not to mention the drop in individual freedoms."

Rachel looked at her watch as an effort to question how long Sean would keep on talking.

Sean smiled and said, "You've got the floor."

"Look—the Green New Deal is a big, bold transformation of the economy to tackle the twin crises of inequality and climate change. It would mobilize vast public resources to help us transition from an economy built on exploitation and fossil fuels to one driven by dignified work and clean energy.

"The economy we have now left millions behind while padding the pockets of corporate polluters and billionaires. The current economy exposes working-class people to stagnant wages, increasing pollution, and stagnant job opportunities. The climate crisis only magnifies these systemic injustices since hard-hit communities are hit harder by storms, droughts, and flooding. Inequality is therefore heightened by the climate crisis by depriving communities of the resources needed to adapt to such conditions.

"Inequality will be increasingly linked to climate change. We can't deal with one without addressing the other. To meet the needs of the climate crisis, a Green New Deal would upgrade our infrastructure, revitalize our energy system, modernize our buildings, and restore our ecosystems. With these changes, a Green New Deal would cut climate pollution while creating millions of family-sustaining jobs, expanding access to clean air and water, raising wages, and building climate resilience. To counteract inequality, GND benefits would go first and foremost to the working-class families and communities of color that have had to cope with the brunt of the fossil fuel economy."

"Sorry, Rachel, but I gotta put it this way. I see the Green New deal as using climate change as a ploy to implement a radical socialist agenda. The Heartland Institute's main argument against the Green New Deal is that its socialism in disguise. It recently launched a website, Socialism.com, that criticizes the Green New Deal as 'energy socialism.' Justin Haskins, an executive editor and research fellow for Heartland and author of *Socialism Is Evil*, is the group's main spokesperson for its claim that the Green New Deal has a hidden socialist agenda. He made two appearances on Fox News in January and wrote several op-eds for conservative outlets to push that line of attack.

"The real experts on this subject see it as all about socialism, not saving the environment. The plan is just plain radical and impractical. It doesn't do anything to reduce global CO_2 emissions. The leading proponents of the activist groups see the GND as transforming our economy and society to a level needed to stop the climate crisis. It seeks to decarbonize the economy, create millions of green jobs, and rectify racial and economic inequality, though a specific policy agenda has yet to be worked out. The Green New Deal, whose backers include Rep. Alexandria Ocasio-Cortez, has polled favorably with registered voters—even though most Americans have heard nothing about it, and those who have don't understand the consequence of it."

Rachel said, "Despite the fact that this plan is not yet fully defined and has no chance of passing through Congress for at least two years, right-wing media have wasted no time in attacking it. Outlets from Fox News to Breitbart News to the *Las Vegas Review-Journal* have spread inaccurate claims about the Green New Deal to stoke fears that it would destroy the American economy and political system. The Heartland Institute, a right-wing think tank known for its climate denial, is one of the most active opponents of the Green New Deal, and it is using right-wing media outlets to amplify its attacks. I don't think we are going to agree on anything with AOC. Shall we move on?"

CHAPTER 26

CORRUPTION

Jackson said, "I know this isn't a pleasant topic, but I think we should take a look at some behaviors by elected officials that could be considered inappropriate or maybe even illegal."

"That's a healthy topic," Rachel retorted with a sarcastic grin.

"And it comes from both sides of the aisle," Sean added.

"It does," Jackson agreed. "I have some notes here; let me just read them. If you dig a little and take an in-depth look at all the past actions and behaviors of all our past presidents, vice presidents, and House Majority and Senate leaders, as well as House and Senate chairpersons, you'll find that many of them have engaged in some behaviors that could be considered conflicts of interest. I want to cite a few of those. Specifically, I'll address Presidents Trump, Obama, and Clinton; presidential candidate Hillary Clinton; Senate Majority Leader Mitch McConnell; and former vice president Joe Biden. They're not bad people, and they're certainly not criminals. However, they have all made decisions or engaged in activities that could easily be construed as conflicts of interest. And it's this type of activity that the media or political opponents can jump on, exaggerate, and attack.

"To be more specific, I'd like to tell you about some research I've done on a subject that should concern us all. I did it for my university paper. I have it here; let me just read it to you. It describes the influence some powerful foreign banks and other foreign sources have on some leaders in the American government. Much of my information comes from books by Peter Schweizer. Other information came from internet research and rumors that reach me here at the Filibuster.

"Peter Schweizer's most recent book, *Secret Empires*, is about how the American political system hides corruption. He also wrote

Clinton Cash and *Throw Them All Out*, a no-holds-barred attack on how the political elite use their power and influence to enrich their friends and families. The key financial players in this game are Chinese banks, which include the four largest banks in the world. The Mitsubishi Bank of Japan is the fifth largest, and JP Morgan is the sixth largest. The values of these banks range from two and a half trillion for Morgan to four trillion dollars for the Bank of China.

"The American politicians involved in this from the left side of the aisle are Joe Biden and his son Hunter, John Kerry and his stepson Chris Heinz, and Barack Obama. On the right side of the aisle, it's Senate Majority Leader Mitch McConnell and President Trump and his family.

"First, keep in mind that, throughout history, family power has been a very effective way to gain financial favor and influence. Furthermore, the explosive growth of global business in recent decades has enhanced the feasibility of insider family-based business activities. In China, for example, the sons and daughters of high-level government officials are known as princelings. They have a clear path to business success; this process is also referred to as cronyism.

"We have some pretty cool princelings here in the United States as well. Look at Hunter Biden, the son of Joe Biden, or Chris Heinz, the stepson of John Kerry, the former secretary of state. John Kerry is divorced from his first wife, Julia Thorne, and is married to Teresa Heinz, the heiress to the Heinz estate—that's the ketchup company. Hunter and Chris have been known to profit from secretive deals they made with the Chinese government while their fathers were doing PR and negotiating with the government. The younger Biden and Kerry, along with another long-time buddy, Devon Archer, formed an investment company, Rosemont Seneca, around 2010. In 2011, while then Vice President Joe Biden was meeting with Chinese President Hu as part of a nuclear security summit, the younger Biden, Kerry, and Archer were meeting with high-level officials at Chinese financial institutions. This was, to say the least, a bit of a unique opportunity for rookie business developers to meet with leaders of the world's largest financial institutions. Their daddies had nothing to do with it, of course.

"The initial deal between the Chinese government and Seneca Capital was first announced in December 2013. It was a billion-dollar deal that was increased by one and a half billion dollars seven months later. In subsequent years, several other deals were made between other Rosemont partnerships and Chinese entities—all while Biden was still vice president. One of these occurred while the vice president and Secretary of State Kerry were meeting with Chinese leadership about China's expansion in the China Sea. Totally coincidental, of course.

"Much to the disappointment of others around the world—in particular, South Korea and Japan—American policy toward China's aggressive move softened after this deal was made. And Rosemont's partnerships were not limited to China. While the VP was overseeing American policy toward Ukraine, Hunter Biden joined the board of directors of one of Ukraine's most profitable and corrupt energy companies. *The Hill* reported that Vice President Biden threatened to withhold loan guarantees from Ukraine if its government did not fire a prosecutor who was investigating a company with connections to Biden's son. So, to sum up, the Rosemont companies, much to the credit of Hunter Biden and his father, Joe, comprise a very wealthy empire. On the personal side, Hunter Biden said that his father counseled him not to worry about hurting the family's public profile with his private life, although he divorced his wife and engaged in a relationship with his late brother Beau's widow, Hallie.

"Much has been written about the Clintons' financial dealings, so I will skip over Bill and Hillary. They had a net worth of half a million when Bill was first elected and claimed to have been sixteen million in debt when he left the office. However, Bill's current net worth is estimated at somewhere between fifty and one hundred million. Obama has gone from three million to forty million since leaving the office. These numbers are all googled estimates.

"Obama, unlike many presidents, was not rich when he left office. He has, however, gotten the hang of the money game since moving out of 1600 Pennsylvania Avenue. His friends are mostly young professionals from Chicago. In his recent book, Peter Shezeer mentioned that 'Obama's Chicago buddies' frequently visited the White House. It appears that these friends quietly absorbed information that allowed them to make timely bets and benefit financially when Obama's decisions impacted American industry. His close friends were a collection of young African American professionals, some well-known, such as Valerie Jarrett, and some not so well-known ones. All are highly educated and motivated peers. One of his buddies was Marty Nesbitt, referred to in the *Chicago Tribune* as 'FOB #1.' Nesbitt, a financial success, was backed by Penny Pritzker, the heir to the Hyatt Hotel fortune. Pritzker and Nesbitt created an offsite parking garage business, acquiring some forty locations. Nesbitt also formed an investment fund named Vistra that focuses on highly regulated industries such as health care, education, and financial services. When he launched his business at the onset of Obama's second term, Nesbitt brought on board several regulators and insiders from the Obama administration, including Tony Miller from the Department of Education and legislative affairs regulator Joe Samuels. The industries targeted by Vistra were the same industries that Obama was targeting for government action. A pattern developed when the Obama administration attacked these industries with government action, leading to substantially lower valuations of those companies. When these valuations dropped drastically, the buyers were Obama's friends. As we might have guessed, these investments recovered, resulting in nice profits for the buyers.

"However, Democrats don't have a monopoly on crony capitalism. Senate Majority Leader Mitch McConnell married into wealth. He was married to Sherrill Redman from 1968 to 1980, with whom he had three children, and in 1993, he remarried, this time to wealthy Elaine Chao. Chao moved to the United States from Taiwan at the age of eight. The Chao family benefits from ties to the Chinese military complex, and they have reaped large profits thanks to the Chinese government. Chao was Secretary of Labor under G. W. Bush and is now secretary of transportation under Trump. In 2004, the couple's net worth was reported to be $3.1 million. Ten years later, it was somewhere between ten and thirty-five million. The Chao family is in the shipping business, and the senior officials at the Chinese banks that financed Chao's ventures are members of the Chinese Communist Party. Senator McConnell's sister-in-law Angela Chao is on the board of directors for a Chinese bank. How do you think this impacts McConnell's views on America's dealings with China?

"Now let's move on to the big leagues: multibillionaire Donald Trump. Many in Donald Trump's wealthy stable of cabinet members have faced some sort of scandal in the president's first term; the corrupt spending habits of Scott Pruitt, Tom Price, David Shulkin, Ryan Zinke, and Ben Carson have all dominated the news at some point. The press had a blast when Rex Tillerson and John Kelly reportedly called Trump a "moron" and an "idiot" respectively.

"But let's look at the Trump princelings: his son Donald, his daughter Ivanka, and his son-in-law, Jared. We all know Donald Trump and his family are real-estate moguls with miles of properties, corporations, and branding deals. Let's begin with Ivanka and her husband, Jared Kushner. Kushner comes from his own real estate empire. Jared's father, New Jersey developer Charles Kushner, was convicted of tax evasion in 2004 under the leadership of then-prosecutor Chris Christie. Kushner served two years of prison time. Jared graduated from Harvard in 2003 and married Ivanka Trump in 2007. Soon after taking over his father's business, Jared put his Harvard education to work, although that expensive education was apparently not that valuable to him. Still new to real estate, he bought a building that covered an entire block of Fifth Avenue in New York City. Apparently, he wanted that big building a great deal, as he paid $1,200 per square foot, twice the previous record of $600. I wonder where the sellers went to school. Kushner financed this purchase with a $1.2-billion-dollar loan from Barclay's Capital. He got an additional $535 million in short-term debt, apparently to make the payments on the loan. Next, he had to sell the company's entire portfolio of rental properties for about $1.9 billion. What was he thinking?

"Jared had projected $120 million annual income from the Fifth Avenue property. He must have been using Harvard freshman math; his actual income was $30 million. He later sold parts of the property to maintain cash flow, but he is still heavily in debt on this investment. He is now serving as an advisor to President Trump. I'm not sure in what capacity, but I hope it's not anything to do with our government's real estate. We have also heard that China is anxious to get to know this White House real-estate princeling. With Trump negotiating with China on trade, you can bet Jared could line up some pretty nice financing in China. I have no idea if that is happening now or not.

"Princelings Eric and Donald Trump Jr. have not joined the White House team. Instead, they settled down to run the Trump family empire. Before Trump was elected, he visited Argentina's president, at which time, a previously stalled building project was granted building permits. Weeks after Trump was inaugurated,

Chinese businesswoman Angela Chen bought a penthouse condo from the Trump organization for sixteen million. The condo had previously been occupied by Ivanka and Jared. The buyer, who Realtors estimate overpaid for the site, has ties to the Chinese government.

"According to Schweizer's book, Trump owed three hundred million to Deutsche Bank of Germany in 2018—as well as hundreds of millions to the Bank of China. The big question here is how the millions that Trump, and other American politicians, owe to Chinese banks will impact policy decisions. In 2017, the Trumps committed to not pursue new deals in foreign countries, but the family business has continued to develop previously negotiated projects. It's difficult to see how Donald and Eric can avoid conflicts of interest.

"Having outlined all these accusations and suspicions, I don't really think any of our elected leaders go into office with the intent of gaining wealth through influence or decisions that would harm the United States. Unfortunately, they are placed in positions where they have abundant opportunities to help their families and friends. What we really need are some clearly defined guidelines for any investments by officeholders and their families."

"I hear you," Rachel said. "I remember some talk about that. I was really disappointed by that story because I voted for Biden and Kerry. They are Democrats, but I know these financial shenanigans are not limited to either party."

Sean nodded. "That's for sure. Republican House Majority leader Tom DeLay resigned for violating campaign finance laws and money laundering, and Congressman Duke Cunningham resigned after pleading guilty to federal charges of conspiracy to commit bribery, mail fraud, wire fraud, and tax evasion. And we can't forget that guy who insisted, 'I'm not a crook.' Richard Milhous Nixon. Oh, and back to the Democrats, I can't leave out the Clintons and how they got their wealth. I think we can agree that there are too many to even talk about."

Rachel said, "I could argue with that Clinton story, but let's just all agree that it happens in both parties and in national, state, and local governments, as well as in business. Excuse the expression, but the little guys are getting screwed across the board.

"Just a minute, though," she added. "I can't let the business world off without mentioning a couple of specifics. The real beauty is the Bernie Madoff scandal. You remember the hedge fund guru? Madoff was essentially running a Ponzi scheme. He even served as chairman of the National Association of Securities Dealers. After the shit hit the fan and he was exposed for fraud, he admitted to his sons—who worked at the firm—that the asset management business was all a big lie. If I recall correctly, the estimate for his fraud was something like fifty or sixty billion. I think he was sentenced to one hundred and fifty years in prison and restitution of more than one hundred and fifty billion, neither of which he will be able to accommodate now he's still in jail—in his eighties. One of his sons committed suicide, the other died of cancer, and the wife lives in a rented apartment. And then there was SAC Capital, run by Steven Cohen, which managed fifty billion in assets at its peak. The SEC was investigating that hedge fund for several years before they raided the offices of some of their investment companies in 2010. A half dozen or more traders were convicted."

"This is not fun stuff to talk about," Jackson sighed. "I think it goes to the heart of our education system; we need to emphasize honesty more! Too often, people see lies as funny and okay. They're not okay. Telling the truth or lying are habits. We've all known people who lie so much that they believe their own lies. We need to teach the importance of telling the truth at a very young age and then emphasize it again in high school and college. It may sound silly to teach college students the importance of honesty, but it's a personal habit people develop when they find they can benefit from lying. Then they become addicted to lying. They need to know that, in the long run, their lives will be better if they make a personal commitment to tell the truth."

Sean smiled. "That's very good. I like that."

"I agree," Rachel said.

"Well," Jackson said, "Sean's one up on the trivia, and we're running out of time. Let's do a couple more. One of our presidents regularly consulted with an astrologer before making decisions or scheduling big events."

Quickly, Rachel blurted out, "Ronald Reagan!"

"Okay." Jackson grinned. "Now we're all even! here's another one. Which president vomited in public?"

"George H. W. Bush!" Sean called out.

"Shit!" Rachel scowled. "Oh, excuse me. Sean's overtaken me. I knew the answer!"

"Sean's back to one up," Jackson announced, chuckling. "But here's an easy one. Ready? Which president had an office worker crawl under his desk?"

"Clinton, Clinton!" cried Sean and Rachel in chorus.

"I heard the start of Rachel's answer first," Jackson decided. "Back to all, even! Next, one of our past presidents, while living in Indonesia, had a pet ape called Tata."

"Obama!" Rachel declared triumphantly.

"Rachel's now in the lead." Jackson gave her a grin. "But before we move on, I'd like to make a few comments about something I often see viewed as a conflict. How can we respect the founding fathers and still abhor the fact that they owned slaves? Well, first, the founding fathers were great men, but I don't like the fact that they owned slaves. They acknowledged that slavery violated the core American ideal of liberty. They believed—and most historians agree—that they could never have succeeded in unifying all the states had they insisted on the elimination of slavery. It was a sad situation, but they still managed to create a government that has been more successful than any other government on the planet. This government has flaws, and one is that it took way too long to free the slaves. In fact, they shouldn't have had slaves in the first place. Some of the founding fathers didn't: Hamilton, John Adams, Thomas Paine, and others. Those who had slaves, like Washington, Jefferson, and Madison, knew it was wrong, but they were farmers— and all farmers owned slaves. Anyone who tried to eliminate slavery would not have survived as a farmer. Their priority was to create a free nation. If they had tackled the slavery problem, they would not have managed to agree on the Declaration of Independence. Their biggest error, though, was their failure to make a plan to free the slaves. They assumed it would be solved eventually. Lincoln made the first big step with the Emancipation Proclamation, but even then, the freed slaves weren't paid; they just worked for room and board. It took Lincoln a long time to free the slaves. Then the southern states continued to fight through segregation. However, since 1860, segregation has gradually been eliminated, although we still deal with some inequality. Lincoln knew slavery was wrong; he wanted to solve the problem without breaking up the union. He seriously considered a plan to ship all slaves to Africa, and he was concerned that they could not survive freedom. Eventually, he realized that emancipation had to be enacted forcefully. History reveals, though, that Lincoln's primary objective in the Civil War was to save the union."

"Wow." Sean looked impressed. "You sure know a lot about the history of the country, Jackson."

"I do," Jackson said. "I've read at least one book on every president. I know them all—at least their names and the years they served."

"So," he continued, "who was president in 1841?"

"John Tyler. He succeeded William Harrison when Harrison died shortly after his election."

"You're right, but I didn't call that a trivia question. Rachel is still one up."

"Who was your favorite president, Jackson?"

"Barack Obama. He wasn't the best, but he did okay. I'm proud of him. He's a good family man, and he did the best he could in difficult times."

"So, who was the best?" questioned Rachel.

"I want to say Lincoln, but the answer is Washington. He was the one person the founding fathers looked to for stability and leadership when the going got tough. Without him, we would never have had an America at all. Okay, enough from me," Jackson said. "Although many of the founding fathers acknowledged that slavery violated the core American ideal of liberty, their simultaneous commitment to private property rights, the principles of limited government, and intersectional harmony prevented them from making a bold move against slavery. The considerable investments of the southern founders in slave-based staple agriculture, combined with their deep-seated racial prejudice, posed additional obstacles to emancipation."

THE GHOST IN THE ROOM

"I think this is a good time to talk about the ghost in the room: the national debt," Jackson said. "The administration, the legislators, and the media all just seem to ignore it. Trump and the Republicans implemented big tax cuts and still increased spending. The Trump administration will be adding five trillion in debt in 2019. If he wanted to cut the budget, what would he cut? He's not going to cut the military budget, and any cut in spending would cost him the election for sure. The national debt just keeps climbing, and if the public and government leaders continue to ignore it, it's just going to keep growing. Sure, they say the debt is dangerously high, but that's just rhetoric. What politician is going advocate eliminating a program that benefits themselves or their constituents?

"President Obama added eight and a half trillion to our debt in eight years, more than all past presidents combined. But not to worry, Democrats—Trump is gonna top that. He's already racked up five trillion, and he has a lot of time to go, especially if he is reelected. Everyone seems to ignore the problem; the media and the public ignore it, so presidents and legislators do too. Why not? Cutting the budget slows the economy and reduces job growth. That's where the people feel it. If a president were to cut spending, the economy would slow down, which would decrease his popularity. American military spending is around six hundred billion, more than any other country in the world. In fact, it's more than the other top ten national military budgets combined, and that includes Russia and China.

"The government's 2019 budget is about five trillion. I don't recall the exact numbers, but most of the budget goes to pay for mandated benefits such as Social Security, Medicare, and Medicaid. Discretionary spending is about 40 percent of the total, and the military takes about 50 percent of that. Interest is about 25–30 percent of discretionary spending.

"The United States spends roughly twelve billion per day, including more than seven hundred million in daily interest. That's more than four trillion per year, for a total that will approach twenty-four trillion by 2020. Few people can even comprehend those numbers.

"Presidential Candidate Elizabeth Warren wants to add a new federal consumer protection agency at an annual cost of more than six hundred million. The agency would be similar to the Consumer Financial Protection Bureau, established in the Obama era. That bureau spent more than one hundred and forty million on a building to house sixteen hundred employees as a result of tripling their original budget. By the way, most of their work is secret. In *Deep State*, Jason Chaffetz explained that our government generates revenue by collecting on four and a half trillion in bonds that it owns. They simply buy bonds by creating new dollars.

"So how do we stop the swelling debt? Is the solution raising income taxes on high-income earners? No. According to Republicans, that will just reduce business expansion and job growth. How about reducing spending on government programs? No. The Democrats argue that cutting this spending will hurt the poor. So, what's the answer? Well, how about cutting waste? Here are a few examples of waste I've read about: What about seventy billion in improper payments in one year, ninety billion in corporate welfare, twenty-five billion in maintaining unused federal properties? What about Congress identifying more than one hundred billion in spending cuts and not doing anything about it. There are many more examples, some absurd, like thirteen billion in aid for Iraq that was wasted or stolen—and eight billion that can't be accounted for at all. And how about two hundred thousand for a tattoo-removal program in California? Some of these make good campaign fodder for politicians, but I hear very little being done about it. Anyway, you get the picture. Let's move on."

"We haven't talked much about education," Rachel said. "America is falling behind. We are still among the top ten most educated nations. If I recall correctly, Israel, Korea, and the UK are the world's leaders in education."

"I think Norway, Finland, and Australia are also in the top ten," Jackson replied.

Rachel continued, "I believe every child should have the opportunity to obtain a high-quality education. That's essential if we hope to maintain world leadership. A Democrat, President Roosevelt, signed the GI Bill of Rights, which guaranteed that the government would pay for education for all veterans. The Truman Commission Report proposed federal subsidies for higher education, laying the groundwork for the community college system. President Johnson signed the Elementary and Secondary Education Act to provide federal funds to schools in low-income areas. Obamacare eliminated Sallie Mae, making student loans more affordable.

"These were all important efforts toward improving education in this country, and all of these focused on people with the lowest income levels. That helps ensure that everyone at least has the basic skills they need to succeed in the labor force. And Democrats believe that every child should have access to high-quality education. That's the pathway to economic growth for individuals and the country. The School of Education at Washington University identified several key points for improving education: acknowledge and address overcrowding, make funding schools a priority, address the school-to-prison pipeline, raise standards for teachers, and put classroom-running and curriculum-building decisions in the hands of the community. These initiatives would promote equity in education and focus resources on lower-income people."

Jackson nodded. "Those recommendations are good, but they're very broad. I still think schools—from elementary school through college—and businesses should focus on teaching children to tell the truth. That may sound very basic, but distorting facts and outright lying seem to become habits, and that starts at a young age. We need to teach young kids that they will benefit from telling the truth and help them make it a habit to do so. Wouldn't it be great if we could count on politicians and businesses telling the truth?"

Sean said, "Well, Republicans have tried to improve education in a variety of ways too. They believe in restructuring higher education so students are better equipped for their desired fields and spend less time working minimum-wage jobs that are irrelevant to their education. They also believe in limiting the federal government's involvement in education. This includes eliminating federal student loans in favor of private loans. Republicans also support school choice and homeschool programs. Overall, Republicans believe strongly in a merit-based educational system that provides students with the environments they want and need to succeed in higher education.

"Republicans also support increasing benefits to students who take more difficult courses. This would be done through partnerships with colleges and universities in an effort to improve science and math programs and to attract math, science, and engineering students to lower-income schools. Oh, and Republicans support abstinence in sex education, believing this is the only sure way of preventing unwanted pregnancies and sexually transmitted diseases. They believe all family planning educational programs should be replaced with abstinence programs.

"First, school advocates say schools and teachers should not be penalized for students' test scores because there are so many more measures of educational success; the same people say that school choice should be stopped at all costs because a handful of studies show slight declines in students' test scores.

"The American Federation of Teachers and the National Education Association are the two biggest lobbyists against school choice. They are trying to turn teachers, parents, and policymakers against the idea of educational choice programs."

Rachel said, "Private school vouchers offer a false choice, and test results show drops in performance when students switch schools."

Sean shook his head, undeterred. "School choice opponents are picking out a few instances showing some children test poorly in their first years using school vouchers. You need to account for the adjustment period any child goes through when they switch school cultures and curriculum. Those same students' scores improve in the second year. Reliable studies find that students who choose vouchers rather than staying in public schools actually perform better in the long run."

Rachel frowned. "What studies? I've read the opposite."

Jackson said, "Well, obviously, performances of students who switch schools will vary depending on the individual school. Not all public schools are the same, and neither are all private schools. I think the important issue is equal educational opportunities."

"Exactly," said Sean. "I like our new Florida governor's plan. Saying it would clear out the fourteen thousand students on the waiting list for the Florida Tax Credit Scholarship, Governor Ron DeSantis called on the Florida legislature to create an Equal

Opportunity Scholarship for students wishing to attend private and charter schools. It could cost up to a hundred million, but it would do a lot of good. Here's what the governor said when he announced his plan at the Calvary City Christian Academy, an Orlando private school that serves low-income, predominantly Hispanic and African-American communities: 'I'm asking the legislature, send a bill to my desk that provides this equal opportunity for those folks who have not had the ability to access a good scholarship. Let's do this. Let's build on the success we've had with the tax-credit scholarship. Let's continue to make Florida an innovation center for education.'"

Jackson nodded. "I feel that all three of us agree on the need for equal opportunity for Americans of all races and genders and from all neighborhoods. That equality has to start with education. What we can't count on or expect to attain is equal levels of success. Different folks have different genes and different abilities. Our own kids have different aptitudes and abilities. In business, you have CEOs, department heads, and different levels of responsibility and leadership on down to the janitor. That should be—and, I believe, for the most part, is—determined by ability and performance. I think it's obvious that a capable child educated in a poor neighborhood school is less likely to become a CEO than an equally capable child who attends a well-funded private school. So, if school choice with vouchers and scholarships lets the poor child attend a better school and become a CEO instead of a janitor, that's a good thing."

Rachel shook her head. "How about just improving the performance of all schools?"

"That would be great," Sean replied, "but it's a little idealistic."

"Oh," Jackson said, "and while we're talking about kids, what do you think of Nancy Pelosi's proposal to reduce the voting age to sixteen?"

"Let me ask you this," Sean answered. "Do you think the people voting should have some basic knowledge of who they're voting for? Should they know something about the issues that are determined by elected officials?"

"Well," Rachel said, "sixteen-year-olds today are more educated and mature than sixteen-year-olds forty or fifty years ago."

"I don't think so," Sean retorted. "Do you really believe that?"

"Yes," Rachel exclaimed. "Education is more advanced, and they have more access to what's going on in the world."

Jackson interjected, "The voting age was changed from twenty-one to eighteen in 1971, and the reasoning for it was that a person who was old enough to serve in the military was old enough to vote. Should serving in the military be the standard?"

"Yes," Sean answered. "Nancy Pelosi is only proposing letting sixteen-year-olds vote to increase the votes for Democrats. I think it's too young. The correlation between serving in the military and being able to vote is the proper rationale."

"I agree," Jackson replied. "However, the decision will be made on a state-by-state basis. In some states, seventeen-year-olds can vote. Many religious issues are left to the states too. Should we have prayer in schools? And how should the Bible be interpreted?"

"That's fine if you think the Bible should be interpreted literally," Sean rejoined. "But evolution contradicts the Genesis story, which says that God created all organisms in their present forms. But you can believe in God without believing that the Bible is literally true."

"I say yes to letting sixteen-year-olds vote and no to school prayer," Rachel declared.

"I would expect you to hold those liberal positions," Sean quipped. "Let's do some more trivia. We need to have a winner."

Jackson sighed. "I'm running out of trivia questions. Oh, here's one. Which president lost the popular vote by 250,000 but won the electoral college by a single vote?"

"Rutherford Hayes!" called Sean proudly.

"All even again," Jackson announced. "Okay, I like this one. He was ambidextrous and could write in Greek with one hand and in Latin with the other—at the same time!"

"Garfield," Rachel said quickly.

"Good one!" Jackson smiled. "Rachel is one up now. Two up will make you the winner, okay?"

"Not going to let that happen," Sean snapped.

"Let's see. The only bachelor to be president was rumored to have had an affair with the senator from Alabama, Rufus King. The two lived together for more than ten years—even though they were rich enough to have their own homes."

"James Buchanan, 1856," Sean announced quickly.

"All even again. You guys are good."

"Okay. It's a tie. I'll do one more for the tiebreaker when we wrap it up in a few minutes. Let's finish up with technology."

"Good point. We haven't talked about technology," Rachel said. "I mean, conservatives attack Democrats for slowing down medical research with government regulations while seeking more FDA restrictions on some kinds of medical research, like stem cell treatments."

"Okay," Jackson countered, "but what about the fact that liberals oppose commercial exploitation of the environment but promote and support biotechnical interventions in human life such as embryonic stem cell research? But before we attack that subject, I want to tell a story."

A guy asks his wife to help him set up a website. She starts to set it up and then tells her husband he needs to choose a password. He pauses and then responds, "'Oh, just use 'my penis.'"

The wife types it in, and then she laughs so hard she falls out of her chair. "It says it's not long enough," she tells him.

CHAPTER 28

TECHNOLOGY

"I love studying innovative technology and its ramifications," Jackson continued. "I think liberals and conservatives can both offer limited guidance for understanding the politics of technology today—both where it stands and where it is heading. Conservatives attack the FDA for slowing down medical research. They seek new limitations on biotechnologies that could alter human life. Liberals, meanwhile, get upset about our exploitation of the environment—but they celebrate biotechnical interventions in human life, even those that involve manipulations of what is natural and sacred. Conservatives express doubt about the future of embryonic stem cell research, but they confidently support big technological projects like missile defense. Liberals claim a special commitment to protecting vulnerable human subjects from research, but they champion experimental techniques for making babies that put the most voiceless subjects of all at risk: unborn babies. On an issue like buying and selling human organs to increase supply, the right and the left both take the middle road: conservative devotion to the market battles with conservative protection of life. With liberals, it's devotion to improving medicine that battles with liberal concerns about the body.

"Both liberals and conservatives sometimes deplore modern life as inauthentic, profane, and harmful. But when it comes to protecting us against the things they fear most—destroying human life for research or exploiting the environment for its resources—most liberals and conservatives turn to more ethical technologies for solutions, whether it is hydrogen cars or adult stem cells.

"Think about what we did before computers and cell phones. Look at how modern medicine can replace body parts. Look at the speed of travel and our advanced military weapons systems. Technology is such a big topic; we just don't have time to get into it.

Some people are concerned that too much technology will eliminate too many jobs too."

Rachel interjected, "My concern is that the rich will keep getting richer, and the poor will keep getting poorer."

"I don't think technology causes that," Sean argued. "I think technology provides more jobs and a better lifestyle for all."

"Well, that's very optimistic of you," Rachel retorted.

"Let's move on to the economy," Jackson said. "One thing about the political debate about the economy is that it's difficult, as we move from one presidency to the next, to ascertain who should take credit for economic changes since economic policy usually has a delayed impact."

"Good idea," Sean agreed. "Bill Clinton claimed he inherited a problem economy from Bush, the elder. Bush the younger claimed he inherited a bubble that was beginning to leak from Clinton. But Obama takes the cake—he claims he inherited Bush's recession, and he wants credit for the current economic boom.

"Actually, this boom was created by Trump's narcissistic and reckless behavior. It's hard to tell how long it will last and what the consequences will be. It may work and may not. If it doesn't work out, I can predict that Obama will not take credit for the bust."

"Yes, but Democrats promote economic policies that benefit low- and middle-income families," Rachel argued. "They believe that supporting policies that promote income equality is the best way to create economic growth. It works because low-income families spend their extra money on food, medicine, and shelter, and that increases demand in the economy more than policies that only benefit businesses.

"For Democrats, the American dream is the right to education, a good job, decent housing, and health care. Franklin Roosevelt introduced the Economic Bill of Rights in his 1944 State of the Union address. And Truman implemented the Fair Deal and presented legislation to support an expanded vision of the American dream. And then, in 2010, the Democrats expanded that dream to include health care with the Affordable Care Act."

"Well," Jackson said, "for as long as I can recall, Republicans have been encouraging budget cuts and seeking to balance the budget. That sounds good to conservatives, but it's easier said than done. They campaign on the need to balance the budget only to find that cuts aren't that easy to make. Government programs are obviously popular with low-income Americans. Democrats, on the other hand, usually try to avoid cuts that will hurt the unemployed or reduce workers' incomes. In economic debates, Republicans are often accused of targeting children, the elderly, and projects that will benefit the people. Meanwhile, Democrats are accused of an addiction to spending, an inability to cut the budget, and a lack of concern for the growing deficit."

"Well, the Republican Party has some very strong views on economics," Sean said. "They believe that every American deserves the right to own, invest, build, and prosper. They accept that reasonable business regulations are important, but they also oppose too many regulations, especially those that increase the cost of operating a business. They want to promote consumers' and businesses' confidence in the economy. And Republicans oppose any policies that are seen as interventionist or that give the federal government control of industry.

"That's because Republicans feel that to many policies and regulations allow the government to pick the winners and losers of the marketplace rather than letting economics and business practices speak for themselves.

"Also, Republicans believe that inflation is a big problem and has the same impact as taxes on the American people. Higher prices diminish purchasing power both at home and abroad. People who have saved money are punished by inflation and increasing prices. Inflation is a major problem for seniors and others who live on fixed incomes.

"For as long as I can remember, Republicans have been proposing budget cuts—and Democrats have been proposing spending packages. For example, Americans have huge student loan debts, and Democrats are proposing free college education. Right now, more than forty million Americans collectively hold around one and a half trillion dollars in student debt, and Congress is right there with them. Even though the current Congress is one of the richest of all time, one in ten members holds student debt, either personally or for a family member.

"I have a friend whose hobby is tracking the behavior of congressmen and women. Out of the 530 current voting members of Congress (that's 431 in the House of Representatives and 99

Senators, minus vacancies), the last report I read showed that ... hold on a second ... I still have those numbers." Sean looked through his notes. "Yes, fifty-three were listed as owing a total of $1.8 million in student loans in their financial disclosures. Of these student debt holders, twenty-eight had a positive net worth, and twenty-five had a negative net worth. As a specific example, California Representative Roy Khanna listed fifty thousand dollars in student loans, but he has a net worth of more than twenty-five million thanks to timely investments and his wife's significant family wealth. How many people who are not politicians have that kind of opportunity?"

"But look at this," Rachel said, sifting through her own notes. "Florida Congressman Darren Soto is one of the twenty-five representatives who, according to the Roll Call Wealth of Congress report, has a negative net worth." She skimmed the report. "He still owes seventy-five thousand and says he understands the responsibility of repayment. He also says he received a valuable education and believes having the ability to attend a top law school was an essential part of his success. And he maintains that, despite his outstanding loan balance, he has a positive net worth." She shrugged. "I'm sure, given where he is, he will find a way. The problem is that most people don't have the kind of opportunities he does. And look what happened when NYU announced that their med school would be free from now on. Applicants have been knocking down the doors."

"Yeah," Sean said. "They can offer free tuition thanks to the retired chairman of Merck, Roy Vagelos, who made a $250 million donation—and also thanks to other donations from successful businessmen."

"That's nice of Mr. Vagelos," Rachel conceded, "but covering one med school is a drop in the bucket. We need that kind of opportunity at all schools across the nation."

"I agree with you there." Jackson nodded. "We need to try to find more ways for students to attend college without going head over heels in debt. I don't see any one solution. What about encouraging students to attend junior colleges? Most of them provide an excellent education, just as good as the first two years at a four-year school, but for much less money. I also think we should also have more programs where work experience is a part of education. Lots of people have told me that work experience was an important part of their education.

"We all agree that we need to improve education and make it more affordable. We disagree about how much we can afford to give away. Congress needs to work across the aisle with some compromise legislation. Let's move along because we are running out of time, and I really want to discuss my favorite issue with you. It's not a new idea, and it's never been received with much enthusiasm. I am talking about a safe, secure, private national ID system. Those who quickly oppose the concept don't seem to think it through and recognize the many benefits of such a system. Some people worry about privacy issues. I understand that concern, but with today's technology, abuses can definitely be prevented.

"We have the technology to create a secure system that could save the government and private companies huge sums of money and lower the crime rate—I mean an effective system that wouldn't invade citizens' privacy—but it could prevent fraud and protect citizens' personal information. Of course, preventing any agency, government, or private source from accessing personal information would be a prerequisite.

"In addition, the system I envision would be introduced as voluntary for American citizens without a criminal record. Noncitizens and people who have committed felonies would be required to carry a national ID. We could also require noncitizens and those with criminal records to carry an accompanying location card so they could be located at all times. The national ID card would be separate from any other ID like a driver's license or Social Security card. It would just be used to verify your identity.

"This would reduce airport security costs as well as numerous other costs where identity verification is essential. Fake ID systems would become extinct. Think of the savings in fraud and identity crimes! Identity theft and fraud cost consumers more than fifteen billion dollars annually, and more than fifteen million consumers are victims of identity theft every year. That's absurd. We're better than that.

"The ACLU has called a national ID a misplaced, superficial quick fix that threatens our civil liberties. I understand their concerns and the desire to protect privacy, but they have not considered what the system could do for individuals and for this country as a whole. Again, the entire system would be voluntary and free. It would help control illegal immigration and illegals in the workforce.

Noncitizens would be so designated on their National ID, reducing illegal employment and illegal immigration. Employers would be required to verify identification and only hire those who are eligible for work."

"That seems logical," Rachel said. "But you couldn't prevent state governments from pushing the limitations you refer to. I can imagine the next step would be requiring a national ID to vote."

"I don't think that would be an issue," Jackson replied, "because, as I said, the legislation would limit the use to ID verification only. And, as I also said, it would be voluntary for citizens. When the benefits became apparent, more people would want and take pride in having the national ID card. What are your thoughts, Sean?"

"I'm listening, but I'm still apprehensive about the idea. I think it would give the government too much power. I am against government lists of those who own or have transferred a firearm for the same reason I oppose any pathway to a national ID. I don't think the government should have the awesome power of monitoring the legal activities of American citizens. That's not a proper role of the federal government—or any level of government, actually."

"Wow, we actually agree on something, Sean!" Rachel exclaimed. "I'm opposed to it too. Forcing Americans to carry around an identification card to affirmatively prove citizenship offends our basic concept of freedom. I'm also opposed to immigration reform using the photo tool in the Interior Enforcement and Employment Verification System."

"I think you're both missing the point of the concept," Jackson protested. "As I said, it could only be used to verify your identity and not to track what you've done or where you've been. I don't see the problem in that. We have so much illegal activity going on in this country. We need to stop the shenanigans with fake IDs. And a national ID could only be implemented if we also establish the technology to prevent false duplication and use by any other person. If Joe Johnson has a national ID that only he could possess—because of this technology—it can only be used to verify that he is Joe Johnson. He would still have to have his other required ID cards. The national card would only verify his identity. And it would be voluntary for citizens; only noncitizens and felons would be required to have one. I think once the national ID was in use, most people would want a card because it would save time at airport security and help prevent crime."

"Hmm," Sean said. "I would consider it if I understood and was confident about the technology."

"I see it as worthy of evaluation," Rachel said.

"Okay," Jackson concluded. "We've run out of time, and I want to end on a positive note. I have your e-mails. I will let you know how I do with my paper. Oh, wait, we do have a few more minutes. Rachel, tell me what you think Obama's key accomplishments are. And then, Sean, tell us Trump's accomplishments."

Rachel smiled and then laughed. "I might take too long." She shrugged. "I will try to make it brief. I know it won't take Sean very long. He's gotta have a pretty short list."

"Oh, you're cute," Sean retorted. "Let's make it legitimate accomplishments and not opinions."

"How about you each do ten?" Jackson suggested.

"Oh, I think that will be a stretch for Sean," Rachel said.

Sean smiled at Rachel. "Okay, tell us what you've got."

"Well," she began, "number one, he passed health care reform, aka Obamacare. If you question that, just look at the polls. The majority of Americans would like to see it retained—with some modifications. Obama also signed the American Recovery and Reinvestment Act in 2009 to spur economic growth, and that was in the middle of the most severe downturn since the Great Depression, which he inherited from Bush, by the way."

Sean interrupted, "It didn't look much like a recovery to me."

"Shush." Rachel gave Sean a friendly poke. "Next, in 2014, he took steps to open diplomatic and commercial ties with Cuba, ending the failed Cold War policy of isolation."

Sean opened his mouth to respond, but Jackson said, "Let's allow Rachel to finish. If we debate every issue, we'll be here all night."

Sean smiled and mimicked sealing his lips.

Rachel continued, "He signed the Dodd-Frank Wall Street Reform and Consumer Protection Act. I think it was in 2009 or 2010. That was after financial practices caused the big 2007–09 recession. He led six nations to reach an agreement with Iran that requires the country to end its nuclear weapons program. Oh, and yeah, he was awarded the Nobel Peace Prize! He instructed all federal agencies to promote openness and transparency as much as possible.

"He secured the country's commitment to a global agreement on climate change. He got Osama Bin Laden. In 2009, injected more than sixty billion into GM and Chrysler, which were struggling, in return for equity stakes and agreements to massive restructuring to save the auto industry."

"I think that's ten."

"I got many more," Rachel said with a grin.

"Okay." Sean rubbed his hands eagerly. "I will give you ten of Trump's accomplishments in his first couple of years, and mine will be real accomplishments."

"I can't wait to hear them," Rachel said with a smile.

"Okay, how about a major tax cut, creating a robust economy, creating more than 4 percent GDP growth, and jobs, jobs, jobs! That's what's important to Americans."

"I could comment on that, but I don't want to interrupt your fantasies," Rachel quipped.

"That's sweet of you." Sean held out his hand, and Rachel accommodated with a shake. They both grinned.

Sean said, "He wiped out wasteful regulations to improve business expansion. He ended the Iran nuclear deal, which would have given Iran an eventual path to nuclear weapons. He enacted beneficial criminal justice reform legislation on opioids and sex trafficking. He moved the American embassy to Jerusalem after the past four presidents promised to do so but failed to follow through. He was the first American president to meet with North Korean leadership, ending nuclear weapon testing in that country. He forced our NATO partners to increase their contributions to military defense. He dispatched American troops to reduce the threat of ISIS. African American, Hispanic, and Asian American unemployment rates reached all-time highs. How am I doing?"

"Great imagination." Rachel smiled and patted Sean on the back.

"I think you've got ten," Jackson offered.

"Oh, I'm just getting started," Sean replied.

"You sound like Trump, and it would be nice if those were all true." Rachel shrugged.

"I find it interesting how you two see some issues in totally opposite ways," Jackson mused. "I think both Obama and Trump accomplished some good things. They just have totally different approaches and different personalities. It's difficult for me to evaluate because I like the Obama family as role models for America, and I am really turned off by the way Trump talks. He has moved boldly and gotten some unique things done, but I don't think Americans want to point to him as their president and hold him up as an example of how to talk. He's always calling people names like Pencil Neck, Crazy Joe Biden, Crooked Hillary, Lying Ted, and so on.

"But what's been really great about this is how the two of you can argue such widely differing views without getting angry. We certainly need more of that in this country, especially in Congress. Okay, let's go back to our trivia game and do the tiebreaker. Whoever gets this next one is the winner, and I will buy you a drink the next time you come to Filibusters."

"So, here's the question. Which president had the youngest First Lady?"

"I got it," Sean exclaimed. "That was the one who married his daughter!"

"No, not his daughter," Rachel replied, "his friend's daughter."

"Yeah," Sean agreed. "But he was the guardian after his friend died."

"I know, I know." Rachel shook her head. "It was … shit, I can't think of his name! He served two nonconsecutive terms."

"I know!" Sean cried triumphantly. "It was Grover Cleveland! His wife was twenty-one when they got married in the White House."

"That's right!" Jackson smiled. "Congratulations, Sean. You're the winner."

"But I helped him with the answer," Rachel protested.

"Let's call it a draw," Sean suggested. He stood up and gave Rachel a big hug.

"Amazing!" Jackson smiled. "You guys have been fantastic—in so many ways—but I need to get this bar ready to open. I really appreciate all the time you've spent with me. I look forward to finishing my paper and submitting it, and I hope you both will come back to see me."

Sean gave Jackson a hug too. "It's been fun," he said. "I think you will get an A-plus!"

Rachel embraced Jackson as well. "I'll be back," she promised.

The Uber driver arrived, Sean helped Rachel put on her coat, and the two left Filibusters together.

CHAPTER 29

SEAN AND BETH

Wednesday was a typical day for Sean. He was up at six and out the door of his Royal Palm home at six thirty. He gazed at the beautiful Jack Nicklaus golf course, which he never tired of, and headed to a breakfast meeting with Scott, his director of operations, followed by another meeting with Mike, a district manager, and a lunch meeting with Ray, another district manager. The afternoon was spent making surprise inspections at several of his restaurants. He verified meal portions, checked food temperatures, examined expiration dates, inspected servers, and had several discussions with servers. At six thirty, he headed home to eat dinner with his kids and then went to his home office to do some paperwork. At eight thirty, he emerged to put the kids to bed, and then he joined Beth in the living room. "Shall we talk?" he asked gently.

"Yes, Sean," she said. "It's time. Do you remember Dr. Blackburn's first name?"

"Jane," Sean responded.

"You remembered!" Beth looked surprised. "She said we should give it a few days to think about her advice and then talk about it in a place where we wouldn't be interrupted. We've both had a few days—three days—without any meaningful conversation." Her phone rang.

Sean looked at her. "Let's ignore the phones."

"I'll turn it off," she said. "So, I think the four terms she wanted us to deal with were criticism, contempt, defensiveness, and ... what was the fourth? Don't tell me. I know: stonewalling."

"You remembered them all except one!" Sean congratulated her. "Give me five."

Beth grinned and slapped his palm. "Yeah, she said we should do something to break the ice before we start. That was good." She smiled again. "And she also said we have to commit to not getting angry."

"I remember," Sean said. "Okay, complaints. I think she said that complaints are about specific actions and behaviors that you don't like in your partner. Criticism, on the other hand, is an attack on the person themselves. I think we're both guilty of that."

"Agreed," Beth said. "I'll take contempt. It goes beyond criticism. It's an intentional effort to wound and demean someone. It's mean. It causes a person to become defensive, deny what they did, or say something like 'It's not me—it's you.' When you accuse me of doing something inappropriate, like implying I could be cheating when I'm meeting a coworker for lunch, I feel like coming back and questioning your relationship with this Rachel woman you told me about. Instead, I should explain my behavior. By countering with a question, I'm just increasing the conflict. That's like saying you're the problem, not me."

Sean nodded thoughtfully. "So, I tend to stonewall. After a few interactions of contempt and criticism, one of us might just shut down, withdraw, stop listening, and stop engaging. We usually have our arguments at this time of night, and then one of us just says, 'I'm going to bed.' We go to our separate rooms, and the next day, we give each other the silent treatment. That only makes things worse."

Beth continued, "The last one was contempt, which involves presenting criticism in a contemptuous way. That automatically causes the other person to become defensive—denying, making excuses. And that only revs things up. I want to add that we should only discuss our disagreements when we won't be interrupted and can talk the issue through."

Sean added, "She talked about how marriages are increasingly difficult today with both of us working, traveling, and being in different environments. I'm in a business environment; you're more in a socialist environment—oops, I mean a *progressive* environment. We have to learn to respect those differences."

"I'm glad you brought that up," Beth replied. "I want to commit to understanding your work environment better. It's not good that I'm involved in critiquing restaurants since restaurants are where you strive to succeed and provide for us. We're both in the restaurant business. I need to talk to you more about what my association friends are talking about, and you need to explain to me why you need to have these meetings at a bar with this Rachel and a bartender.

"The institution of marriage arguably carries a heavier weight of pressures and expectations today than it has at any time before. Spouses don't just partner up for purely economic and procreative purposes. They expect to be romantic lovers, best friends, co-parents, and sometimes even business partners.

"Balancing all of those roles might seem like a burden, and it certainly can be. Husbands and wives may both be working—and not just one job, but several. There are kids to raise and schedules to juggle. Family members can end up feeling like ships passing in the night.

"But modern marriage is also an incredible opportunity—one that, if managed right, can be an unending source of joy and satisfaction. It's you and your spouse against the world, building your own world. If you want to plan and tackle life's greatest adventures side by side, you have to stay in sync and work effectively as a team."

"It's … it's time to go to bed," Sean said with a smile, offering his hand to Beth. They walked together to their bedroom, both realizing their marriage had just transitioned into a new phase.

CHAPTER 30

RACHEL AND JAKE

Rachel sat on the living room couch at her home in Coral Springs. She was alone; Jamie's gun lay on the couch by her side. The twins were at a friend's home, which Rachel had arranged to accommodate her plans. Nervously, she took several deep breaths, rehearsing what she would say when Jake got home. Tense anticipation sent a chill through her body. She wondered if she should tell him how she had found out about Sandy Sowden? It really didn't matter now. She heard the garage door open and then close, and she walked to the kitchen.

After several anxious seconds, the door opened. Jake entered and looked up to see Rachel pointing the gun straight at his face. "You son of a bitch. I know what you've been doing. You're sleeping with Sandy Snowden every night I'm out of town. The gun is loaded this time."

"Stop it, Rachel." His tone was conciliatory. "This isn't you."

"Tell me how many times," she demanded.

"Stop, Rachel, stop!" He flinched reflexively.

Rachel pulled the trigger. There was a flash and a loud shock wave. The smell of chemical residue permeated the air.

Jake's hands flew to his chest, and he dropped to his knees.

Rachel, now frightened, looked at the gun. "No, no!" she protested. "It was a blank cartridge!"

Jake realized that only the shocking sound of the exploding empty cartridge had caused him to drop to his knees in surprise. "You bitch!"

Rachel, relieved now that she saw Jake was unhurt, said, "Get out of my house!"

He began walking toward her. "*Your* house? Like hell."

"I've already called the police. I called when you pulled in the driveway. They were expecting my call and are on their way. I've already filed for divorce, and I have a restraining order. Your belongings are in those suitcases." She gestured at his suitcases, neatly stacked in the corner of the kitchen. "Get out of my house. Here's your gun. You'd better get out of here now."

Jake, recognizing defeat, stuck the gun in his belt, picked up the suitcases, and strode out the door. She knew he wanted no part of the police.

Rachel pulled out her cell phone and dialed the number from memory. "Steven, I need you. Now. Come to my house immediately." Rachel was ready to begin a new life.

PART III

From: Jackson Lewis
To: Rachel Patterson and Sean McCarthy

I look forward to seeing you both the next time you're in DC. Here's a copy of my paper for review and comments, which I submitted to Lake Geneva University online. I hope you will agree with my conclusions. I received an A and was recognized for submitting the best report for the semester.

Getting Logical
Jackson Lewis

The Republicans do it; the Democrats do it. As soon as a president is elected, the opposition party attacks, investigates, and sometimes even attempts impeachment. The result is legislative gridlock. Why can't we fight like hell during the campaign but then accept the election results? Why do we want the winner to fail? Presidential failure costs all Americans. We can argue our positions on the issues, but why not be willing to seek compromise? Let's get logical!

The best example of selfish political posturing is our government's inept management of our decaying infrastructure. Certainly, the common-sense justifications for upgrading our infrastructure are no-brainers. Doing so enhances our economy and creates jobs, and it's a fundamental obligation of our government. Yet Obama's efforts were thwarted by a Republican-majority Congress, and Trump's promised infrastructure plans were stymied by Nancy Pelosi and the Democrats. Why? It's because a president who upgrades infrastructure, like Eisenhower, gets a political boost. Allowing that to happen is a no-no in today's political climate.

Our American government and political climate have seen some drastic changes in the past twelve years. Think about it. Before 2008, who could have imagined that a young African-American with the name Barack Hussein Obama II would be elected president and then followed eight years later by a previously bankrupted but successful, wealthy businessman with a locker-room mouth, who would be threatened by impeachment despite a booming economy and who would then face more than twenty opponents to his reelection, including a thirty-eight-year old, gay, small-town mayor? Wow!

Angry rhetoric, distortions of the facts, and the desire to win at all costs are par for the course in American politics today. However, deep concern prevails among citizens and historians. Can our 230-year-old nation survive these mean-spirited clashes year after year—or will we have to call for a Constitutional convention to rewrite a constitution that has survived for more than 230 years?

I have hosted and engaged in a deep analysis of this question, not with traditional experts, but with the two very intelligent and highly educated mainstream American individuals. Rachel is a progressive, and Sean is a conservative. I am mostly self-educated, am an avid reader, and have the privilege of speaking with many of our American legislators and various government staff members on a daily basis. For more than forty years, I have been the bar manager of Washington DC's most popular pub, Filibusters, and this has given me the opportunity to discuss key government issues directly with members of what has been called the government swamp.

Somewhat to my disappointment, these two individuals and I have been unable to arrive at compromises on many of the issues that we debated, but we have been able to express our differences in civil, candid discussion and in a professional manner. In this paper, I will summarize our discussions and also offer some personal opinions about how we could use logic to develop compromises.

The fundamental thought processes and histories of conservative versus what has recently been referred to as progressive or liberal thinking are the foundation of most disagreements about the basic issues that concern Americans. Both views are promoted with the sincere belief that they are on the right side of history. As I see it, striking the proper balance between these two visions—within the framework of our existing Constitution—offers the best hope for America's future.

The election of Donald Trump in 2016 was a shock to the world and an unbelievable development to the Democrats. Their disbelief and embarrassment have been increased by Trump's egocentric, boastful behavior, and he was himself shocked by the results. His tweeting, name-calling, and use of locker-room language added poison to the Democrats' wounds. Irritated by Trump's label of "fake news," the liberal-dominated media joined the Democrats in an all-out war on Trump.

The Democrats smelled a rat and adopted a primary agenda for their House majority: finding the culprit and hopefully undoing the election through impeachment. Trump's business dealings with Russia and his attempts to make friends with Russian dictator Vladimir Putin provided sufficient reason for Democrats to appoint a special prosecutor to investigate the suspected Trump-Russia collusion in the election. Unfortunately for Democratic leaders, after $30 million and an almost three-year investigation, along with the convictions of numerous persons associated with Trump on various grounds, Prosecutor Robert Mueller was unable to find Trump guilty of collusion or any other crime. As could be expected, the Democrats were again shocked and then proposed the impeachment of Prosecutor William Barr. At the same time, the Republicans began to investigate accusations that the Democratic Obama administration had spied on Trump. And the beat goes on.

However, none of these investigations, many of which are still ongoing, have ever solved anything. In fact, the investigations are really just mean-spirited political posturing on both sides. In this report, I will summarize my thoughts—from a moderate, logical, unbiased point of view—regarding the progressive and conservative debates in the American political landscape. So here it is: "Getting Logical."

The foundation of any nation is the economy. The saying "It's the economy, stupid" was coined by Clinton campaign strategist James Carville during Clinton's successful 1992 campaign against sitting President George H. W. Bush. The economy has almost always been the key factor in presidential elections. If the economy is strong, the incumbent usually wins. The opposition party can always find reasons to criticize, but if almost anyone who wants a job can find one, home lending is available, and inflation is under control, then most people, whether secretly or openly, don't want to upset the apple cart.

Looking at the results of the past four presidential elections over the past twenty-seven years, we find good news and bad news for both parties. Bill Clinton managed to attain the best economic growth with a GDP of 3.8; the GDP was 1.8 under George Bush and 1.9 under Obama. Trump has taken it back above 3 for the first time since Clinton's tenure. Of course, however, we also need to consider the ghost in the room, something politicians don't like to talk about: the United States' multi-trillion-dollar national debt. It's not hard to boost the economy by spending money the government doesn't have. Bill Clinton had the least troublesome numbers on this measure as well: American debt increased by $4.4 trillion during his administration. Under Bush, the debt was $5.3 trillion, but it soared to $11.6 trillion under Obama.

Meanwhile, Trump, who advertised his intentions to wipe out the national debt, is on target to add $9.1 trillion, bringing total American debt to more than $30 trillion. How are we going to pay off that debt? You can only dig a hole so deep before it caves in. This brings our discussion to the topic of free education.

When my friends and I discussed the controversy over student loans and proposals for free college education, as I expected, Rachel (the progressive) favored free college education for all young people who seek it. Sean (the conservative) opposed this because of the enormous cost; such plans would push our national debt, which is already at a dangerous level, even higher. For myself, I have to ask what we are trying to achieve and what is financially feasible. We want to develop new generations of highly productive, talented young people who can achieve a comfortable lifestyle while contributing to an American economy that stands strong internationally.

To that end, I will propose guidelines for a compromise between these typical liberal and conservative positions. We can't achieve the objectives described above with a system that discourages education because of a cost structure that burdens young people with huge amounts of debt at the beginning of their careers. Nor can we afford to incur huge national debt by providing free college to anyone who seeks it. What we need is a compromise between these two extremes.

We need a clearly defined, merit-based system whereby qualified students can earn full tax credits on the income they will earn after graduation. Students who qualify for the program on the basis of merit could be identified by a congressional educational committee; the requirements for the program should include maintenance of a specified grade point average, an acceptable attendance record, and the use of a curriculum approved by the educational committee. Perhaps the program would be further limited to tuition at junior colleges and only offered to families with incomes under a specific level. For other students, loan programs could still be offered, but loan payments would be deducted directly from the students' income taxes after graduation.

The objective, as much as financially feasible, is to encourage and provide education opportunities for low- and middle-class young people who are serious about earning an advanced education. Again, I recognize that the specifics of the plan would have to be established by a congressional educational committee.

My friends and I also discussed health care, which presents some of the same issues. I agree with progressive Democrats that free health care, along with free college education and more food stamps, would be great. But how are we going to pay for it all? Where would that take the soaring national debt? One of the two dozen Democratic candidates for 2020 suggested that the government send everyone $1,000 a month. How fun is that? Many people would not even need a job. What do you think that would do to our national debt?

This question of how much we can afford to give is the root of the differences between Democrats' and Republicans' economic management. We need to take care of the unfortunate, make health care available to everyone, and provide growing income opportunities for the middle class. Ideally, the progressive approach uses government programs to achieve those objectives. Higher taxes on the wealthy seems like an obvious answer. The problem with that, however, is that the United States has a capitalist economy based on free enterprise. Opportunities for profit and the creation of wealthy families and retirement benefits are the driving forces behind economic development.

We would like to see all these benefits for the poor and middle classes. The problem is that not everyone has the talent, drive, and ambition to invent products and create enterprises. As a matter of fact, many don't have the desire to be leaders, work long hours, or take risks. Personally, I'm happy with my job. I earn a respectable living and have no desire to become wealthy.

Consequently, as I see it, we need to frame our economy so that it provides sufficient incentives for those who do have the skills to build new enterprises. A successful economy based on free enterprise will never offer everyone the same income and benefits. High performers must be rewarded if you want them to perform. The caveat is that the means of achieving—and the extent of wealth and privileges—need to be monitored for fairness.

Health care is the issue that concerns Americans most. We are a wealthy nation, but we are one of the few nations in the world that does not offer universal health care. Our health care is also the most expensive in the world. So, let's look at it logically. Our multilayered system is very inefficient. Huge insurance companies need sales personnel and administrators. Most Democrats think the government should create a universal plan, such as Medicare for all. However, more government doesn't appeal to Republicans; they believe private enterprise is more efficient.

The best solution would involve a joint effort by Democratic and Republican legislators to find a way to streamline the system under the management of the competitive free enterprise. Too much money goes to doctors' and hospitals' liability insurance. Too much waste occurs when patients abuse the system by overusing it, and too often, patients visit expensive doctors when nurses could conduct the first step to evaluate their health care needs. One example is Marathon Health, which provides health care services for large employers. They offer in-house medical facilities managed by trained nurses. However, these are only a few ideas. Much more could be achieved through a joint effort by Democrats, Republicans, and experts in the medical field.

The abuse of entrusted power for private gain, better known as corruption, is a favorite topic of the media. Corruption is difficult to define and often disputable. When you have a president like Donald Trump, whose previous career involved international investments, where do you draw the line?

But what about Joe Biden? He has tended to be soft on China, and he has visited China for various negotiations accompanied by his son, Hunter, who at the same time was seeking and then obtained a business loan from China Bank. Our government needs to develop a clear definition of unacceptable conflicts of interest.

Meanwhile, how much should we spend on national defense? Many Democrats tend to favor cutting the military budget, which they consider excessive, and express concern that the United States is promoting an arms race. However, the purpose of the American military policy has always been to protect our citizens and to maintain good, healthy relations with our neighbors. And today, in the nuclear age, every country is our neighbor. Unfortunately, not all countries are peaceful. Therefore, I have long supported maintaining our country's military as the strongest in the world while seeking worldwide elimination of nuclear weapons systems.

Year after year, decade after decade we have dueling opinions on our military involvement and financial commitments in Middle East confrontations. Do we need to maintain military presence and give financial support as a strategy to keep the battles over there or should we bring our troops home and let the Middle East them fight their own battles? Many who opposed Trump in 2016 feared he would start a major war. Yet in 2019 he faced criticism for bringing troops home. Dealing with that strategy is a no win situation.

Another topic, the abuse of drugs, tobacco, and alcohol, can be depressing to discuss. However, this abuse costs our nation more than $750 billion annually. More than 400,000 tobacco-related deaths occur each year; alcohol is connected to 88,000 and illicit drugs to 80,000. Those numbers don't even include the divided families and losses in productivity and education related to this problem that is scorching the very core of our nation. Furthermore, this is not a partisan issue; it's an issue that Congress could work together to solve in order to save dollars and lives. To start, more could be done in our education system, from elementary school through college, to help guide young people away from the ugly path of substance abuse.

Our discussion group all agreed on the need for higher teacher salaries. However, conservative Sean and progressive Rachel disagreed on the issue of merit pay. I tend to agree with Sean on this one; I believe educators should be rewarded for superior performance.

Sean is a gun owner and supports the National Rifle Association (NRA). I also own a gun, but I feel the NRA promotes gun sales too aggressively. I don't see how you can deny the logic that more guns on the streets lead to more deaths. You only need to research the countries with strict gun laws to see that most of them have fewer gun-related deaths. It's not complicated; it's simple math, and denying that fact is illogical. I appreciate the Second Amendment and enjoy having my gun safely stored and locked in my home. Why would anyone object to a background check to help keep guns away from those who could pose a danger to others? A group session of the NRA, gun owners, and legislators representing both sides could, without a doubt, come up with some manageable regulations to save lives. However, the NRA fears that giving an inch will lead to more inches, and they have the political lobbying power to prevent every Republican from voting for any new gun legislation that includes restrictions. Have you ever heard of a Republican congressperson or president who opposed the NRA? They wouldn't be in office very long.

Can the problem of America's leadership in the industrialized world's per capita gun deaths be solved? No matter what we do, will limiting gun rights eliminate gun deaths? Are assault weapons the problem? Could we pass enough gun laws to eliminate mass shooting and lower murder rates? Will we still be debating these questions in 10, 20, 50 years? Can we come up with a fix? If we pass new laws, such as certified serial number with traceable registration, what happens to the millions of guns already on the street and illegal guns sales? Can we collect all unregistered guns?

We have a whole lot of questions and few good answers. When will we hear about the next mass shooting? How many gun deaths will there be in Chicago this coming weekend? So what do we do? Just say we can't solve the problem? Or do we make it easier for more responsible people to buy a gun to protect ourselves from bad guys and the mentally ill?

"Okay, enough questions. It's time for answers. The cold hard fact is that the problem cannot be solved soon, in five years, or in ten years, or more. We have to accept the fact that gun deaths will always be with us. Are enough people in America really willing to look at the facts? What sacrifice are gun owners willing to make to save American lives? Would American political leaders be willing to vote against the NRA? Are the majority of Americans willing to look at the undisputable facts? Or do they love their guns so much that they will never accept further controls? Yup, it seems to be an insurmountable task.

"Let's look at it logically. For the sake of discussion, accept that the US will have approximately 25,000 US citizen gun deaths in 2019. Then, for a moment, accept that we could find a way to save 1,000 of those lives. How much would that be worth? Would you be willing to sacrifice some inconvenience and cost? How much are lives worth? Your answer may be that you will never give up any rights to the second amendment. I doubt that would be the case, especially if it was your own family.

"Consider the following for a moment, for the purpose of an example. Imagine if we required all guns to have serial numbers matching the permit user's license, we only sold specified sporting guns to licensed owners who must be over 18 years of age, and all guns were required to be safely stored when not in use and concealed in the owner's residence with the licensed owner responsible for the whereabouts of the gun, subject to a fine for violation. Second, we engaged in a long-term plan to recover and destroy all illegal guns. Okay, you don't like the idea. Think about it. Don't just say it could never happen or that it wouldn't work. It would work. It worked in Australia, UK, Japan, Norway, and New Zeeland. The question is, are you willing to sacrifice a minor inconvenience, and do you have the patience to see the gradual saving of lives over the long term? Is the inconvenience worth the lives? It's either yes or no?

"You can't deny the fact that gun controls and the number of guns per 100,000 population in nations around the world determine the number of gun deaths per 100,000 population. Nine nations combined (Australia, Denmark, France, Germany, Israel, Japan, Ireland, Sweden, and the UK) have far fewer guns per 100,000 residents and far fewer gun deaths per 100,000 residents than the US. Some gun advocates claim those statistics are skewed because 60% of US gun deaths are the result of suicide. That is not a relevant statistic, because there isn't a meaningful statistical relationship between gun population and suicide. In any case, the US still leads the way in gun deaths without counting suicide. Guess which of those countries with fewer gun deaths have more restrictions on gun ownership than the US? All nine of them do. Now look at Brazil, Columbia, El Salvador, Venezuela, Honduras, Columbia, Jamaica and other South American countries. They all have more guns per capita, easy access to guns, and the gun laws they do have are not enforced very well. Consequently, they are the world leaders in gun deaths per 100,000 residents. The facts are conspicuously obvious. What kind of nation do we want America to be? What would your position be if a member of your family was shot while in school, walking down the street, or shopping?

"The NRA gun lobby and its members refuse to consider these facts. They cling to the second amendment's reference to the right to bear arms. A case can easily be made that the authors of that amendment didn't intend to see the proliferation and use of guns that we have today. Gun advocates are programed by the NRA to deny the problem, and Americans who recognize the problem have gun advocate friends or family that they don't want to argue with. So, they grumble a little at the report of each mass shooting and then forget about it. Our elected politicians can't fight the issue for fear of losing NRA support for their job. Republicans can't survive in office unless they support the NRA.

"Now for a grand slam *Make America Safe* plan: require a certified, traceable national ID and a serial-numbered and traceable gun permit for gun owners. No, that's not too much government control, it's saving lives. The national ID would be voluntary for citizens who had not committed a felony or had mental health issues, but having the ID would be beneficial for security access, immigration control, and saving on the cost of crime. I realize this proposal will be seen as a next to impossible undertaking, but it's not impossible. We just have to realize that the world has changed, and we have to either adjust or accept a continuation of the unnecessary loss of thousands of lives year after year.

"Gun advocates often cite states or cities with stricter laws on guns or bans on them failing to have an impact on gun violence. Of course that happens. If someone in those cities or states wants a gun, they just go to the next city or state to obtain it. The only controls that will be effective are national controls and national laws. Then, pro-gun people say guns will still come in from Mexico. That's correct, but it will be fewer guns, and improved immigration and border control will lessen that problem. We can't eliminate the problem; we can only decrease the problem and save some lives. What are lives worth? It keeps coming back to, what are you willing to do to save lives?

Our discussion trio was initially split but then came close to an agreement on the issue of abortion. Democrats, of course, mostly support a woman's right to choose abortion under almost any circumstances. Conservatives mostly support the right to life, which they believe begins at conception. The compromise position is sparing the right to life after some point during pregnancy. Four months is the most commonly agreed limit. I think a compromise should be found by a mixed group of congresswomen, pediatricians, and representatives of pro-life organizations. We all agreed that a live baby, outside the womb, regardless of intent or circumstances, should have a right to life.

In our discussions, I also raised the question of what I refer to as the fourth power. The original three branches of our government, as established and defined by our founding fathers, are the executive, judicial, and legislative branches. However, unofficially, a power has gradually emerged over the years since our Constitu was written. This power is the media. It doesn't have any offic authority, but it has become very influential as it expanded from radio and television to the internet. Radio talk shows seem to have more conservative anchors, while television and print media—aside from Fox News—are dominated by Democrats. Personally, I flip between CNN and Fox News and also often watch the evening news on CBS, NBC, or ABC.

Earlier, I mentioned the influence of the NRA on Republicans. On the other side of the aisle, the Democrats also have a boss: the unions. Have you ever heard an elected Democrat oppose unions? I don't think so. I agree that employees need representation to prevent unfair labor practices and ensure fair wages. But like many Republicans I know, I have reservations about union management. Are they looking out for the workers or for themselves? Like many organizations, unions have good and bad leaders, and historically, they have included some criminal elements. Furthermore, I don't believe union management should address company management policies that don't relate to employee treatment, working conditions, or compensation.

Unions bring us to the issue of the minimum wage. Historically, Democrats have continued to push for a higher minimum wage. That's understandable; that's their job. Minimum wage, while generally not an issue in manufacturing, is a constant topic of discussion for small businesses, especially in the restaurant industry, where many teens and part-time workers are employed. The problem with increasing the minimum wage, however, is that it had been very low for years and then took a big jump. This large percentage increase is problematic for employers and often forces them to increase prices to cover the cost or suffer losses. As a bartender, I am not personally concerned because I earn most of my income from tips—all of which I report on my taxes, of course. (I say that with a smile). The solution is to agree on a bare minimum with an annual CPI increase.

Sean, a restaurant owner, brought up another issue. The economic model of restaurants, especially fast-food restaurants, is to provide inexpensive food quickly. Such restaurants rarely offer full time jobs for adults supporting families. Most employees are pa time, and for many, it's their first job. With this economic mc pushing wages too high will push prices so high that the concept is no longer viable. Closing down fast-food restaurants would reduce the options for quick, cheap meals.

When our discussion came to selecting candidates for president, I asked this question: If you were delegated the task of selecting a teacher to educate your children or a doctor to perform surgery on a member of your family, would you prefer to seek the advice of randomly selected people off the street or the advice of a group of experts from those professions? The answer, of course, is obvious and logical. Why, then, wouldn't the two political parties use experts to select their presidential candidates? I proposed a system that would enable both parties to find a qualified candidate. In the 2020 election, the Democrats started with more than twenty candidates aged thirty-eight to over seventy. In 2016, the Republicans selected a candidate who had never worked in government and spoke like he was in a locker room. What if each party established a seven-member selection committee? The members of the committees should have knowledge and experience in national and international management. They would then interview candidates and choose one. The committee should be selected from a cross section of experienced, successful leaders in fields such as business, education, international affairs, the military, science, history, technology, and economics. This group could undertake an unbiased search for the ideal presidential candidate. In the general election, the American people could then choose between two ideal candidates, one selected by the Democrats and one by the Republicans. The corporate world is known to be more efficient and to have better managers than the government; I don't think that would be the case if corporations had campaigns and primaries to select corporate leaders. Unfortunately, given the well-established game of party politics at conventions and primaries, such an efficient, logical idea is unlikely to ever happen.

We also discussed immigration at great length. All three of us agreed that we want to see immigrants come to this country; immigrants have been the foundation of America. However, the immigrants who form this foundation didn't come to America by climbing under or over a fence; they came through immigration control with identification and an acceptable plan for a place to work and live. We all find the mess at the Mexican border incredible and absurd; our inability to manage our own border is an international joke. We need a barrier—some type of technical system or a wall, whatever it takes to control who comes into our country. Rachel, the progressive liberal, wants to allow anybody who wants to come except criminals. Sean wants to be more restrictive by limiting immigration to those who can fill available jobs. If Rachel and Sean could come to an agreement, why can't Congress? Well, they don't have time. They are too busy trying to find reasons to impeach the president or a member of his staff. And Republicans are spinning their wheels too. They want to expose the Democrats for spying on the 2016 Trump campaign. Apparently, that's more fun than immigration reform. I have yet to hear a responsible person say we don't need immigration reform, but the government continues to fail to do anything about it.

The government fails to solve any of these problems because our representatives in Washington spend way too much time attacking each other, feeding the media with controversy. They seem to want opportunities to be on camera. Think about it: The Democrats appointed a special prosecutor to investigate Trump for collusion with Russia, and when he couldn't find sufficient evidence after spending $25–30 million, they sought to convict Trump for obstruction of justice. Then they began screaming for impeachment. Not to be outdone, the Republican attorney general appointed a prosecutor to investigate why the Democrats started the entire investigation in the first place. Of course, the president is adding fuel to the fire with silly name-calling. Regardless of our political positions, we can all agree that our representatives in Washington need an attitude adjustment.

One of the big political firestorms of 2019 was the Twitter and press conference battles between President Trump and the progressive group of Ilhan Omar, Alexandria Ocasio-Cortez, Ayana Pressley, and Rashida Tlaib. I think I can assume my liberal friend, Rachel, would defend the progressives and Sean McCarthy would defend President Trump.

Actually, they are both wrong. The four congresswomen have been infuriating the Jewish community and discomfiting the Democratic leadership with their expressions of anti-Semitism, and it has been condemned in a Senate resolution. Of course, since they have also been critical of Trump, the president has taken the bait, tweeting back with statements, which opens him up to being accused of racism. This type of rhetoric never accomplishes anything and takes time that could be used to accomplish some constructive legislation on health care, climate change, infrastructure, immigration, education, the homeless problem, and drug trafficking.

A popular topic for newscasters, politicians, and political journalists is China's effort to overtake the United States as the world's largest economic power. Operationally, they have a big advantage. They don't have elections, and they don't have to deal with political gridlock to the extent that we do. However, they also lack the ingredient that has made the United States the world's leader. They don't have our incentive-based free-enterprise capitalist economy, and their citizens are not free to choose their leadership.

Why does America lead the world in reserve currency, technology, medical research, robotics, medical innovation, military, computers, artificial intelligence, oil and gas, universities, literature, theater, movie production, fast food, wealth per adult, billionaires, Olympic sports, wilderness preserves, and more? These are the reasons so many people want to come to America, and they are the reason I don't want to see us move too far toward socialism.

The predominant issue in past presidential elections has been the condition of the economy and whether or not we are involved in an unpopular war. The 2020 election seems more likely to be decided on the voter's judgment of the personal character of the incumbent president and his opponent and whether we want to see the United States become more of a socialist country or continue with free enterprise and capitalism. When the time comes to vote, I will take a logical approach to analyzing which candidate I think will make the best decisions in leading our nation to a healthy economy and world leadership.

In our discussion group, the grand finale was a conversation about a safe, noninvasive personal identification system that could solve many problems and save our government and business community billions of dollars. The first reaction to this idea is usually a concern that the government would know too much about us. I agree that it wouldn't work unless it could only be used to verify identify and not to track where people are going or where they have been. Furthermore, it would be voluntary for citizens. Only noncitizens and persons convicted of a felony would be required to have the card. The government would also supply the national ID card at no cost. The cost savings from crime prevention, simplified airport security, and other security improvements would more than cover the cost of the system's design and management. All three of us agreed that a carefully planned national ID could be the most important innovation that our government could implement.

In closing, as I contemplate and attempt to objectively and logically evaluate this continuous, complex and frustrating political challenge we Americans face between the advocacy of progressive socialism and conservative capitalism, I recall watching the CNN and Fox News coverage of the Trump-directed celebration at the National Mall on July 4, 2019.

I flipped between the coverage of CNN and Fox. The CNN panel of five was primarily critical with the view that demonstrating our military strength with the costly exhibition of our military was inappropriate and typical Trump boasting. They emphasized that all the money used in the cost of the display should have been spared and used to provide more help and assistance for what they described as horrible conditions for children and families at the US-Mexican border.

The contrasting point of view was emphasized by the Fox discussion group, in which they expressed the importance of demonstrating appreciation for those who have served in our military since the Declaration of Independence, the saving of our citizens and the world from evil dictators, and enabling the safe existence of this nation, which so many people around the world want to come to. If not for our great military, we would not be the nation that millions are storming our borders to come to.

Both points of view have merit, depending on your political party preference. For the sake of our future, we will need some logical compromising rather than stubborn political profiling to keep this great nation together—and the media can be instrumental in creating that environment.

In the 2020 election, Donald Trump, assuming the Democrat's impeachment efforts are unsuccessful, appears ready to continue to move forward with his controversial tweeting to the public, bold decision-making, and continuing with conservative options. In fairness, he has demonstrated some willingness to compromises on some issues.

Among the Democrats who have a chance to win the nomination, Elizabeth Warren and Kamala Harris represent the push to a more socialist direction, and Joe Biden, based on his past record, represents the cautious, middle-of-the-road approach to governing. Biden is most likely among the Democrats to work for left leaning compromise. In fact Biden has to stay left campaigning to get the nomination. However, I wouldn't be too surprised to see Hillary Clinton come in as a late entry. A dark horse is Mayor Pete. A bright young alternative against Trump could be formidable. Watch the campaigns, analyze logically what you think is best for your family's future, and vote.

When we completed our interview sessions, we decided that we had set a good example of what it will take to save the foundation of this nation: maintaining the two-party system and discussing issues objectively and fairly, without anger. We also need to get logical and be willing to compromise. Conservative Sean and progressive Rachel walked out of Filibusters together as friends. They have different opinions about American politics, but they learned that they could find ways to compromise. They got logical.

POLITICAL
DATA INDEX

(Government statistics are at varied dates and subject to change)

Federal, City and State Government

US House of Representatives: 235 Democrats and 197 Republicans
Senate: 51 Republicans and 47 Democrats

Governors: As of 2019, there are 27 Republicans and 23 Democrats holding the office of governor.

City Mayors: (top 50 by population), we have 33 Democrats, 14 Republicans and 3 Independents.

Our Economy

Unemployment GDP Inflation

1993	6.5%	2.8%	2.7%	Clinton
1994	5.5%	4.0%	2.7%	Clinton
1995	5.6%	2.7%	2.5%	Clinton
1996	5.4%	3.8%	3.3%	Clinton
1997	4.7%	4.4%	1.7%	Clinton
1998	4.4%	4.5%	1.6%	Clinton
1999	4.0%	4.8%	2.7%	Clinton
2000	3.9%	4.1%	3.4%	Clinton
2001	5.7%	1.0%	1.6%	Bush
2002	6.0%	1.7%	2.4%	Bush
2003	5.7%	2.9%	1.9%	Bush
2004	5.4%	3.8%	3.3%	Bush
2005	4.9%	3.5%	3.4%	Bush
2006	4.4%	2.9%	2.5%	Bush
2007	5.0%	1.9%	4.1%	Bush
2008	7.3%	-0.1%	0.1%	Bush
2009	9.9%	-2.5%	2.7%	Obama
2010	9.3%	2.6%	1.5%	Obama
2011	8.5%	1.6%	3.0%	Obama
2012	7.9%	2.2%	1.7%	Obama
2013	6.7%	1.8%	1.5%	Obama

2014	5.6%	2.5%	0.8%	Obama
2015	5.0%	2.9%	0.7%	Obama
2016	4.7%	1.6%	2.1%	Obama
2017	4.1%	2.4%	2.1%	Trump
2018	3.9%	2.9%	1.9%	Trump

Resources for Table: US Government

Personal Tax Rates for 2019

Tax Rates by Income
10% $ 0–$9,525
12% $9,526–$38,700
22% $38,701–$82,500
24% $82,501–$157,500
32% $157,501–$200,000
35% $200,001–$300,000
37% $300,001 or more

Income Earners Paid Percentage of US Total Taxes
Bottom 90: 30.5%
Bottom 50: 12%
Top 50: 97%
Top 1: 37.3%
Top .001: 2%

Do you spend more than you make? The government does.
The government collects more than $27,000 per household in taxes and spends more than $35,000. The difference is federal debt.

Where it goes:
Poverty programs: $6,483
National debt interest: $3,054
Veterans' benefits: $1,556
Justice department: $557
Health research/regulation: $533
Highways/mass transit: $493
International affairs: $422
Federal tax programs: $1,500

Where it goes:
National defense: 20 percent
Social Security: 20 percent
Medicare, Medicaid, and children's health insurance
Safety net programs

National Debt of Last Four Presidents

Donald Trump: Added $5.088 trillion first term (and projected at $9.1 trillion for two terms)
Barack Obama: Added $8.588 trillion
George W. Bush: Added $5.849 trillion
Bill Clinton: Added $1.396 trillion

Top Ten Countries by Revenue (2017)

Rank	Revenue	Expenditures	Deficit	% of GDP
1 US	6,028,001	6,807,161	-887,204	-4.6%
2 China	3,312,308	3,787,245	-474,937	-4.0%
3 Germany	2,200,000	1,900,000	300,000	2.6%
4 Japan	1,678,000	1,888,000	-210,000	-4.6%
5 France	1,334,000	1,412,000	-78,000	-3.1%
6 UK	1,077,300	1,120,000	-43,000	-1.1%
7 Italy	884,500	927,000	-43,000	-2.3
8 Canada	623,700	657,000	-34,000	-2.1
9 Brazil	618,853	779,532	-160,679	-7.8
10 India	544,422	725,052	n/a	n/a

Top 10 Causes of Death in the United States

		Deaths Per Year	Percentage of Total Deaths
1.	Heart Disease	635,260	23.1
2.	Cancer	598,038	5.9
3.	Accidents	161,374	5.9 percent
4.	Chronic Respiratory	154,596	5.6 percent
5.	Stroke	142,142	5.18 percent
6.	Alzheimer's	16,103	0.8 percent
7.	Diabetes	80,058	2.9 percent

8. Influenza and Pneumonia	51,537	1.88 percent
9. Kidney Disease	50,046	1.8 percent
10. Suicide	44,965	1.64 percent

Preventable Causes of Death in the United States

Tobacco: 480,000 with 41,000 coming from secondhand smoke. Tobacco is expected to kill 7.5 million people worldwide by 2020 (Reuters).
Alcohol: 88,000 people (approximately 62,000 men and 26,000 women) die in the United States from alcohol-related causes annually.
Drug Abuse: 72,000

Immigration

The latest estimate by Pew Research indicates 10.7 million unauthorized immigrants are in the United States. That's about 4 percent of the American population. In 2018, ICE arrested 105,140 illegal immigrants who were convicted criminals.

Gun Deaths per Year

Country	Gun Deaths per 100,000	Significant Gun Laws
Jamaica	35	Minimal
Bahamas	35	Minimal
Colombia	20	Minimal
United States	19	Minimal
Mexico	11	Some
Canada	2	Yes
Greece	1.5	Yes
Sweden	1.6	Yes
Denmark	1.5	Yes
Ireland	.8	Yes
Greece	1.52	Yes
Germany	1	Yes
Poland	.26	Yes
UK	.23	Yes
India	.3	Yes

Japan	.06	Yes
Hong Kong	.07	Yes
South Korea	.08	Yes

Military Power

Nation	Personnel	Aircraft	Tanks	Naval Assets	Budget
United States	2.3m	13.7k	5.8k	415	587B
Russia	3.3m	3.8k	20k	352	446B
China	3.7m	3k	6.4k	714	168B
India	4.2m	2.1k	4.4k	295	51B
France	388k	1.3k	406	118	35B
Japan	312k	1.5k	700	131	44B
UK	233k	856	249	76	46B
Turkey	743k	1018	2,445	194	8.2B
Germany	210k	698	543	81	39.2B
Egypt	1.3m	1,132	4,100	319	4.4B

Where Do We Get Our News?

Fewer than 20 percent of Americans now get their news from newspapers, and 80 percent get the news from television or the internet. ABC with David Muir is the leader for the six o'clock news hour, attracting about 8 million viewers.

On cable news, which is on twenty-four hours, Fox News is the leader. They attract more prime-time viewers than CNN and MSNBC combined. The two most popular individuals are Fox's Sean Hannity (first) and MSNBC's Rachel Maddow (second). Others, in order, are Tucker Carlson on Fox, Andrew Cuomo on Prime Time CNN, Ingraham Angle on Fox, The Five on Fox, and Anderson Cooper on CNN.

T R I V I A
Did You Know?

George Washington (1789–1797) had some dental problems—so he had some teeth made. They were made of hippopotamus bone, lead, brass, screws, gold wire, and animal and human teeth.

John Adams (1797–1801) had an excellent vocabulary, but when he got angry, he said some pretty obnoxious things. For example, he called George Washington "a mean-spirited, low-lived fellow, the son of a half-breed Indian squaw, sired by a Virginia mulatto father." He said if Washington became president, "murder, robbery, rape, adultery, and incest would be openly taught and practiced, the air will be rent with the cries of the distressed, the soil will be soaked with blood and the nation black with crimes."

Thomas Jefferson (1801–1809) was an amazing writer, but not so much when it came to speaking. He hated public speaking so much that he only gave two speeches in his presidency, one per term. He had his State of the Union speeches presented as written documents to be read at Congress by a clerk.

Note: Jefferson and Adams died a few hours apart on the same day: July 4, 1826. It was also the fiftieth anniversary of the adoption of the Declaration of Independence. John Adams was ninety, and Jefferson was eighty-three.

James Madison (1809–1817) was a big man in stature. He wrote the US Constitution, was involved in writing the Federalist Papers, and sponsored the Bill of Rights. Physically, however, he was not so big. He was five foot four and weighed one hundred pounds.

James Monroe (1817–1825) was our fifth president. Due to his penchant for outdated Revolutionary War-era dress, Monroe's nickname was "The Last Cocked Hat." His first term was called the Era of Good Feelings because of the national unity that followed the end of the War of 1812. He ran unopposed for his reelection, something that has only happened one other time in American history (George Washington).The last surviving founding father, Monroe died on July 4, 1831, five years after both Jefferson and Adams died and fifty-five years after the Declaration of Independence was signed.

John Quincy Adams (1825–1829) was the son of our Jefferson-hating second president. John Quincy Adams was known for skinny-dipping in the Potomac River every morning. A reporter took advantage of this information and sat on his clothes until he would grant her an interview.

Andrew Jackson (1829–1837) had a talking parrot who only became a problem one time. The parrot had to allegedly be removed from Jackson's funeral because it wouldn't stop cursing.

Martin Van Buren (1837–1841) was the first president born in the United States. He was nicknamed "Old Kinderhook" because he was from an upstate New York town called Kinderhook.

William Henry Harrison (1841–1841) was president for one month. He died of pneumonia, which he acquired while celebrating his inauguration on a very cold day.

John Tylor (1841–1845) was vice president when Harrison died, but there was a disagreement as to what powers he would have. He managed to convince Congress that he should become president. This paved the way for the Twenty-Fifth Amendment, which made the line of succession official.

James Polk (1845–1849) is considered by many to be the best one-term president in American history. He was a strong leader during the Mexican-American War. He added a huge area to the United States from the Oregon Territory through Nevada and California.

Zachary Taylor (1849–1850) viewed a Fourth of July celebration on the grounds where the Washington Monument would later stand. While viewing the event, he snacked on a bunch of cherries that contained bacteria. That was a problem. He died a few days later.

Millard Fillmore (1850–1853) was Taylor's successor, and he married his schoolteacher. Historians don't have much else to say about him.

Franklin Pierce (1853–1857) was not very popular while in office. His own party refused to nominate him for a second term. His reply to being cast aside was: "There is nothing left to do but get drunk." He often drank too much and was allegedly arrested for running over an old lady with his horse.

James Buchanan (1857–1861) was the only bachelor to be president but was not home alone. He lived with Alabama Senator William Rufus King for more than ten years, despite being rich enough to have their own homes. Andrew Jackson called them "Miss Nancy and Aunt Fancy."

Abraham Lincoln (1861–1865), a tall drink of water, served tall drinks as a bartender. He was also a really good wrestler, winning all but one of approximately three hundred matches.

Andrew Johnson (1865–1869) and his brother ran away from home as teens. They had been assigned to a tailor as indentured servants. The tailor offered a ten-dollar reward for their capture. They were never captured. Johnson made good use of his experience, making all his own suits as president.

Ulysses Grant (1869–1877) was supposed to be in Lincoln's theater box on the night of his assassination, but he changed plans at the last minute. He regretted not being there for the rest of his life because he believed he could have stopped it from happening. Other fun facts about Grant: he couldn't stand the sight of blood, which is ironic considering his Civil War history, and he dismantled the Ku Klux Klan during his presidency (they unfortunately regrouped decades later).

Rutherford Hayes (1877–1881) was the victor of one of the most disputed elections ever. He lost the popular vote by less than 250,000, but he eked out an electoral college win by a single vote, earning him the nicknames "Rutherfraud" and "His Fraudulency." His abstinence from drinking, smoking, or gambling also had some calling him "Granny Hayes."

James Garfield (1831–1881) was ambidextrous and could write in Greek with one hand and in Latin with the other—at the same time! He was shot a few months into his presidency by an assassin, and he died eleven weeks later. Doctors tried using a newly invented metal detector by Alexander Graham Bell to locate the bullet, but the metal bedsprings kept messing up the results, leading the doctors to cut in the wrong places. On top of this, the doctors also introduced bacteria into Garfield's body with their unsterilized, prying fingers.

Chester Arthur (1881–1885) wanted the White House completely redecorated, but he needed money to pay for all the new furniture. His solution was to sell off twenty-four wagon-loads of historical relics, including a pair of Lincoln's pants and one of John Quincy Adams's hats. The redecoration wasn't the only luxury he took; he also owned elaborate clothing, including eighty pairs of pants, which earned him the nickname "Elegant Arthur."

Grover Cleveland (1885–1889) was the twenty-second president. Upon the death of his law partner, Cleveland became the legal guardian of his friend's eleven-year-old orphaned daughter. Ten years later, they were married at the White House, making her the youngest First Lady ever at the age of twenty-one—and making him the Woody Allen of the nineteenth century.

Benjamin Harrison (1889–1893) was the grandson of President William Henry Harrison. He was called the "human iceberg" by some for how stiff he was with people. Maybe people misread anxiety for stiffness. He was the first president to have electricity in the White House and was so scared of being electrocuted that he refused to touch the light switches and was known to go to bed with all the lights on.

Grover Cleveland (1893–1897) was the only president to be elected in nonconsecutive terms.

William McKinley (1897–1901) considered carnations his good luck charm and wore them everywhere. On September 6, 1901, he gave a little girl the carnation from his lapel and was shot by an assassin a short time later. He died the following week.

Teddy Roosevelt (1901–1909) was the twenty-sixth president. On Valentine's Day in 1884, both his first wife and his mother died.

William Howard Taft (1909–1913) was most known for his waistline and supposedly getting stuck in a bathtub (historians say this didn't really happen). People don't talk about his stuffed animal enough. Toy manufacturers believed teddy bears would fade out and wanted a replacement. They came up with Billy possum. Unfortunately, the origin tale has nothing to do with Taft sparing a baby possum and everything to do with him scarfing down a huge possum dinner one night. Despite rude anti-Teddy Bear postcards, Billy Possum did not catch on.

Woodrow Wilson (1913–1921) was the twenty-eighth president. In 1919, incredible stress led to Wilson experiencing a series of strokes. He was left partially paralyzed and almost blind, but he stayed in office until 1921. He relied heavily on his wife, Edith Bolling Galt, a descendant of Pocahontas, for help, leading to her nickname as the "Presidentress."

Warren Harding (1921–1923) had quite the wandering eye. He had an affair with his wife's close friend, Carrie Fulton Phillips, which was revealed through a series of love letters. He also messed around with a woman named Nan Britton. She wrote a book called *The President's Daughter* about how her daughter was Harding's. In 2005, DNA testing proved that he was the daddy.

Calvin Coolidge (1923–1929) was known as Silent Cal. He was once seated next to a young woman at a dinner party, and she told him she had a bet she could extract at least three words of conversation from him. "You lose," he replied. An animal lover, he had two pet raccoons, Reuben and Rebecca, who would sometimes run around the White House. He also had someone rub Vaseline on his head while he ate breakfast.

Herbert Hoover (1929–1933) liked animals as well. The Hoovers had two pet alligators that ran around the White House grounds. He is most remembered for being president during the 1929 stock market crash.

Franklin Roosevelt (1933–1945), our longest-serving president, feared the number thirteen. He refused to have dinner with thirteen people or leave for a trip on the thirteenth of the month. He was considered one of America's greatest presidents and possessed the greatest presidential secrets. His movements were limited, and he had to use a wheelchair, which was unknown to a majority of Americans.

Harry Truman (1945–1953) had an early romance. He met his wife, Bess, in Sunday school when he was six. He made the decision to use the most lethal killing weapon in war history when he called for the atomic bomb to be dropped on Hiroshima on August 9, 1945, killing more than a hundred thousand people. The rationale was to end the war and stop more killing.

Dwight Eisenhower (1953–1961) thought Shangri-La, the name for the presidential retreat, was too fancy a name for a Kansas farm boy. He changed it to Camp David.

John F. Kennedy (1961–1963) was the twenty-eighth president. His father, Joe Kennedy, said his son Jack was "careless and lacked application." However, he still got $1 million on his twenty-first birthday (all nine brothers and sisters got the same), and he went on to graduate from Harvard.

Lyndon Johnson (1963–1969) saved himself for the presidency with a potty stop. During World War II, on a flight to a dangerous mission, the plane he was in stopped for a potty break. Johnson missed the takeoff, and the plane crashed on its mission—and all the passengers were killed.

Richard Nixon (1969–1964) is widely known for the Watergate scandal. Most people do not know he was a skilled player of the piano, clarinet, saxophone, violin, and accordion. He could play those instruments without learning to read music. He also loved to bowl so much that he had a one-lane alley put in the basement of the White House.

Gerald Ford (1974–1977) wasn't born Gerald Ford. His birth name was Leslie Lynch King Jr. He was the only president to never have elected president or vice president by the voting public (Vice President Spiro Agnew resigned, followed shortly thereafter by President Nixon). Ford, Michigan's only president, was a football star at the University of Michigan, where he played center and linebacker. He actually turned down offers from two professional football teams.

Jimmy Carter (1977–1981) appeared in *Playboy* magazine and said, "I've looked on a lot of women with lust. I've committed adultery in my heart many times. This is something that God recognizes I will do—and I have done it—and God forgives me for it." It was during a presidential campaign too, which made the outcry even more pronounced. Carter refused to apologize.

Ronald Reagan (1981–1989) was a Hollywood star before turning to politics. He regularly consulted with an astrologer, Joan Quigley, before making decisions or scheduling big events. In 1982, while he was on a horseback ride with the queen on the grounds of Windsor Castle, the queen's horse is said to have had a bout of prolonged flatulence. The queen reportedly said, "Oh dear, Mr. President, I'm so sorry!" Reagan supposedly replied, "Quite all right, Your Majesty. I thought it was the horse."

George H. W. Bush (1989–1993) inspired a Japanese word, "Bushusuru," which means "to do the Bush thing." The thing was vomiting in public, which Bush did all over the Japanese prime minister in 1992. He also skydived from an airplane when he was ninety years old. He has been called by many to have had the most qualifications to become president. He was captain of two high school sports teams and was president of his class, he won a distinguished cross as a military hero, was a representative to China, was elected to the US House of Representatives, was an ambassador to the United Nations, was chairman of the Republican National Committee, was director of the CIA, and was vice president for eight years.

William Clinton (1993–2001) has two Grammys (one for Best Spoken Word Album and another for Best Spoken Word Album for Children). He is also the only president known to have had a staffer under his desk while he was on the phone.

George W. Bush (2001–2009) is the only president to have been the head cheerleader in high school. He attended Phillips Academy in Andover, Massachusetts. Bush grew up in a politically involved family. His father was president, his brother Jeb was a governor, and his paternal grandfather, Preston, was a senator.

Barrack Obama (2009–2017) had a pet ape called Tata while living in Indonesia. His teen work experience was at Baskin-Robbins. Rumor has it that he doesn't like ice cream now.

In high school, he used to be called "O'Bomber" for his basketball skills.

Donald Trump (2017–?) loved himself more than any past president. He said, "People love me, I am rich, I am smart, I am the best, we are going to win so much you will beg me to stop." He has the most rank vocabulary of any president, and he may be the only president who never drank alcohol or smoked.

CPSIA information can be obtained
at www.ICGtesting.com
Printed in the USA
FFHW020906141119
56054388-62027FF